DUST & GRIM

DUST & GRIM

CHUCK WENDIG

ILLUSTRATED BY
JENSINE ECKWALL

LITTLE, BROWN AND COMPANY
New York Boston

Text copyright © 2021 by Terribleminds LLC
Illustrations copyright © 2021 by Jensine Eckwall

Cover art copyright © 2021 by Jensine Eckwall
Cover design by Karina Granda
Cover copyright © 2021 by Hachette Book Group, Inc.

Little, Brown and Company
Hachette Book Group
1290 Avenue of the Americas, New York, NY 10104
Visit us at LBYR.com

First Edition: October 2021

Little, Brown and Company is a division of Hachette Book Group, Inc. The Little, Brown name and logo are trademarks of Hachette Book Group, Inc.

The publisher is not responsible for websites (or their content) that are not owned by the publisher.

Library of Congress Cataloging-in-Publication Data
Names: Wendig, Chuck, author. | Eckwall, Jensine, illustrator.
Title: Dust & Grim / Chuck Wendig ; illustrated by Jensine Eckwall.
Other titles: Dust and Grim
Description: First edition. | New York : Little, Brown and Company, 2021. | Audience: Ages 8–12. | Summary: Soon after meeting her eighteen-year-old brother, Dustin, for the first time, thirteen-year-old Molly learns their shared inheritance, a mortuary business, serves monsters.
Identifiers: LCCN 2020053070 | ISBN 9780316706230 (hardcover) | ISBN 9780316706247 (ebook) | ISBN 9780316706223 (ebook other)
Subjects: CYAC: Supernatural—Fiction. | Brothers and sisters—Fiction. | Funeral homes—Fiction. | Monsters—Fiction.
Classification: LCC PZ7.W469133 Dus 2021 | DDC [Fic]—dc23
LC record available at https://lccn.loc.gov/2020053070

ISBNs: 978-0-316-70623-0 (hardcover), 978-0-316-70624-7 (ebook)

Printed in the United States of America

LSC-C

Printing 1, 2021

To the Childe B-Dub,
Heir Apparent to the
Monsters I've Created

contents

PART ONE:
MOLLY AND THE MYSTERIOUS
FAMILY BUSINESS

PART TWO:
MOLLY AND THE
MONSTROUS INHERITANCE

PART THREE:
MOLLY THROUGH THE
MOTHSTEAD GATE

part one

MOLLY

AND THE

MYSTERIOUS

FAMILY

BUSINESS

1. how I met my brother

"OUR FATHER IS DEAD AND I HAVE COME TO DISCUSS MATTERS OF HIS estate."

The girl, age thirteen, stared across the table at the young man, age eighteen. His hair was raven black, slicked back as if each strand had been pinched by hand and lined up like cooked spaghetti. Hers was a messy scribble of fading color, fire red dipped in lavender. He wore satin pajamas the color of copper patina, swimming with little paisleys; she wore a raggedy gray T-shirt with an X formed of teal lightning bolts, the symbol of her favorite superhero of the Sovereign Super Universe, Zap Girl. (She had declined to wear

Zap Girl's mask to this meeting.) He was scowling. And sweating a little. She was baring her teeth in a smile. His lip was cleft, as if someone had taken a pair of tiny scissors and cut into them the way you might cut through paper or cardboard—long-healed but hard to miss. On her, a pale patch of scar marked her chin like a hyphen—that from a fall five years ago when she'd tried (and tried, and *tried*, and totally failed) to learn how to skateboard.

They had a few things in common: porcelain skin, a scrutinizing glare, a familiar v-shaped dent above the bridge of each nose that deepened as they stared each other down.

"I'm sorry," the young man said, his voice snipped as if with nail clippers, "who are you again?"

She rolled her eyes. "Told you. I'm your sister."

"Molly," he said, repeating the name she'd given him. "Molly."

"And you are…?"

The girl watched as the young man, her brother, turned his gaze toward the other man, the large fellow sitting to her right. That man was a lumpy dude stuffed into a cheap blue suit. His body shape was that of hot dogs lashed together and swaddled in deer leather. He ran a mitt through a wave of thick, blond hair as he said:

"Gordo." He jerked a thumb toward the girl. "I'm her lawyer."

"And my uncle," the girl clarified. "Sorry. *Our* uncle."

Against the far wall, a window-unit air conditioner hummed and clicked: *tick tick tick tick, vmmmm.*

The young man stiffened. "I don't have an uncle. Or a sister."

"Bad news." The girl winced. "You do."

"And my father…"

"Yes, he died."

The brother seemed flustered. Like he was trying to figure out if he believed this and if he should care. "I suppose I should ask how?"

Molly shrugged. "Looking at his phone while crossing the street. City bus came up and—" She clapped her hands hard against each other. "Goodnight, Steve-o."

"Ah. I'm…sorry? For your loss."

Molly's middle tightened. *I won't be sad, I won't be sad, I won't be sad.* Steve wasn't worth getting sad over, she told herself. Instead, she hardened her jaw and said, "Don't be."

"Ah. Okay then. And so *what* is the point of this visit again?"

"Thought you'd never ask." She thrust her index finger in the air and gave it a lasso whirl. "I get half of this. The house, the property, the funeral…thing, er, business, whatever. Half of *all* of it."

"Half of it," the young man repeated. "Half of all of it."

"Bingo, dingo. For the money. I need the money."

His lips cinched tight like a coin purse. "And you need money why?"

"I gotta pay for costuming school and, to do that, I need money. Money that's rightfully mine."

Gordo jumped in: "But which is, ahh, tangled up in *alla this*."

The young man forced a trim, thin smile. "Let's begin again. It's early in the morning. My name is Dustin Ashe. You are Molly—"

"Grim. Molly Grim."

To the man: "And you're, ahhh, Gordo, her uncle."

"Yup." The big man nibbled a thumbnail. "Your uncle, too."

"Could you explain *how* exactly we are all related?"

Molly gave Gordo a look. He gave her a loose, slumpy shrug of his big shoulders, so she took the wheel. "Your mother was Polly Ashe. She married Steven—Steve, Stevie, Steve-o-roonie—Grim. But Steve-o bailed when you were what, like, five? Six?"

Agitated, Dustin used the fingers of his right hand

to pluck at the fingers of his left hand—perhaps a kind of soothing gesture. "Yes."

"Do you remember our mom being pregnant with another kid?"

His eyes roamed the room—though Molly guessed he was really looking inward, at his own memories. "I do," he said crisply. "But she…she never had the baby. She lost it." Under his breath came a panicked mumble: "I mean, I always *assumed*."

Molly grinned.

"Wait," he said. "No. *No.* You're—"

"That baby."

"Impossible."

"No, just *improbable*."

He steepled his fingers and leaned forward. Dubiousness knitted his brow. "You're saying that she gave you up to him? My—our—father? Gave him a newborn baby and let him"—Dustin walked his fingers across the table like a jaunty little man—"go?"

"That does seem to be the case," Gordo said, piping back in.

"Why?"

Molly shrugged. "Who knows. Especially since Dad was a real turdbutt."

Steven Grim had rarely spoken of Molly's mother,

but when he had, he did so the way a religious person might talk about an angel: someone almost supernaturally pure. Of course, to Molly, her mother—*their* mother, she supposed—was no better than any regular, crummy human. The lady was certainly jerk enough to abandon her own daughter with Steve the slacker.

"What I *do* know is this," Molly continued. "Half of all this is mine. So we're going to have to figure that out. If you want, you can pay me the value in, like, *cash money,* and then I'll be out of your hair. *Or* we can just sell the place—"

The already pale Dustin went paler. White as fireplace ash. "We can't sell this. This is—" He swallowed whatever it was he was about to say. "This *was* Mother's place. You can't—I can't—*we* can't—"

Molly shrugged. "No, no, it's cool, you need to think about it."

"He needs to think about it," Gordo said. "We understand that."

"We *understand* that," Molly repeated. "In the meantime, I'll just stay here. It's a big house. There's gotta be a guest bedroom."

Gordo chuckled. "Probably *five* guest bedrooms."

Dustin stood up so fast that the chair behind him teetered, then fell to the floor with a clatter. It seemed to startle him further. He had the look about him of a jittery rabbit. Or maybe some kind of polecat? A very nervous polecat who had to pee.

"I need to see proof of this," he declared, leaning his clenched fists on the table. Was he trembling a little? Molly thought that he was.

Gordo was ready. He spun his alligator-skin briefcase around, popped both latches, and drew out a file. He gave the paper inside it a haphazard spin and it glided across the table, *fwipping* against Dustin's knuckles. The young man looked at the paper, then back to Molly, then back to the paper. His eyes flicked between them probably a dozen times. As if he didn't believe it. Because he probably didn't.

Oh well. Sorry, brother.

"You can't stay here. It's not—I'm not—*no.*" Dustin looked like a robot about to short-circuit. He continued, stammering as he spoke: "I—I can't be responsible for her. She's young. I—I'm not a *caretaker.* There's school—"

"It's summer," Molly corrected sweetly.

"And I don't even know *who* her caretaker is—"

"She's emancipated," Gordo said.

"Emancipated."

Molly nodded. "Yep. Like, basically an adult."

"How? She's too young."

"Magic." Gordo wiggled his fingers like a stage

magician. At this, Dustin stiffened. "Legal magic, anyway."

"I'm going to call my lawyer."

"Great," Molly said, putting on a sad face that she told herself was just an act. "That's cool, super cool, that your first instinct after meeting your long-lost sister is to call your lawyer."

"And let me do more magic and predict the future," Gordo said. "You're gonna call that lawyer, and that lawyer's gonna tell you I got you in a barrel going over a waterfall, Dusty."

"Dustin. Not Dusty."

"Uh-huh. Point is, we're prepared to sue. Forget Molly's financial claim on this home, property, and business. You denying her a simple bed? A place to rest her weary head? Oof. Not gonna look nice in the courts, Dusty."

"Dustin."

"It'll be a huge disruption for you. Not to mention… costly. Lawyers, court fees, the loss of business. They might even have to send inspectors out, go over this place with a fine-tooth comb, a black light, a no-stone-left-unturned attitude. I mean, double *oof.* All because you couldn't give your little sister a place to stay while we sort out the finicky bits."

Something went out of Dustin then. Like the soul

gone suddenly from a dead pet. "Fine. Yes. There's a—a room upstairs. I can—I can have it ready in a tiff. A *jiff*, I mean. Just, just…give me a bit."

With that, he spun heel-to-toe and whirled out of the room.

"Well, that was fun," Molly said.

2. baggage

"MY BROTHER SUCKS," MOLLY SAID MINUTES LATER AS SHE STOOD IN THE driveway (also: the parking lot) with Uncle Gordo. She grunted as she hauled a steamer trunk out of the back of a broad-chested Cadillac. The trunk, onto which she'd painted in hot pink the word *kosupure*, thudded onto the gravel, kicking up some summer dust. "You could help, you know."

"I am helping. I'm helping with the law." He shrugged, then feigned a dramatic wince. "Besides. Bad hips. Sorry."

"Uh-huh." She hoisted her backpack out next, slung it over her shoulders. "Anyway. Wow, that

Dusty dude—like, hello, judgy much? A total Judgy McJudgypants! What a jerk. I mean, the first time I meet my brother, he's just a big *snoot* about everything."

"Reminds me of your dad," Gordo said with no small bitterness. "He always judged me. And he had no room to judge, lemme tell you. But it's early in the process, relax. We *did* surprise him, and we're asking a lot. *A lot* a lot."

"Dustin thinks I'm trash. He lives in this big old house and I'm just road garbage to him. Like a dead possum."

"You're not a possum."

"I didn't *say* I was a possum, I just said—"

"I get it," Gordo said, obviously tired of her. "Do you want him to respect you, or do you want the money?"

I want him to like me. That, an uninvited thought. A trespasser traipsing around her brain. Molly scowled. "So what's the play here?"

"The play? The play is we wait. He'll relent. He has to. Your dad owned half of this place." At this, Gordo twitched visibly. "When your mother inherited it from her family or whatever, she put Stevie's name on the deed, too. That's *his* name over there—" He pointed to the wooden sign hanging in front of the house: ASHE AND GRIM SOLEMNITIES.

"*Our* name on the sign."

Gordo grinned. "That's the attitude I like to hear. Forget your dad. This is about you. About us."

"You didn't like my father very much, did you?"

A visible tension seized him. "Not a fan, no. He got himself into scrapes, but he always turned up heads, like a bad penny. I had to fight tooth and nail for everything. Him? Luck seemed to fall into his lap. Blessed little Stevie."

"You're not wrong, Unc." It was like with rent. Steve-o-roonie was always, always, *always* late with the rent. But by the time the landlord—an old dude who had the body of a broken broomstick—came around to make a fuss, her father seemed to find the money. Someone "owed" him, or he "found" an old baseball card he could sell, or he won just enough on a scratch-off lottery ticket. Every time. Though he never managed to find extra cash when Molly needed something, like new X-Acto blades or EVA foam. Only way she afforded any of it—the gear, the makeup, the hair dye—was usually to sell his stuff to the pawnshop. Which he'd then buy back. And which she'd steal and resell again.

"I'm never wrong."

"I don't miss him," she added suddenly. But she wondered if she really meant that? A little part of her did miss him. He was fun, and funny. He'd seemed to love her, maybe. He'd just loved himself more.

Well, whatever. Like Uncle Gordo said, *Forget your dad.*

Boom. Done. Forgotten.

Molly looked around to take stock of her new—temporary—home. The house here loomed over everything. A pointy-headed Victorian with narrow shoulders, it had the presence of a surly vicar or a grumpy bishop. Beyond that was a wooden outbuilding—a black barn with an Amish hex over the doors—its style out of sync with the house. Beyond *that* were the rolling hills of this part of Pennsylvania, and beyond *those* waited a sprawling dark forest of pine and oak. *Oh, cool, creepy woods,* Molly thought. She told herself: *Remind me never to go there.* Behind them, the driveway snaked through swaying meadows of tall grass and blotchy wildflowers, leading to a ribbon of country road.

It was all very *remote.* Molly had grown up in the city, a bustling, busy place. This was quiet. Too quiet. A weird thought struck her: *If something were to happen to me out here, would anyone even know?* She shivered at the thought.

Something moved out on the country road just then, catching Molly's eye. Sunlight glinted off a vehicle, a pickup truck, boxy and old. It turned off the road and bounded down the serpentine driveway, dipping and bumping into every divot, ditch, and pothole that Molly and Gordo had also hit on their approach. It roared up to the house, lurching as the driver applied the brakes at the last second. A cloud of dust came in behind it, like a filthy ghost.

"Who's this?" Molly asked. "Dustin's lawyer?"

"Don't think so. Looks like Vivacia Sims," Gordo answered. The Black woman who stepped out of the truck wore a corduroy blazer over a white tee. She was tall and thin. Severe in every way—like whoever had drawn her had done so with an X-Acto knife, not a pen or a brush.

The lady didn't give them one look before hurrying up to the house with long, confident strides. The door slammed shut behind her.

"And who exactly is Vivacia Sims?"

"She helps run this place. You saw him—Dustin is young. Too young to really"—he flapped a rubbery hand in the air—"manage anything. So she does it. She was a friend of your mother's."

"You know a lot."

Grumpily, he said, "I do my homework. I'm a real lawyer, you know."

"Who just so happens to have his face on bus-depot posters. And on late-night infomercials." She affected his New Yorker cadence, one she did not herself share: *"If you've been the victim of a messenger-bike accident—"*

"Now who's being judgy?"

"*Fine.* Sorry." She shifted uncomfortably from foot to foot.

"Besides, I've met Vivacia. Been some years, but she was a cold fish back then, and I'm guessing she's one now, too."

"We need to worry about her?"

Her uncle shrugged. "We need to worry about everything. I did my homework, like I said, but there's some stuff that doesn't line up here. This is a funeral home, but they don't seem to do a lot of business. They got a license for a cemetery service and a cemetery—but you see one anywhere? 'Cause I sure don't. And there was some paperwork wrapped up in Orphans' Court proceedings that I couldn't get unsealed by the county seat."

"Okay. So?"

"So it's just weird."

"And is that bad for my getting a piece of all this?"

He seemed to think about it. "We'll see. This is a pretty open-and-shut case." His tone, though, told Molly that he wasn't confident on that point, which made her nervous. Up until now, he'd assured her everything was hunky-dory. "But while you're here… do a little detective work."

"Detective work."

"Yeah. *Snoop around.* You're nosy."

"I'm not nosy."

"I caught you going through my office desk a week ago while I took a whiz."

"Fine, I'm nosy."

The two of them met when her father died. There was a reading of a will, which left Molly basically nothing at all—and that's when Gordo showed up, said he was her father's brother. He told her that Steve didn't have much to give, no, but her mother? Polly Ashe? That was a different story. When Polly died unbeknownst to Molly, that triggered what she owed to Steve—but Steve, for whatever reason, chose not to claim it. Gordo said he could help Molly with that claim. With that, he helped get her emancipated and then started her on the path of, in his words, "getting what's yours."

They sold what few possessions Steve-o-polis had, which helped pay for her motel room and a storage unit not far from Gordo's office. She'd never seen where her uncle lived—Gordo was pretty private about that for some reason. But it had been easy to snoop through his office. He drank a lot of coffee, which meant he took a lot of pee breaks—and whenever he did, she went through his stuff.

Just then, the door to the house opened anew.

There, framed half by shadow, stood Dustin. Behind him, even deeper in the darkness of the house, stood the woman. Vivacia.

Dustin waved Molly over. "I have the room ready," he called.

Oh boy. Her stomach gave a lurch. This she would have to do by herself. She'd tried on the car ride over to get Gordo to stay at the house with her, but he'd said it wouldn't seem right—and besides, she could snoop a lot more if he wasn't there. So, off he'd go. Leaving her here. Alone.

"Go get 'em, kid," Gordo said, his eyes shining.

3. quatresomething tessewhoozit

THE WALK THROUGH THE HOUSE WAS HASTY. DUSTIN MOVED LIKE A MAN on a mission: a monorail silently and urgently gliding along. He walked in a curious way, his hands clasped at his middle and his shoulders pinched forward, his head leading the way in front of his feet. And he moved *fast*, walking on the balls of his feet. The old floorboards did not groan beneath him, and in fact, they seemed to barely register his presence at all.

Molly did not see hide nor hair of the woman, Vivacia, who had disappeared by the time Molly got up the front steps. She did note that everything in the house seemed to have its particular place—the rooms were meticulous in their arrangement. Old photos on the walls seemed to hang perfectly level, and there wasn't a speck of dust to be found, nor the smell of must and mold one might expect in a home of this age. In fact, the place was a panoply of smells: here, rose; there, lilac; past the kitchen, a whiff of pineapple; and then on the steps, a most curious and intensely strong smell, that of fresh soap. Basic, run-of-the-mill soap. But the scent was *so strong* that it formed almost a full sense reaction, as if she were standing there, washing her hands, instead of climbing an old wooden staircase.

Then the scent was lost to another mundane, more expected odor: that of basic orange oil slicking the wood.

At the top of the stairs, Dustin turned sharply into the room at his right. Molly followed.

And then she did a double take.

The walls were—

Well, they were an assault to her eyeballs, for one. The room's wallpaper was made up of four-petaled shapes intersecting like chains, their gilded lines cast against a royal blue so deep you could swim in it. And they went on and on in every direction, each four-petal flower about the size of a cup lid. Almost 3D, even though it was clearly two-dimensional. It was dizzying.

Like a camera lens that couldn't find its focus, her eyes couldn't get ahold of any one part of it. A buzzing arose in the back of her head. Her stomach boiled with sudden queasiness.

"Quatrefoil tessellation," Dustin said, unprovoked.

She blinked. "What?"

"The walls. The pattern. Tessellated quatrefoil. More Edwardian than Victorian, I confess."

"Oh. Okay."

"I saw the look on your face. It can be a bit much."

"Yeah. It is. Do you have another room I can sleep in?"

Dustin hesitated. "No."

The bed was a narrow thing, with a white frame whose bedposts were topped with brass fleur-de-lis. "I kinda toss and turn at night," she said. "I'm afraid I'm going to impale myself on those."

"You could get a motel," he said with a bit of a sniff.

Defiant, she thrust out her chin. "No. I'll stay here. And I don't have any money anyway, remember?"

"Fine."

"What's the smell?" It hit her suddenly. It was fruity and rich. And *strange*. One she'd never encountered before.

At that, he seemed to momentarily loosen up. "Lilikoi. Passion fruit." A small smile found his face. "It's a

Hawaiian fruit. Well, not Hawaiian specifically, but I associate it with that."

"Hawaii."

"That's right."

"You don't seem like a *Hawaii* kinda guy."

A flinch. "I am. I'm quite taken with it."

"So you've been there?"

Another flinch.

"No."

"No?"

"No."

"Then why are you taken with it?"

"I just am," he said, his tone as sharp as a poke from one of those fleur-de-lis. "I'm fond of the *idea.* I don't have to explain it. Never mind. The rules of the house are simple: You are not to interfere with funerary business; the funeral parlor at the back of the house is off-limits; you are *not* to interact with any of our clients; you are *not* to eat any of the food out of the refrigerator, especially any of the fruits and vegetables—I use them for smoothies and such; you are to stay in your room after ten PM except to use the bathroom across the hall, and this is because the floorboards are very *creaky* and *groany* and I will be awakened by their complaining."

Here, he paused, only to continue before Molly could reply. "You are not to change the décor in any way; I have chosen it all quite deliberately. I don't care for *popular music*, so none of that; no flushing anything down the toilet except for toilet paper and one's… expected biological leavings; the cellar is *off*-limits; the forest is *off*-limits; the attic is *off*-limits; do *not* feed any of the stray cats, not anything, not ever; no scented candles; actually, no candles at *all*; you are not to bother Vivacia or myself; and you are *not* to interfere with funerary business."

Molly huffed. What a load of junk. "You said that last part twice," she grumbled.

"Because it is the most important part."

"You don't like me," Molly said plainly. *And I don't care.*

"It's not—it's not that. I don't know you. You're an intruder—"

"An intruder!"

"I don't *mean* it like that, but you are a trespasser of sorts."

"A trespasser. Ouch." *Okay, maybe I care a little.*

"Ugh," he said, gesticulating in agitation. "What we do here—" He paused, as if trying to arrange his thoughts and put them into his mouth correctly. "What we do here is *very* important, Molly. The dead and the bereaved deserve care and empathy for what they are going through. Death is difficult. We all must be laid to rest in the ways that we feel are best for ourselves and those around us—family and friends and society. And it is our job, as masters of solemnity, to be the theoretical final stop for those who come to us. We give them peace. We give them a forever home. We rejoin them with the cosmos, if you will. That is no small thing, Molly Grim. No small thing, *indeed*."

She blinked. What Dustin had just said, he really meant it, didn't he? He cared a whole lot. It almost made her feel bad, but she wasn't going to let him know that, no way. And she certainly didn't want to reveal that this place, and what Dustin did, was actually sorta fascinating and that she had a hundred different questions about bodies and graves and graveyards, and did they *really* pump people full of embalming fluid, and were dead people's eyes fake, and were cremated bodies like fine ash or more like kitty litter, and, and, and. But she held her tongue because, though he cared very much about this place, he cared not at all about her, and that made her mad.

So she resolved, instead, to violate all the rules on his list. Just because she could.

Curtly, she said, "Ugh. Whatever. We done with the lecture, Dad?"

"I'm not your—" He scowled. "Yes, we're done. Dinner is at five. *Always* at five. I'll see you then."

4. a girl needs her armor

"YOU WERE RIGHT, UNC. THIS PLACE IS WEIRD," MOLLY SAID A FEW minutes later as she juggled her iPhone from one hand to the next and popped the lid of her suitcase. She stared into its colorful, motley depths, trying to figure out what she would wear to dinner. What would Hina Harumi wear? Or Stargirl? Or Katja, the Last Dryad? Then she thought, of *course*, she should go as Leia. Leia from Cloud City. Leia at an uncomfortable family dinner with Dear Old Darth Dad.

"It's fine," Gordo answered.

"It's not *fine*," she said, pulling out pieces of her Leia getup. "Dustin is a real oddball. Probably sits in the dark. Surrounded by taxidermied squirrels. Eating weird, stinky tropical fruits and hard-boiled eggs and plotting *sinister plots.*"

"You got an active imagination. He's your brother. It's *fine.*"

"Unc, I have to sleep in this creepy house. They prepare *dead bodies* here! There might be dead bodies in here *right now.*" She wasn't really creeped out by that, though. She kinda wanted to see it, actually.

"I don't think they got any dead people in there, Moll. Like I said, doesn't look like they do much business."

"How long do I have to stay here?"

"Until something happens."

"Aaaaaand how long will that be?"

He sighed. "I dunno. Dustin will have to go over their books. He'll have to figure out how to pay you. He'll call a bank. He'll call his lawyer. Maybe he takes out a loan. He'll relent. You'll sniff out some *secrets.* It'll be great."

"And then what?"

"And then you go about your life. You said you wanted to go to that fancy art school with the...the dress-up program?"

"Costuming."

"Whatever. So you go to that fancy art school. Or you travel. Or you buy a cat. You seem like a cat person."

"I'm not a cat person. They have parasites." That, too, was a lie. Molly liked cats fine. It just felt good being…whatever the word was that her teachers used to use…*contrary.* Like she didn't have to agree all the time or do what other people said.

Exasperated, Gordo said, "Fine, *no cats.* I gotta go."

"You'll call me if you find anything out?"

"I'll call you if I find *any*thing out. Same if you find something."

She hesitated. "Okay. Fine."

"Snoop around."

"I know."

"Do your nosy thing."

"I know."

"You know, you know. Yeah, you know. Okay. Goodbye."

Molly hung up and stared at her phone, trying to figure out why she suddenly felt so tired. "Ugh, get it together, Molly. In a few hours, we're going to dinner with Darth Dustin."

And with that, she began assembling her outfit.

Again, the same table from this morning, where she sprang her trap on him. Dustin sat there, perfectly still, in a crisply pressed, flower-print shirt with a collar so sharp

Molly thought it might cut his throat. He said nothing when she sat down to join him. But it was as if sitting were the on-switch to a peculiar mechanism: When her bottom touched the chair, Dustin began moving mechanically—lifting his napkin, unfolding it, placing it in his lap. Then he picked up his fork and examined it the way an alien might regard a piece of primitive human technology.

In front of the siblings were plates of food, if it could be called that—this was food for rabbits and caterpillars. Greens, mostly, with a few slices of cucumber and some cherry tomatoes the shape of round, fat thumb tips. There was something else Molly couldn't identify, too—strips of some raw pale-green veggie that gave off the faintest scent of licorice when she poked it. She made a face.

"It's fennel," Dustin said, eating diligently and delicately.

"*You're* fennel," she said, a sudden, childish outburst that didn't even make sense but felt good regardless. With some regret, she realized she should've gone with *Your FACE is fennel*, or perhaps for maximum rudeness, *Your BUTT is fennel*.

To this, he said nothing but continued to eat with little, purposeful bites. As if each bite were a mission he must not fail. Molly detected some anger there, too. The tightness in his jaw gave it away.

"Why are you dressed like that?" he asked suddenly.

"I'm Leia."

He hesitated. "I thought you were Molly."

"No. Leia. Like, *Princess* Leia. This is her Bespin Cloud City dress."

"Bespin Cloud what? I don't follow." His chin lifted with additional suspicion.

"Prin-cess Lei-a. That doesn't ring a bell?" The impossibility struck her: "Oh, dude, you've never seen *Star Wars*, have you?"

He didn't answer. He looked into the depths of his salad.

"Of *course* you haven't," she said.

"I'm a busy person."

"Nobody is so busy they haven't seen the *cultural touchstone* that is *Star Wars*. That's like saying, 'Oh, I don't know what a frog is,' or, 'Why no, I've never eaten a hamburger.'"

He flinched and made a small, throat-clearing sound.

She sighed. "You've never eaten a hamburger."

"I'm a vegetarian."

"Whiiiiiich explains this bird's nest we're eating."

"It's not a bird's nest," he said sharply. "It's quality, healthy food the likes of which I suspect you are not used to eating. Let me guess, your preferred meal is… instant ramen? Mac and cheese? Chicken nuggies?"

That last one he said with a truly snooty tone, nasally and weaselly in equal measure.

"You're a very judgmental person," she snapped.

"Says the pushy little creature who acts like I'm some…some kind of *pariah* for not having seen your *space wizards* movie."

"Pushy little—what? Did you just call me a *creature*? I'm a person. A human being. Ever heard of those, robot? Or were you not programmed with that knowledge, either?"

He stood up suddenly, the fork clattering against the plate. "I am *not* a robot. It takes a certain kind of mind to handle the pressure and the responsibilities around this place. The kind of responsibilities with which you've never had to reckon."

Now *she* stood up, too. "Oh, I've reckoned with a lot, *bro*. I didn't just have a whole house and business handed to me on a silver spoon."

"Silver *platter*."

"What? Whatever, shut up. I've got more responsibility in my left pinkie than you do in your whole bony body, and—"

Just then, she heard a thump upstairs. Dustin heard it, too. He looked suddenly panicked, and in her head, Molly did some quick calculations—only to realize that directly above them on the second floor was the room in which she was staying.

Oh, you conniving little weasel, she thought, and then took off for the stairs.

She bolted up them and slid into the sharp turn to her room, catching herself on the doorframe to see the woman, Vivacia, with Molly's trunk overturned, its contents emptied on the bed.

"My stuff!" Molly cried. She darted in and began gathering bundles of colorful clothing into her arms. "You can't *do* this."

"I can and I am," the woman said, her voice thrust through with a vein of cold iron. "You are in his house, and in our business. It's only fair that we should see who you are and what you've brought into this place." She held up a massive pile of iridescent fur. "What is this?"

Molly snatched the fur away from her. "It's a costume. Chi-ku, from Peculiar Arena Ultra? The card game?" Molly *ugh*ed. "It's a possum-unicorn creature and—it's a work in progress, okay? Put that down! Put all of it down!"

Vivacia suddenly held a pistol—a Han Solo DL-44 replica blaster—in her hand the way one might hold a pair of mystery underwear. She frowned and tossed it aside, then drew out a Captain Marvel T-shirt, then an Aerith-from-*Final-Fantasy* wig, and finally, a pair of shoulder pads from which emerged something that looked half like knives, half like feathers. *"Careful,"* Molly said angrily. "Those are part of my Hina Harumi getup. Hello? From *Zero Flower,* the anime?"

"What's all this?"

That question came from the doorway. It was Dustin. He peered in, confused.

"You," Molly seethed. "You planned this. Distracted me with dinner while she was up here rifling through my things!"

"I didn't. I swear. I didn't know. Viv, tell her—"

But the woman said nothing. She reached again into Molly's trunk but stopped short when Molly hissed at her like a feral possum.

(Maybe she was a possum, after all.)

"Put down the cosplay, lady."

"Cosplay," Dustin repeated, like it was a foreign word.

"Yeah, you know? Cosplay?"

Vivacia sneered. "A child's hobby. Dress-up, except instead of Disney princesses it's...all *this.* Pop-culture mess."

"Viv," Dustin cautioned quietly.

"It's not a mess!" Molly shouted. "And it's not for children. It's a whole *thing.* Comic-Con and TV competitions and there's a community—you can be anybody you want and—" And she felt all the more frustrated even trying to talk about it, like it was making her sound *more* childish, not *less*. "Ugh! Never mind. Just back away from the trunk, lady. It's mine. It's not yours."

The next words Vivacia did not say so much as she *spat*: "Funny, that. Because all this is *ours*. And not *yours*. And yet here you are, greedily grabbing at what belongs to someone else. Do you see how it feels now?"

"Viv," Dustin said again, louder this time.

The tall woman shot him a look but kept going. "You're a thieving magpie, just like your *father*, and we don't like you poking your beak—"

Dustin said it a third time, more urgent: "*Viv.*"

At that, the woman made an exasperated sound and pushed past him out of the room. It was like watching a storm shoulder its way back to the sea.

"I'm sorry about that," he said after a few moments. "Viv can be…severe."

"Get out," Molly said.

"What?"

"I said, *get out*." When he remained, she said even louder: "Get out! Or I'll call the police. Do you want that? I can tell them whatever I want. I'll tell them Viv hurt me. Or that I heard voices. Maybe you're keeping people here against their will. They'll have to open this whole place up. They'll have to *search* it from top to bottom. Do you want that?"

Panic made moons out of Dustin's eyes. "No. I... I'll leave you alone." Almost robotically, he turned the other way and eased the door shut behind him. Molly, now by herself, began gathering up her clothes—and her costumes, which easily outnumbered articles of actual clothing by a whole lot—and shoving them angrily back into her trunk.

As she did, she promised herself:

You snoop on me, I'll snoop on you twice as hard.

I'll find out what you and that witch are hiding here.

And then half of it will be mine, bro.

5. molly the shadow

AND SO, SHE FORMED A PLAN.

Initially, Molly thought, *Oh, I just have to sneakily sneak around like a little mouse,* but when she tried that over the next couple of days, she found herself thwarted at every turn by Vivacia. The woman appeared in every doorway, every dark corner, every room Molly entered, like a summoned ghost, urging Molly out of rooms, locking doors before she could get to them, standing bodily in her way again and again. Other times she simply followed Molly about, like a creature that only moved when you weren't watching it. The woman trailed her like a shadow.

That's when Molly realized:

I can be a shadow, too.

So on the third day, after several awkward plant-meals with Dustin and very little sleep in her dizzifying room, she changed her tactic. Instead of trying to creep around and poke about the house, she ducked Vivacia and found Dustin, becoming *his* shadow, much to his increased agitation. He trembled in her presence like a cold chihuahua.

It probably didn't help that she was kitted in the full, all-black costume of Cav Leer, Ninja Detective (it was super easy to turn a black T-shirt into a ninja *fukumen-zukin*, or hood-and-mask). And wherever Dustin went, Molly went, too, explaining to her older brother that she would be with him for his entire day of work here at the so-called Solemnities Parlor. He told her no, of course, which was the perfect time to threaten him with police intervention again. (Vivacia was not swayed by such casual threats. Dustin, however, was candle wax to that particular flame.)

He seemed spooked by the very idea of her trailing him. Which was, of course, her point. Suddenly he was forcibly animated, like a pizza-arcade animatronic—and he began narrating what he was doing. "And now," he said, unlocking a pair of cherrywood pocket doors with a heavy brass key, "I will…go into the funeral parlor, and…I will…" But here he struggled.

"Have a funeral?" Molly asked.

"No," he said, stepping into the room. It was a simple Victorian parlor, curiously less flashy than the rest of the house. As if death preferred vanilla.

"Will you have a funeral tomorrow?" she asked.

"No."

"Day after?"

"No!"

She took a sniff. The musty air hung still and heavy, greasy with motes of dust. "So, like, what do you do in here?"

"Well, I—I could clean."

"It *is* a bit dusty."

"Yes."

"Like you haven't used it in a while."

"That's—that's not it at all. We use it. It's just old. An old house sheds more dust than newer homes."

"Uh-huh."

He stopped suddenly. "Why are you dressed like that? Like a—what are you?"

"Ninja."

"Why are you dressed like a ninja?"

"Why wouldn't you want to dress like a ninja?"

He sighed in exasperation and waved her off. "Anyway, now," he announced, obviously eager to get out of this conversation, "I will go into the *office* and perhaps do some…paperwork. Good. Excellent." Quickly, he headed toward a wooden door that said OFFICE, unlocked it, and revealed a cramped, one-desk room piled high with papers and folders. It clearly used to be a bathroom—Molly could see an outline against the wall where a sink once stood, the wallpaper around the cutout gone all bubbly and warped.

With no small amount of awkwardness, Dustin adjusted some papers. He opened the desk's middle drawer, removed a pen, and fiddled with it.

"You don't know what you're doing," Molly said suddenly.

"That is quite the accusation. I know everything about what I'm doing."

She tapped a piece of paper atop a teetering tower of other papers. "Without looking, what is this?"

He didn't miss a beat. "It's a funeral-planning form. It goes in a packet with body-release forms, claim forms, short- and long-form death certificate request notices, plus cremation-authorization releases, burial-assistance request forms, and other possible administrative necessities."

"Oh," she said, disappointed.

"Yes. *Oh*."

"And you know how to fill them all out?"

"I do," he said, but only after some hesitation.

"Uh-huh," she said suspiciously.

"I don't *get* to fill these out. I know how—I do! I'm just not allowed to."

"Whyzat?"

"Because I await my funeral director license."

"Don't you need some sort of, like, college for that?"

He sighed. "I graduated high school at fifteen and then did a two-year mortuary science program, all the while completing my necessary apprenticeship under Viv. But there is a final test, and a considerable fee, and I have to receive the licensing board's approval, which couldn't happen until I was eighteen. And now"—he swallowed, visibly—"I am."

"Oookay. So you just have to take a test."

"I don't want to fail."

"So what if you do?"

"I can't disappoint her."

"Viv?"

Dustin didn't say anything, and that's when Molly knew: *He doesn't want to disappoint his mother.* Or *their* mother. Whatever. "Was Mom hard on you?"

"No, not at all. I just…she's gone and I want to do right by her."

"So take the test, pass, and then you get to officially run this place."

"Yes. Yes! I must be fully prepared. Taking over can't be rushed or taken lightly…" he trailed off.

"So you're kinda scared of success the same way you're afraid of failing."

At that, he made a screwed-up face. "Well, that's not true."

Now Molly answered his screwed-up face with one of her own. "Then what's stopping you?" She stopped to think for a second. All she knew about Dustin was that he liked weird food. And Hawaii. "Is it because… if you succeed, then you're trapped here? No Hawaii? No fun?"

Again, he scoffed. "Pish. No! I have a legacy to fulfill. I know who I am and…and what I want." But to her, he didn't sound convincing.

"Mmkay." Molly decided to test the fences in a different direction. "Soooo, mortuary science, huh?"

"Indeed."

"That mean you get to, like, fill dead bodies with preservative goo?"

"It will mean that, yes. When required of me."

"And you do this in a mortuary?"

"Yes," he said, sounding both concerned and irritated by this line of questioning.

"*And* there's a mortuary here? In, like, *this* building?"

"Yes, and I'm not taking you there."

"But you are."

"But I'm not."

"Wanna bet?" Chaos gleamed in her eye.

"I won't accept your threats anymore, Molly."

She shrugged. "Oh. Okay. Seems like I have no power over you anymore. Well, poop. Oh. Hey, by the way, totally unrelated, I bet that board would be reaaaaaal hesitant to give you a fancy license if I told them you were doing all kinds of weird stuff in here. I wouldn't even have to call the police."

Dustin froze. His breathing quickened.

"You wouldn't dare."

"You overshared, bro. There are some things you just shouldn't tell me. If only you'd known." She clapped her hands. "Now! Onward, to the mortuary!"

6. onward, to the mortuary

THE WANNABE FUNERAL DIRECTOR AND THE NINJA GIRL ENTERED A DARK room that buzzed to life at the flip of a switch. Its bright lights painted a white concrete-block room and white tile floor with garish fluorescence. They also lit up a black metal pull-down door at the room's far end, like you'd find at a garage. Next to that, a metal table with a long white fiberglass tray on it—big enough, Molly realized grimly, for a body—and next to that, a boxy machine with a bunch of buttons and dials that looked like it was about forty years old. Like a console on an Imperial Star Destroyer. On the other side of the room were metal racks and shelves, a series of white-fronted drawers, plus a large fridgey-freezery-looking thing. Which, as it turned out, was exactly that.

"That holds the deceased in storage," Dustin said. "Two at a time only, as we are a small operation. Those who have passed on are brought through that garage door—there's a small loading dock on the far side of the house, you see—and then they wait in storage until... well, we do what must be done."

"Where do they get buried? You got a cemetery here?"

He flinched. "No, of course not."

Didn't Gordo say they had a license for burial plots? Hmm. "So they get buried wherever."

"Not *wherever*. There are many fine cemeteries around the county."

"Uh-huh."

Molly wandered across the room, noting that it smelled strongly of antiseptic...but also, musty. She trailed a finger along the fiberglass tray, and the pad of her finger came away with dust. Then she ninja-stalked her way to the strange machine in the corner, and it was only now she saw the rubber tubes coming out of it—and next to it, a glass jar full of something brown, the label long worn off. "Oooh. Is this the...whaddya-callit...*embalming* machine?"

"It is. Don't touch it."

She lifted a hose, and at the end of it was a long, pointed tube with a sharp needled end. "Oh, dude. You stick this in the, ahh, and then you do the, uhh—"

But Dustin was having none of it. He moved fast on the tips of his toes and snatched the hose out of her hand. "I said, *don't touch it.*"

"Relax, bro, I'm not gonna break anything."

"Don't call me *bro*," he said as she ninja-ran past him. "Please."

Already she was whipping open drawers. Inside she found a wicked metal saw and made a face when she realized what it was used to cut. She started to pick it up, but Dustin swept over to her, plucked it from her grip, and eased the drawer shut with his knee.

"I don't think that thing cuts down trees," Molly said in a stage whisper.

"Why are you doing this?"

"Doing what?"

"This. *This.* Coming into my home, my place of work, and, and…causing chaos."

"Chaos? What I want is *order.* I'm on the side of the law here, dude. I tried to get my cut the right way. It's you and Viv who don't wanna play by the rules."

"You don't understand. This place is important. You don't know *how* important. I've worked very hard for all this. You can't just come in here—"

She thrust her chin up, her face right in his, and stared him down as if her eyes were ninja blades, drawn and threatening. "Oh, I see. You think you deserve this. But news flash, *bro*: What you inherited wasn't all yours. It's partly mine. And you think you worked for it? Well, I *suffered* for it! You got to grow up with Pollyanna Ashe, who, like, had a job! She probably even loved you! Meanwhile, I got stuck with Steve-o-roonie. Dad never had a job for more than two weeks. I didn't have a bed most times—I slept on the *couch*. We had cockroaches the size of rats and rats the size of poodles! You know what kinda guy Steve was? He took the first slice of pizza and the last slice of pizza and most of the slices in between. He said he loved me. But he never showed it. If Polly had a good heart, Steve had a rotten one."

At all of that, Dustin seemed to go a bit slack. "I'm sorry."

"You should be. The only nice thing Steve-a-reen-o ever gave me was a surprise inheritance. First time I ever heard about our mom or having a brother was when Gordo showed up three days after Steve died with my emancipation papers. I don't know why Steve never tried to get some cash out of the family business himself. But he didn't and here we are. This place is my ticket to something better."

Dustin looked at her with sad eyes that flashed

intermittently with genuine frustration. "What is this *something better* you want?" he asked, wary.

"Like I told you on day one: costuming school. It costs money." And she thought but did not say, *Also, I don't really know what I'm doing.* There was a lot you could learn on YouTube, and you could get pretty far with junk you bought from pawnshops and consignment, but she needed a teacher. Luke needed Yoda. Rey needed Luke.

"Is that why you…dress up as you do?"

Molly looked down at her ninja costume and, for a moment, felt foolish. But then why should she? This was what she loved. And it was nice to feel like she could be somebody else, a person who mattered, a hero, a villain, a character of consequence. *Anybody else other than yourself,* a little voice told her. *Someone whose parents loved her. A ninja kid with a loving ninja mom and dad.*

"I dress up because I like it. And it lets me practice my skills. It isn't just sewing, you know. It's sculpting foam, cutting PVC pipe, making material from clear resin or whatever. Lotta tools involved. Sergers, 3D printers, even just, like, a screwdriver or soldering iron. It's learning history: how a sword looks, how people used to dress. It's *design,* too—figuring out how this stuff is supposed to look and how it can be made and worn practically."

Confusion flashed across Dustin's face. "Okay. But to what end? What comes after costuming school? What will you do with all this?"

She made a gross face. "I dunno. I mean, there's costuming for movies and TV shows, or I could just, like, start an Etsy store or whatever. But it's not always about what you can *do* with it. It's not always about money. Money is just the means to an end—it's not the reason to do the thing."

"That's how I feel about this place."

"This dusty, musty old place."

"Hrm. Well. Yes." Then, changing the subject: "You know, I suppose I do know a bit about…costuming."

Molly arched a curious eyebrow. "Like what?"

"Those who go to their final rest sometimes require certain kinds of outfits. Certain garb or ceremonial… attire. Makeup, too. Some of our clientele are quite, ah, peculiar."

Her curious eyebrow arched even farther upward, trying very hard to hover above her head. "Peculiar how?"

"I—"

The door to the mortuary swung open, and Vivacia came in like a rolling storm. Her eyes fell to Molly first and she said, "*There* you are—" But then, upon seeing Dustin, her face registered confusion. "Did she break in? Steal your keys?"

"No," he said. "I brought her here."

"*Why?*"

"She was, well, she wanted to see the business and I figured—"

"You figured what?" Vivacia hissed.

He shot a glance at Molly. "Can we not do this? Now? In front of her?"

At that, Vivacia said to Molly (with considerably forced politeness, as if the very effort caused the woman pain): "Would you give us a moment, please?" Then she stepped aside from the door and practically pushed Molly through it.

Molly, cast back into the funeral parlor, found the door slamming in her face. It clicked, suddenly locked. And behind that door, their voices kicked up in a hushed argument—the words were not discernible, but the *topic* was plain:

They were arguing about her.

Which made her angry, but only for a moment.

Because if *they* were in *there*—

And *she* was out *here*—

Then nobody was watching her, nobody at all.

And that meant...

It was time to snoop.

7. the door behind the door

THE HOUSE WAS BIG, BUT ONLY IN THAT OLD VICTORIAN WAY. IN REALITY, most of the rooms were small. And so Molly set herself to racing through the place as fast as she could, now less like she was in a stealth video game trying to sneakily sneak about, but rather, more like she was in one of those video games where you race against the clock or try to dodge your eventual pursuers—less *Assassin's Creed*, more *Five Nights at Freddy's*.

She ran on the fronts of her feet, heading out of the parlor area entirely to start upstairs (better to be as far away from Dustin and Vivacia as possible, because eventually her two adversaries would stop arguing and come find her). There, besides her own room, she found three other guest rooms, each containing the same elements in different arrangements (garish wallpaper, old radiators that looked like wrought-iron accordions, tiny beds, creaky floorboards). She found no televisions, though she did discover an iPad charging station—probably the only piece of present-day technology in the house.

So far the upstairs was supremely boring and was not hinky, wonky, or suspicious in any way that she could swiftly decode. Boring, too, was the bathroom up here: octagonal pink tile on floor and walls, with a bumpy popcorn ceiling. Its only interesting feature was a claw-foot bathtub with claws that were truly beastly, even monstrous. And, curiously, each foot was unique: One looked like the talons of a falcon or an owl, another looked as if it belonged to a wolf, the third as if it were a massive raccoon paw, and the fourth wasn't a clawed foot at all, but rather, something *hooved.*

Just the same, it was only a tub. She'd already taken both a bath and a shower in it. (Admittedly, Dustin had very good taste with the waterfall showerhead, but way too many tropical soaps and shampoos.)

Back out into the hallway Molly went. *They'll come up any second,* she knew. So, what? Go back downstairs? She felt sure she was missing something up here—even after looking underneath the beds and behind the radiators and opening each drawer of every antique dresser. She stared down at her feet, trapped in the paralysis of indecision when—

She noticed something.

Two spots on the carpet here: rumpled, rectangular imprints on the hall runner.

As if something had been placed there. Something heavy.

Idly, she looked up.

There.

A door waited above her head. A trapdoor, if you could call it that—okay, fine, that suggested something *sinister*. A hatch? Was that a better name for it? Whatever. It was pretty obviously how a person would get into the attic. And she didn't have time to climb up there now.

So she went down the stairs, this time trying to be silent in case her footsteps reverberated anywhere else through the house. She darted through the kitchen, nearly pausing to peek into the pantry and fridge (*Am I hungry? I'm hungry*, she thought, but then realized now was not the ideal time to steal a snack), then kept moving toward a door she suspected must lead to the basement. Or was it a cellar? Old houses had cellars, right? She grabbed a tarnished doorknob and pulled—

Only to find a second door inches behind the first.

"Uh…okay then," Molly said, perplexed.

This inset door, newer than the first but still made of old and oiled wood, was locked *three* times. Two of those locks were dead bolts on *this* side of the door, easy to undo, indicative that the door was locking something *in* the basement rather than keeping someone out. The third lock on that door was a padlock, but not a small and modern one. No, this was an old iron padlock, its keyhole cartoonish and comical, with a circle at the top and a skirt-shaped triangle beneath it. Around that keyhole was inscribed, somewhat clumsily, a half moon. And around that half moon were etched outlines—almost like one would draw waves of vibration or sound in a comic-book panel. *A trembling moon,* Molly thought idly. Along the sides and back of the chunky padlock were other symbols: a sun with a beaming face, a circle with a cross in the center, another circle with what looked to be devil horns, a simple five-pointed star. And then right underneath the keyhole was a final symbol:

A comet with a fiery tail.

With a gingerly hand, Molly touched the padlock.

"Whoa!" she whispered.

The metal seemed to gently vibrate, as if with its own energy. Not electricity, exactly, but something *else.*

And then, the half moon, the *trembling* moon, began to glow.

She gasped and pulled her hand away.

The glow ceased.

Her heart rate picked up. What was going on? What was behind this second door? She quickly scolded herself: *It's nothing, Molly, calm down.* She reached out with a tentative hand and again touched the lock—

And again, it hummed and buzzed and the symbol came to life and light, emanating a soft glow. *A moonglow,* she realized. It was almost comforting... until, along the side of the padlock, the other symbols started to glow, too, each a different color, until finally the comet lit up last, and that one with an unearthly *red* glow, the glow of hellfire, the glow of molten lava.

Molly pulled her hand away as if it were hurt. She'd felt something strange—something she could only describe as being in her blood. A song calling to a song, an echo bouncing around a cave and back upon itself.

"Hello," said a voice. Molly wheeled around (in her head, it was *very* ninja-like) and found Vivacia standing there, with Dustin just behind her, almost as if he were trying, but not really committing, to hide. The greeting sounded oddly mechanical and definitely forced.

"Hello," Molly said, slow and wary. Then, without meaning to, she blurted out: "A door behind a door, huh? With a pretty weird lock. Not that I care. Things should be locked. Secret things. Not that the things you're hiding are secret, and not that you're even *hiding* anything, and—" *Stop talking, Molly. Stop your mouth from blabbering.* "Yeah. So…hello."

"Molly," Vivacia said, "I wanted to say—"

But Molly's tongue kept wagging. "What do the symbols on this old padlock mean? Like, the comet, let's say?"

Dustin and Vivacia traded a conspiratorial look.

"The comet is a symbol," Dustin said.

"Yeah, I know, that's why I said, *the symbols—*"

"No, I mean, it's a symbol with meaning, is all. Comets were once associated with death, though later with bad luck—it was believed a comet heralded the Black Death of the Middle Ages. And so comets were then inscribed in places as a symbol of good luck, or a symbol against death and harm, or even a symbol indicating a good death and not, well, a bad one."

"Sure, okay, but, like, why…is it on a padlock locking a door?"

Another conspiratorial look between them.

Vivacia answered with an obviously fake smile: "It's just a decoration. A mood. We want to invoke here a feeling of transition to the heavens, to the stars. That's all it is, Molly."

"Yes," Dustin said, seeming to swallow a hard knot. "That's all."

Except it was a lie, Molly knew. It had to be. If they cared about that sort of thing, this whole *place* would be decked out in suns, moons, planets, comets. But it wasn't. It was just this little lock that buzzed in her grip and glowed a little when she touched it. She thought to ask about that, too, but feared she'd sound out of her gourd.

"Okay," she answered.

Viv pulled her gently away from the cellar door, talking as she did. "Molly, I wanted to say *sorry* if I came on a little *strong* earlier. I am glad to see your taking an interest in Dustin, our house, and *the business*, and hopefully it will give you a clear perspective on how—"

Here, Molly repeated the next words in concert with Vivacia:

"*Important* it is," they said in unison.

Dustin smiled stiffly. "As Viv said, we apologize."

"Okay," Molly said. *You are both acting very strange*, she thought.

"Okay," Dustin said.

"Okay," Vivacia said.

"Oookay."

8. the lady's bribe

OF COURSE, ONCE CAUGHT, MOLLY WAS USHERED BACK TO HER ROOM. A bit too forcefully, she felt. They're hiding *something*, she knew. She felt it for sure. Weird doors. Strange business. They were acting all uptight and nervous.

That night, Molly paced her room, back and forth, back and forth, confusion and anger and the sheer *mystery of it all* biting at her heels like a frothing terrier. She'd known this house would be a weird place—it was part *mortuary* after all—but buzzy, glowy locks? Two people who hated her now acting like friendly robots?

Her phone vibrated with an incoming text: *vbbt.*

It was from Uncle Gordo.

FOUND ANYTHING?

(Of *course* he texted in all caps.)
She texted back:

> found some doors and
> a creepy padlock

BREAK INTO EM

> dude i'm not a thief

> did **you** find anything

GIMME A FEW DAYS

And that was the end of their conversation.

The next few days passed with little fanfare—*and* little opportunity for her to do much searching. She tried to sneak off to the big black barn out back (which now she noted had an odd steeple jutting up from the far side of it, as if it were once some kind of curious farm church), but either Dustin or Vivacia were on her like owls tracking mice. They *had* grown friendlier to her, which felt less like a nice thing and more like a trap—a show they were putting on to not spook her, and maybe even to stop her from snooping around any more than she already had.

Ugh, how was any of this trying-to-snoop even *helping*? These people didn't want her there, and even if she'd maybe kinda sorta hoped that Dustin would think it was cool to have a long-lost little sister, he'd made it pretty clear that wasn't the case.

Feeling useless and frustrated, not to mention bored and annoyed, she excused herself from a dinner of mushrooms. (She knew there was more on the plate than just that, but mushrooms, Molly knew, had the texture of human ears and, no, she would not be eating *those*, thank you very much.) She instead snuck a bag of dehydrated pineapple slices from the pantry, chomping on them as she went upstairs to her room, unsure what she should do. Sneak out when it was dark? Lately, whenever Molly had tried to creep down at night, Vivacia was there, a secret sentinel, casually awake and reading a book.

This time, as she entered her bedroom, she once more found the older woman.

Vivacia sat on a high-backed chair in the corner, which definitely hadn't been there before. How long had the woman been here?

"Have a nice dinner?" the woman asked, glancing at the bag of pineapple slices.

"Mushrooms" was all Molly said.

"I don't like them, either."

At least we have something in common.

"So," Vivacia continued, "you've been here, what, a week now? Have you found anything interesting?"

"Why? Is there something to find?"

Vivacia stiffened. "Of course not. But the property is pretty. It's an old house. It's an odd business. Certainly one can find interesting things. For example, I found an arrowhead the other day."

"Coooool," Molly said in a way that indicated she, in fact, found it boring. (Even though an arrowhead *was* cool, she just couldn't give this lady the satisfaction.)

"Yes, very cool."

"*Super* cool."

The woman cleared her throat. "We've gotten off on the wrong foot."

This again.

"Have we? Because I feel like it was the foot you wanted." Molly wrinkled her nose because that didn't sound right. "I just mean, I think you knew what you were doing. You didn't want me around. *Don't* want me around, even though now you're pretending like you do."

"It's not that we don't want you here. It's that the grieving process for the bereaved is—"

"I get it. It's, like, *really* serious. But I think it's more than that. I think you're hiding something. Probably some kinda scam. Maybe a weird cult." Molly paused, and she just couldn't help herself when she said: "Maybe something out in the barn or the woods."

At that, Vivacia lost her cool. Her calm veneer cracked and for a split second, she looked genuinely rattled. *Gotcha*, Molly thought.

The woman quickly regained her composure, then eased her ankles apart and pulled out from underneath the chair on which she sat a black leather bag—like an old-timey doctor's bag.

"Here," Vivacia said.

"A bag?"

"More about what's in it."

Hesitantly, Molly inched closer. When she grabbed the bag, she did so quickly, as if the woman might suddenly attack—she half-imagined Vivacia coming at her with a syringe or a pair of scissors. Or maybe a bag to throw her in, then toss her into a furnace downstairs like a proper witch would do.

Molly pitched the bag atop the bed and, keeping one wary eye on Vivacia, popped the snap-latch at the top.

Inside was money.

Lots of money.

"It's two thousand dollars," Vivacia said. "And you'll get more. A thousand a month for as long as I can spare it. That's twelve thousand a year—well, thirteen thousand this first go. Quite a lot of money for a girl your age."

"It won't buy what I want."

Vivacia raised an eyebrow high enough that it could've been a hat. "Art school."

"Art school for costuming. Room and board is thirty grand a year. More than double what you're offering."

"Ah."

"Yeah."

"This is more than you had before. It'll get you some of the way."

"Some of the way isn't all the way."

"I'll…see what I can do. Would that be enough?"

"Enough to what? Send me on my way?"

"Yes, precisely."

"Didn't you just tell me 'it's not that we don't want you here'?"

While Vivacia sputtered, Molly thought about the offer. This money *was* more than she had. More money than she ever imagined having, to be honest. Maybe she could apply to the school and qualify for aid and this *would* be enough. But a darker part of her thought, would she even get *into* art school? Maybe fighting for her inheritance was a waste. She could make a go of it on her own, no mortuary, no costume school. Start over. Thirteen grand a year would buy a lot of supplies. Of course, she didn't have a place to live....

And then, there was the other thing: that stubbornness all up inside her. Like a second spine made of steel rebar instead of bone. Why should Dustin have all this? Their mother discarded her but kept him. Molly was *owed*. And if Vivacia was trying to buy her off, it meant Molly and Uncle Gordo really *had* struck a vein of precious material, right? Vivacia and Dustin were hiding something. *Protecting* something.

"I'll think about it."

"You'll think about it," Vivacia repeated, wryly.

"That's right."

Vivacia reached for the bag. "You don't get to keep this until you make up your mind. It's yours then, and not before."

Pouting, Molly relinquished her grip. "Ugh, fine."

With that, Vivacia stood, said her good night, and left the room. Molly plopped down onto the bed. Her mind raced between the pole positions of *instant money* versus *what I'm owed*. Back and forth, back and forth. So she got up to fritter about with her clothing and cosplay, mixing and matching outfits, pondering a gender-bent Han Solo, or how to figure out the Dark Mode unlock-edition outfit from the Hina Harumi video game import: *Zero Flower: Sun Petal Samurai.*

But it wasn't like she had tons of costume ingredients on hand, no puffy paint or glue guns or foam, and it wasn't like she could go to a thrift store (oh, the costume ingredients you could find at thrift stores!), *and* her portable sewing machine was in the storage unit (that Uncle Gordo had begrudgingly paid for), anyway.

Once more, the thought of money crept into her mind, tantalizing her. Costuming wasn't cheap. *I could take that money. I could do cosplay design and sales on my own. Start an Etsy store. Forget school. Just go and live my life....*

But she hated giving up. And Hina Harumi sure wouldn't give up. Harumi battled the *literal stars* (made manifest and possessed by demons, of course) to find her best friend Jura and rescue him from the void.

Eventually the sun went down. Sighing, and finding little joy in tonight's cosplay ruminations, Molly flopped back onto the bed, turned off the lamp on the bedside table, and buried her head under a pillow, as if that would somehow smother all the thinky-thoughts, as if those thoughts were external and not inside her own skull.

She flung the pillow across the room.

She waited in the dark for her brain to quiet.

And that's when the wall whispered something to her.

9. what the wall said

LOOK IN THE WOODS.

Molly bolted upright and spider-scrambled her way to the foot of the bed. The whisper had come from behind her, somewhere above or near the headboard. She squinted against the darkness of the room, trying to see something, *anything.* There. Did something move? She was sure that it had. The sense of a shadow climbing up the wall...

"Who's there?" she hissed. "Is someone there?"

She waited a moment, then thought, *This is banana-pants, nobody is there, you're hearing stuff.* Still, she kept listening. Looking.

Nothing.

Maybe it was Vivacia. That would be a thing she'd do, wouldn't it? Try to scare Molly away? Make her think this old house was chockablock with ghosts? But why would Vivacia tell her to look in the woods? Unless the woods was a trap.

Maybe she's gonna try to kill me. That was a dark thought. But if Vivacia was afraid Molly wouldn't take the money, maybe the woman would try to get rid of her in a more *dramatic* fashion.

Her pulse racing, Molly fumbled for her phone and texted Uncle Gordo:

> **maybe we should look
> at the woods**

She waited for a response. None came.

Eventually, after a long time of sitting in the dark and waiting for something else to happen, she hid under the covers and fought her way to sleep.

Morning came, and her phone buzzed.

After taking a quick look under her bed and glaring at the walls around her, Molly opened an all-caps text from her uncle—

PLAT MAP

Well, that sounded like pure nonsense. So Molly typed back two nonsense words of her own:

whale thermos

WHAT DOES THAT MEAN

donkey feathers

STOP TALKING NONSENSE

onion grass

But she quickly followed that up with:

wait no that's an actual thing nm

A PLAT MAP IS A REAL THING
IT'S A PEOPERTY MAP
PROPERTY NAP
PROPERTY MAP!!!1!

Okay, settle down, dude, jeez.
Three dots in a bubble popped up as he typed something else.

Except, it wasn't something he was typing; it was something he was *sending*. An image, as it turned out—a scan of some kind of document. Handwritten and old, almost like a blueprint.

Ohhh, she realized. It was a map of *this* property—the one on which the Ashe & Grim Solemnities business sat. The map showed the house structure and also the barn out back. The lines of the property were kind of a...rhombus. Was that right? A rhombus? Maybe not. A rhombus had equal sides, but this wasn't that—it was an erratic, odd-angled shape, like a rhombus that had been stepped on. Weirder still was a small bit at the north end of the property, well past the house and the barn. It was like someone had taken scissors and cut out an erratic chunk. A specific niche of acreage snipped out.

> **what's with this funky bit
> at the top of the map**

She waited. No response. No response. And then—
The phone rang. Gordo.
As soon as she answered it, he started talking:
"—figured it was easier to just call you. I hate texting. I got thick thumbs. Anyway. That part at the top, the cutout? Initially, it looked like Dustin—and your parents before him—didn't own that bit. But I couldn't find who the owner was. No records at the county courthouse. I

was able to figure out a parcel number, though—that's the number an individual plot of land gets, and if you want to subdivide it, you need a new parcel number—"

"I'm bored now," Molly said, keeping her voice low in case anyone was listening.

"Kids today, I swear, you got the attention spans of punch-drunk fruit flies. I'm trying to say I figured out the parcel number of that *funky bit* and was able to track it to a land conservancy—"

"I don't know what that is, either, but I'm close to plunging into a *boredom coma.*"

Gordo grunted. "Bear with me, okay? A *land conservancy* is a nonprofit group that buys up land and, I dunno, protects it or something. Usually from development. Rural purity and all that hot garbage."

"So the weird section is owned by some land-conservation group, whoop-de-doo."

"Not just some group—the POCLC. The Pact of Consanguinity Land Conservancy."

"Fancy name." Molly reminded herself to look that up: *consanguinity.* Cool word. Wasn't *sanguine*, like, a blood thing?

"Fancy name for a lotta *nothing.* I researched their conservancy—I thought, maybe they're a 401(c) nonprofit. Except they conserve only *one* parcel of land. The one at the north end of this map."

"Okayyyyy."

"And guess who sits on the board."

Molly flinched. "Vivacia Sims." Her eyes flitted toward the door, as if speaking her name were enough to summon her. Like the devil.

There came a pause before Gordo snorted. "Oh, you figured it out."

"Well, I mean, I knew it wasn't Dustin. And when you were all, like, *dun-dun-dun, guess who, blah blah blah*, I pretty much figured you weren't going to be, like, *Beyonce! Whoa!* And since that tall Valkyrie lady was just going through my stuff and I'm mad at her, well—her name came out of my mouth. So it's her, huh."

"It's her."

"She offered me money, you know. To go away."

He cleared his throat. "How much?"

"Two grand plus a thousand a month after that."

"She's got that much to spare, they gotta be sitting on a gold mine. People hide three things: affairs, dead bodies, and money."

"I'm hoping it's just money," Molly said. *But I guess they have dead bodies, too.* "So what does all this mean, exactly?"

"I don't know what it means. But you can find out."

She guessed. "You want me to go there. To the place. With the thing."

"Yes. Looks to me like this parcel of land coincides with the tree line—you told me we should check out the woods? Well, this is it. The woods."

Look in the woods, the wall had said....

"How far away from the house is it?" she asked, deciding she really didn't want to go near the spooky woods. "Looks like a long walk."

"It's not even a mile. You're young. You'll be fine."

Molly hesitated. A week's worth of guilt and exhaustion hit her.

She sighed. "Like, okay, Uncle Gordo, what if we *don't* do this? What if we just see what we can wrangle out of them and go on our merry way? I don't want to stay here anymore. It's creepy. And I'm starting to feel bad—I don't think their business is healthy. They're not *doing* anything. And the house itself can't be worth much. Dustin doesn't even seem to care about the money, he just cares about... making his mother's ghost proud of him or something."

Gordo paused. "You're right. The property ain't worth much. The land might be useful to farmers, and maybe we could squeeze a little coin out, but Dusty and Viv are gonna fight selling it. And that means we end up cutting some kind of deal where they portion out the money in drips and drops. And a judge will say you're not even eighteen yet and might suggest putting the money in a private trust until you're an adult, and—"

"Whoa, what?" Molly asked, taken aback. "You just called this place a gold mine. You said this was all shut-and-dry."

"*Cut*-and-dry. You mean, cut-and-dry. Or open-and-shut."

"Gah. Whatever! You said it was fine!"

"And it is. Or will be. If we can find something they've been hiding, something that gives us a little leverage…that's juicy. We can dangle that in front of them. In front of a judge. We need a *dangler*."

"A dangler."

"A dangler, yeah."

"That sounds like a dingleberry."

"I like how you always remind me I'm talking to a *child*."

"You're a jerk, just like Dad."

"Oh ho ho, your dad was King Jerk. Don't you dare even compare me to him."

She rolled her eyes. "Fine. I'll go into the woods."

"I'd go before dark."

"Why?"

"Well. Dark forest and all that."

"What, am I going to get eaten by something?"

He chuckled a little. "You never know, little girl. You never know."

10. ninja smoke bomb

AND NOW CAME A NEW PROBLEM: HOW, EXACTLY, TO SNEAK OUT OF THE house?

Initially Molly thought, *Gordo.* Just have him show up with some fake documents that needed to be looked at and signed, and that would distract Dustin and Vivacia enough that she could slip out of the house like a mouse under the door. Problem was, despite trying to get him to stay when she first arrived, Molly didn't really *want* Gordo here now. Honestly, she'd always found him sorta...off-putting. After three months of meeting with her uncle and tolerating his heavy cologne, the swish-swish of his corduroy pants, the rough and unpredictable throat-clearings, well, she was pretty much over it, though grudgingly grateful he had kept her out of foster care. More important, though? She wanted to do this on her own.

All day she kept going round and round in her head about strange locks on strange doors, about whispers in walls and that tantalizing bag of money. It was that thought, in fact, she kept coming back to:

Vivacia's offer.

Did Dustin know she'd made it?

Molly bet he didn't. Vivacia was running this show. Which Dustin clearly *needed* her to do—but also, it seemed to chafe him a little, didn't it? That was a tiny fracture in their relationship. And even the smallest crack was a vulnerability—like how a huge stone wall could be pulled apart by the shoots and runners of unruly, reaching plants.

So the plan was to capitalize on any conflict between them (even if she did feel a smidge bad about it).

Molly waited until dinnertime. It was just her and Dustin again. She wore another pared-down Hina Harumi getup: this time, her Crimson Diplomat outfit from Series 4 of the manga. When Molly had first read the book, she'd found it a little boring—but now she kinda dug it? It was less about fighting and more about negotiating peace treaties between the Seedcap Nation and the Thorn Broker Bank while also trying to drive a wedge between Prince Aven Kitsune and the Thornwitch, who were totally in love. (When Hina finally drove them apart and the Thornwitch confronted her, Hina said, in translation: "Now you are reminded that my power is not contained to the blade." Ironically, then they fought. With blades.)

Dustin, for his part, wore a pastel-blue Aloha shirt. And dinner was yet again a complex salad—bits of apple and mango, poppy seed passion fruit dressing, and something called "frisée," which looked a bit like a scribble, like something you'd see over the head of an angry cartoon plant. Molly took small bites of it and found...

...that it wasn't bad? She wouldn't say that out loud, of course. No need to give Dustin any satisfaction. Instead, she poked at him a bit:

"Why are you wearing that?" she asked.

"What?"

"That outfit. It's what you always ask me, so I figured I'd turn the tables."

He seemed taken aback. But not in an offended way—rather, in a thoughtful one. "I suppose..." he started, then stopped. "I suppose it's aspirational."

"Aspirational how?"

"I just…sometimes want to…"

"Be somewhere different? Be some*one* different?"

He leaned back, rigid as a broomstick. "This line of questioning again, is it?"

"That's not an answer."

He stabbed at a rectangle of mango (a mango-tangle, Molly decided) and it slid off his fork. He stabbed harder at it and it slid off his fork *again*. He sighed sharply and, instead, just *sat* there.

"It's cool, bro. Don't tell me if you don't want to," Molly said, deftly sliding her fork *underneath* a piece of mango with unpracticed gentleness. She popped it into her mouth, defiant and more than a little cocky. Time to poke harder at Dustin's edges—in particular, the edges of his relationship with Vivacia. "By the way, tell 'Viv' I'm not taking her deal."

He narrowed his gaze and leaned forward. "Taking what deal?"

Gotcha.

"Oh. She…didn't tell you?"

He pursed his lips. "Tell me what?"

"About the money." The look on his face was written large, like the advertisement on a billboard: He didn't know squat about any of this. *Time to press my advantage,* she thought, just as Hina would. "Last night, Viv offered me a bag of money and said I could get one of those bags every month. All for the low, low price of me leaving you two alone. I assumed you had to be on board with it—"

He stood up suddenly, the chair complaining against the wooden floor.

"I have to go speak with Viv," he said curtly.

And then he whisked himself out of the room.

The woman was still here, Molly knew—Vivacia would be waiting nearby, as spiders often did when hungry for prey. Except now, Molly liked to imagine herself as the spider. One that hunts other spiders.

Moments later, she heard the muffled sound of arguing—it wasn't far away. Sounded like Vivacia was in the sitting room. As before, their voices were restrained, like they were trying to keep it quiet. Only one sentence broke through with some clarity:

"But she's my sister."

It sounded, what, almost protective? It couldn't be. Dustin hated her, and she hated him. *Or so you tell yourself,* said that annoying little voice in her brain. No, she must be misreading his tone, she decided.

It almost made her feel bad about what had to happen next.

Right outside the room, she had stored a secret something:

A sword.

The weapon was Hina Harumi's demon-haunted hell-blade, Astrogoth. The short sword had a black blade etched with molten runes, and a hilt sculpted with swirls of red and black. Okay, fine, it wasn't *real*, not in the sense that it was a functional weapon. Molly didn't have any actual weapons. But this was one she'd made for her variety of *Zero Flower* costumes—it was a combination of open- and closed-cell foam, with a core of kitespar. Not a bad boffer weapon. Light, but it worked. Not that she was into the fake combat stuff, but it had some heft.

It looked hella cool, anyway.

She figured, if she was going to go traipsing into some woods a few hours before dark, it made sense to have something she could *pretend* was a weapon. And if she hit hard enough, it would at least give any attacker a good swat.

So, demon-haunted foam weapon in hand, and with Dustin and Viv still arguing two rooms away, Molly set out.

Outside, the afternoon had already stretched out like a languid cat on a windowsill, its paws nearly touching evening. Molly twirled her foam blade—a move she'd practiced many a time, hoping one day to demonstrate it at a proper comic convention, where everyone around her would *ooh* and *ahh* and give her that cool nod like, *you're one of us.*

On light and quick feet she headed behind the house, toward the black barn with the strange steeple. As she passed it, she saw that the broad doors were chained shut—again with a padlock and another celestial symbol. This time, a seven-pointed star—the top point of which curved in on itself like a sickle blade. This only confirmed for her a suspicion she hadn't put proper words to yet: This was weird, and it seemed very possible, even likely, that Dustin and Vivacia were running some sort of kooky cult.

It was the only thing she could think of. Freaky weirdos with a forbidden barn and a door whose locks were marked with strange symbols? Freaky occult-looking symbols? Had to be a cult. *Had to be.*

That thought confirmed for her that what she was doing was right. It obliterated any guilt she felt. Dustin and Vivacia weren't running a business but serving as judgy-pants cult leaders who were probably waiting for some UFO to take them away from this world—and they'd convinced an eager bunch of acolytes of that very lie and were milking them for cash.

Sweet, sweet cash.

Molly wanted some of that cash.

Half of it, to be specific.

Because she *deserved* it.

And now, as she poked at the barn padlock with her sword before going on her way, she decided she knew exactly what she would find in the woods: the cult's true church. Or temple or sacrificial grounds or monkey shrine or whatever and wherever it was that they did all their *culty stuff.* A stone circle or a weird boulder altar or maybe a giant wicker goat or something. Freaks.

She spied then a pair of black cats poking their noses around the corner of the dark barn, their raised tails above their heads forming question marks. The two cats quickly disappeared when spotted. Molly thought nothing of it and kept going.

She walked through the meadow grass. Wildflowers swayed in the breeze. Bumblebees bumbled. Shimmering clouds of gnats guided her way—appearing before her and dispersing as she walked closer, only to re-form again ten feet ahead.

Up one hill, and down another.

Ahead, the forest loomed.

It was a pocket of trees—a copse, wasn't that the word? Back in sixth grade, when she was trying to be fancy and use big words, she'd described a group of trees as a *corpse,* and her teacher, Miss Margill, had said, "No, dear, it's a *copse,* c-o-p-s-e." But Molly wasn't having any of it and swore up and down for days that it was *corpse*, like the dead body.

(Molly could be quite stubborn. Especially when she was wrong. She knew this. And yet. *And yet*.)

This copse (c-o-p-s-e) of trees looked almost as if some divine being had taken a giant mower and cut down the trees around it, leaving only field and meadow on either side. The trees here (all deciduous, none evergreen) were tall and healthy, growing up and out, giving the small pocket of forest the look of a curious bouquet. The copse couldn't have constituted much more than an acre or two. Wouldn't take her long to walk through, she guessed.

Whatever was in there, she'd find it fast.

Molly put a bit of spring in her step. She felt newly excited, as if she'd discover something in the trees that would put this problem of hers to rest. All she had to do was find the cult's strange *cult playground* and she could be all like, "Okay, *bro*, you either gimme my sweet, sweet cash or I'll tell the world about your creepy UFO goat cult! I'll call the police! The newspapers! I'll slather it all over Instagram, sucka!" (Not that she talked like that. But she kinda wanted to when the time was right. Better to practice now.)

As she got closer, though, the trees almost seemed to grow taller. And their shadows—stretching out toward her—seemed to get *longer*. As she drew near, Molly expected the woods to look like something out of a fairy tale, a series of big, pretty trees between which she could hop and skip. But it was a snarl. A thorn-tangle! Through the toothy undergrowth, she caught glimpses of fallen trees and turtle-backed boulders. Spears of sunlight pierced the canopy, pinning down patches of forest floor. She peered deeper, hoping to see... well, what she hoped to see she didn't quite know. But as she looked, the whole thing seemed to swim and distort in her vision. Her gaze swept suddenly to the left, as if her eyes were on a carousel, but the rest of her was not.

Dizziness swarmed her and she staggered back from the forest's edge.

"Well," she said to no one. She blinked a few times. The spinning had stopped. "That's that. I didn't see anything. I'll go... I'll go tell Gordo."

No one, and nothing, answered. It did not confirm her plan or deny it.

She told herself to turn around. To go back to the house. Molly *willed* herself to do that—mentally, she sent the command down to her legs: *Get working, slackers. Pick one foot up! Then the next! Move, move, move.*

And yet—

She didn't budge.

Instead, she stayed where she stood, staring into the woods.

The sun seemed to sink beyond the forest. A wind whistled between the trees. On it, a faint sound, like a wind chime.

No, she realized.

Like the jingling of keys.

A smell came with it. A verdant, heady scent—like fresh, wet moss crunched in your hand. Then a second smell intruded, twining with the first: the pickled sour smell of something dead.

(c-o-r-p-s-e)

And finally, her name came whispered to her on the wind.

"Molly…"

"Hello?" she said. Her voice was smaller than she meant it to be. She'd tried very hard to be brave and bold—but the sound that had come out of her was little more than a squirrel fart. And again, her name returned to her—

"Moooooolllllllyyyyyy…"

Gingerly, she took a step closer.

And another.

And another.

She found her hand drifting toward the forest, toward the tangle of briar that prevented her from entering—

And as she gently, barely touched a coil of thorny brush—

It crackled, as if she'd startled it. And then like a retreating snake, loops of bramble and rose thorn began to untangle themselves, retracting into the darkness.

With that, a path opened before her.

Did that…just happen? she asked herself.

It seemed that it had. That or she had hallucinated it.

You could go back.

Take the money.

Forget this place.

But something urged her forward. A desire to know, perhaps. Or maybe, just maybe, something deeper in her. A song in her blood that demanded to be heard.

With that, Molly took a deep breath, held her demon-haunted boffer blade in front of her, and stepped into the dark woods.

11. the path, the door, and the fivefold lock

WANDERING THROUGH THE FOREST FELT LIKE A DREAM TO MOLLY.

She did not recognize it.

And yet the forest seemed certain that it would be recognized. The way you remembered snippets of a dream the day after you wake from it.

You've been here before, it seemed to say, to *demand*, even though she was sure she hadn't.

The thick, overgrown understory of the forest seemed to move out of her way as she walked forward. The path opened or, perhaps, had always *been* open, and only she could see it. Or remember it.

All the while, the forest continued to whisper her name. Not, Molly realized, in her ears—but in her *head.*

Around her, oak trees loomed tall but not straight. Many seemed to gently bend toward one another—branches plaiting together, their green leaves dappled with the fading light of day.

Birds jostled between their branches. Red birds on one side. Blue birds on the other. Little chips and chirps coming from both.

Molly crept through the woods. The sun began to drift, going from bright white to pale gold as it sank ever downward.

She knew the forest should be at its end by now. The grove of trees was not eternal—it shouldn't have taken more than a few minutes to get out the other side. But onward it went. And time seemed muddy. She couldn't tell how long it had been since she'd entered. Was it only five minutes? Ten? An hour?

Molly fumbled with her phone to check the time.

The battery was dead.

"Not now, phone," she cursed. Was it all that texting with Gordo? Her iPhone *was* an older model. And junky. *Dangit.*

And then, when she looked up again—

A wall loomed suddenly ahead of her. A considerable

wall, at that. Easily three times her height, it was con-
structed of old, dark, uneven stones slick with moss
and wedged in against one another.

It hadn't been there before.

Molly was *sure* of it. She'd stopped to look at her
phone, and there had been no wall. When she looked up?

Wall.

Big wall.

A wall that went left and right, west and east, into
the trees. A wall with no end, and more to the point, no
beginning.

"Huh," she said.

The top of the wall featured the same black stones
used in the bulk of its construction—but instead of
being laid flat against one another, at the top their
points faced up.

Like jagged, broken teeth.

Molly went to the wall and put her hands on it. She
thought to climb it, but how? The soft, cold moss afforded
her no handholds. Every damp clump slipped through her
hands. And none of the trees had branches that extended
out over, or even near, the top of the wall. (*As if they were
scared of getting too close,* she thought idly.)

So Molly picked a direction—right, because she was
right-handed—and followed the edge of the wall.

Her hand, sliding along the wall as she walked, felt a sudden interruption in the stone. She hadn't even realized the wall had changed, so lost was she in her own thoughts. But what had she bumped?

A hinge.

Two of them, actually, and rather prodigious at that. They were made of black iron, each connected to a tremendously large wooden door. A door so large, in fact, it would best be described as a *gate*—as high as the wall and wide enough to accommodate Gordo's Cadillac. At the far side, she spied a massive iron band barring the door shut. And on that band—

"A lock," she said to no one.

"*Mollllllly*," the forest whispered in return.

She shuddered. "That's weird. You should stop that!"

"*Sorrrrry*," the forest answered.

Well, at least it's a polite *menacing voice.*

Grimacing, her arms dotted with chill-bumps, Molly went to the lock and examined it. No celestial symbols marked this lock, not exactly—but there were *five* keyholes, and they were arranged in an almost star-shaped pattern. The base of each keyhole pointed in its respective direction, outward from the center. Old-timey keyholes for old-timey keys.

Her fingers drifted over the lock, and she felt the faintest electrical charge buzz through her. Similar to what she'd felt with the padlock earlier—but much bigger and buzzier. Molly yanked her hand away.

And then, in the door itself, she saw something else: two handprints painted in a red so close to the color of the door they were almost hard to see. She tried to put her hands over them but found that she couldn't—because they were reversed. The thumb on each pointed not toward each other, but away. She could put her hands on the handprints only by crossing her arms. When she did so, she expected...well, what? She didn't know. But nothing happened. No tingle as she'd felt with the lock.

Above the door, thick with bundles and pockets of moss, was a name:

MOTHSTEAD.

Beneath it, the image of a large, strange moth—graceful in its curves, with a swooping set of twin tails, as if from a kite.

"*Molllyyyyy...*" came the voice again.

It came from the other side of the door. Molly swallowed hard.

"What do you want?" she asked. "What do you want me to do?"

For a few moments, there was nothing.

And then, a single word breathed like wind through the keyholes:

"*Run.*"

12. the stubborn girl

THE LOCK TOLD HER TO RUN—OR PERHAPS IT WAS THE FOREST, OR whatever waited on the other side of the big wooden door—and when something like that happened, most people would run.

Wouldn't they?

It'd be one thing if the mysterious voice told you to do a handstand, or eat a bad egg, or rub mud on your butt. But something so primal, so declarative as *run*—well, you wouldn't want to stick around to find out what you're running *from*, would you?

To reiterate: Most people would run.

But it is with great obviousness that it must be pointed out: Molly was not most people.

Because Molly, in the care of her father, Steven Grim, had been left alone. A lot. Her father worked a job until he got bored and either quit or was fired. He gambled. He went to bars. He dated totally replaceable randos. He barely spent any time with his daughter, leaving her out-of-school education to a single device:

A used flat-screen television with a handful of dead pixels.

Steve wouldn't spring for cable, but he did spring for internet, and between Netflix and the YouTube app she downloaded to the TV, Molly began a pop-culture education in earnest. One that was only hastened by that time they lived two doors down from Javi's Pawn Shop, where the owner let her borrow an old DVD player and a wheezing PlayStation 3. This let her play a host of old anime movies and video games. Plus the pawnshop had comic books, too, and a rack of old fantasy paperbacks, so sometimes she'd park herself in one of the teetering, dusty aisles of old fax machines and Christmas decorations and ninja stars, and there she'd read, and read, and read.

She didn't have many friends.

But she had books, and games, and YouTube, and

movies, and comics. *Those* were her friends. And one thing she learned again and again from her friends:

Heroes didn't run. Heroes got up when they were knocked down. Heroes *stood in the path of evil.*

Plus this door—this *locked* door—was exactly the sort of thing she was looking for if she wanted leverage over Dustin. And so, Molly did not run. She needed more information. She needed something to hold over his head—a dangling (dingleberry-ing?) sword of Damocles.

Instead, she whirled to face the forest, her foam sword in hand. She gave it a twirl. She bared her teeth. *Time to look the part and pretend to be a hero.*

And then—

Nothing.

Her body tensed up. She felt like a spring unsprung. The air vibrated.

But…still nothing.

"Wh—" she started, and then stopped, because it felt very strange to speak to a disembodied voice. "Why should I run?"

Through the keyholes, the voice said, after some hesitation: *"They're coming."*

She blinked.

"They who?"

"The sentinels."

"The sentinels," she repeated.

"*Yessss*," the voice whisper-hissed. "*The door-wolves.*"

"The door-w—"

Through the trees, she heard the crackle-snap of a lone twig breaking. *Kkkt!* Every molecule in her body tightened. Door-wolves? What the heck were *door-wolves*? Her knuckles went bloodless around the hilt of her (very, very fake) sword. Ahead of her, more brush crackled. The understory shook, a shush of something moving through the tangle.

Two shadows emerged.

The first wolf was lean and lithe, its fur the soft brown of an acorn. Its legs were long, too long—impossibly, monstrously so, twice the length of what you'd expect from the average dog or wolf. The second wolf was smaller, walking low to the ground, with braided muscles rippling underneath its thick white coat.

Molly swallowed hard. Her teeth chattered, as if she were cold—but she realized it wasn't the temperature. It was fear running laps through her body.

The two wolves paced back and forth, trading places.

Behind them, the sun began to set. Darkness spread inward across the forest like an oil spill. Night was coming fast—too fast.

"Go away!" Molly barked, recalling that she'd read the best way to scare off a bear or a cougar was to appear larger and louder than it—pretend to be a bigger, meaner beast. Thus indicating more trouble than an attack would be worth. "Shoo!" She raised her hands above her head and swished the blade. "Raar!"

Then, that dizzy feeling swept over her again. She felt *weird.* Off-balance more in her own mind than her own body. Molly blinked—

And when she did, the wolves looked... *different.*

The first, with the long legs, now stood even *taller* than before—and its fur was not fur, but rather—*this can't be right,* Molly thought—thorns.

Its coat was a bristling carpet of long green thorns.

Its teeth were like the pointy tips of tree roots. When it opened and closed its mouth, she could hear the *crunch* of dry leaves, the *crackle* of brittle branches.

The second wolf was thicker, and its coat seemed almost... ephemeral, as if it both *was* and *was not* there. It gave the sensation of a white curtain moving in front of a bright window. A coat made of illusions, or dreams. Shimmering. And its teeth were like jagged white pebbles. Clacking together, *clackity-clack, clickity-click.*

The dream-wolf said, not out loud but in her head:

DREGIL, DO YOU SEE WHAT I SEE?

The thorn-wolf said, also in her mind:

YES, LAC. I SEE THAT SHE SEES.

SHE SEES US AS WE ARE, the dream-wolf said.

CURIOUS. CAN SHE HEAR US, TOO? the thorn-wolf asked.

Molly nodded. "I…I can."

AHHH. SHE CAN, the dream-wolf—Lac?—said.

The thorn-wolf—Dregil?—chuckled dryly. SHE IS A SPECIAL ONE, THEN. BUT SHE IS NO MOSQUITO.

AND, Lac said, SHE IS NO TRICKSTER. NOR A WILL-BENDER, A HAG-CHILD, OR A POOR LITTLE GULL.

OH MY, LAC. YOU MUSTN'T USE SUCH IMPROPER TERMS. BUT YOU'RE RIGHT. SHE IS NOT THESE. SHE IS NOT ANY OF THE PROPER CELESTIALS.

The dream-wolf seemed to shrug with its muscular front shoulders. REGRETTABLY, YOU ARE RIGHT. I BESEECH YOUR FOR-GIVENESS, BROTHER.

THANK YOU, SISTER.

Brother, she thought. *And sister.*

Then, an additional, intrusive thought: *Like Dustin and me.*

PERHAPS SHE IS ONE OF THE RARA AVIS, LAC.

PERHAPS SHE IS A RARE BIRD, PERHAPS, PERHAPS. IT COULD BE THAT SHE IS BLOODED, YES.

At that, Dregil, the thorn-wolf, took a hearty, rigor-ous sniff of the air.

YES, THAT IS IT. SHE IS BLOODED.

The dream-wolf, Lac, nodded. SO BE IT. SHE BELONGS.

AND YET, Dregil said, teeth bared, WE MUST DO OUR PART.

"What?" Molly said nervously. "Nobody needs to do any part. We're good here. I'm good. Are you good?"

WE ARE SORRY, Lac said, staring at Molly. WE ARE WHO WE ARE. WE ARE SENTINELS. AND YOU ARE A TRESPASSER.

AND TRESPASSERS, Dregil said, ARE PREY.

"No! Nonononono I'm not—I didn't mean—I—"

Through the keyholes, one last exhortation:

"Run, Molly. Run."

YES, Dregil said. RUN.

OR FLY, Lac said, chuckling. BLOODED LITTLE BIRD MUST FLY.

But Molly did not know *where* to run, and she sure couldn't fly. The wolves were right in front of her. She certainly couldn't open the door or climb the wall. They'd be on her like ants on a glob of ice cream.

GO! the thorn-wolf barked.

Molly yelped. She picked a direction—*back the way I came!*—and sprang into a hard, if clumsy, sprint along the wall's edge.

The wolves laughed, almost musically, and chased after.

13. the chase

MOLLY WAS NOT FAST. SHE WAS A BIT NIMBLE, IF ONLY BECAUSE OF HER size and her frame. But nimble enough to outrun a pair of wolves? Worse, a pair of wolves who were clearly, *clearly*, not of this world?

Not so much.

And she knew it. The moment she leaped into a run, she already feared her fate was sealed. These beasts were of the forest—no, they were of *this* forest. Molly realized that now: This was not a normal place, the wall was not normal, nor was the door. None of this was normal.

And the wolves were going to get her.

As her feet pounded the forest floor, leaves and branches crackling underfoot, she could *feel* the presence of her pursuers. Close now, and getting closer with every moment. The beasts panted and laughed—a cruel *chuff chuff chuff* sound as they gave chase.

Along the length of the wall she sprinted, until suddenly she darted hard to the left—ducking the arch of a fallen oak that leaned against a stout, white-barked birch. One of the wolves grunted and huffed in what seemed to be frustration (*Good!* Molly thought), though the other didn't lose a step. This was their territory. She could not win against them. As she ran, birds flew out of the underbrush, taking to higher strata of the forest as if to say, *get me the heck outta here.*

And that's when she figured it out.

The forest was their territory—but not all of it. Only the ground was theirs. Go up, and it belonged to the birds.

And now it belongs to me, Molly thought.

She skidded her heel out, suddenly darting right this time. Then right once more. And then right a third time. The wolf behind her had a hard time adjusting, snapping at the air, snarling, and she thought, *I did it. I'm getting away.* Ahead she saw the same arch she'd passed under only moments ago: the oak against the birch.

Almost there, she thought.

And then, ahead, something charged at her through the brambles.

It was a wolf that blended in perfectly—the thorn-wolf who called himself Dregil. The beast's maw was wrenched open the way a shark might open its mouth, its gaping throat getting wider and wider, the jawbone unhinging, crackling. Molly screamed and leaped into the air—

Her toe out—

Sword swiping down—

The foam tip *thwapped* the beast on the nose.

The wolf yelped, his jaw snapping shut from the surprise of the hit. He shook his head and stared into the middle distance, as if pondering the indignity of what had just happened. And as he bowed his head for a second, Molly landed on the creature's haunches and used them as a springboard to leap to the fallen oak. She caught it with both hands, her sword dropping from her grip as her arms wrapped around the trunk. Hurriedly she scrabbled with her feet, hauling herself up the collapsed tree to the healthy one it leaned against—

The two wolves were already at the base of the oak. She watched them take her fallen sword in their mouths and then wrench their heads in opposite directions, tearing her blade in twain, as if it were nothing at all.

And then the beasts attempted to resume their pursuit, claws scrabbling against the tree—

"Get *away*!" she shrieked. And though she knew her words had no true power, it certainly *seemed* as if they did: The two wolves could not gain good purchase on the steep angle of the fallen tree. They clambered up the log again and again, only to slide back down, strips of rotten bark peeling away under each assault from their long-clawed paws. They snarled and thrashed as Molly afforded one last panicked look back.

Then it was time to go, go, go.

She scrambled from one branch to the end of another—the next tree over required a bit of a climb up, then a scary jump over (*don't fall, don't fall, don't fall*). Blessedly, she made the leap, hugging the new tree as if it were a long-lost relative.

(*A long-lost relative who actually wanted to meet me*, she thought with some bitterness.)

(*Dustin, you jerk.*)

From this tree, to the next, to the one beyond it. Onward, Molly went. Sometimes she could simply step from one branch to another. Sometimes it meant a climb or a jump. But it wasn't long—really only three or four trees, in fact—before she saw the open hill and meadow, and in the distance, the glowing windows of a house in the dark.

She knew this meant going back down to the ground. And she knew what waited for her there:

Two wolves. Two *impossible* wolves. A coat of thorns on one, a coat of dreams on the other. She waited, watching the brush below. Listening, too. But after a while, she heard nothing and saw no presence of the beasts that hunted her—and so she tried to balance her quickness against her quietness as she clambered down this oak tree, using the branches as the rungs of a (very uneven) ladder.

Her feet hit the ground and she was off like a bottle rocket. Ten steps and she crashed through the brush, into the open grass.

She went another fifty feet, then finally looked back.

The forest had closed itself up again. No path was present. The thorns formed a dark, shadowy thicket.

But from within, she saw two pairs of eyes watching her, glowing like fireflies, before winking out.

The house appeared quiet as Molly approached it. Again, time felt slippery, like an eel fighting in her grip. How long had it been since she left? It felt, in part, like she'd only been gone fifteen minutes, but another side of her brain screamed that it had been fifteen hours, fifteen days, fifteen years. A weird fear ran through her that she'd step into the house and find it empty, its inhabitants dead or moved on, or she'd see Dustin sitting on a chaise lounge, aged into his forties, looking as dour as ever.

She checked her phone before remembering it was out of battery—

And yet, it lit up. Not dead at all, still had 37 percent battery.

It was ten PM.

Which meant, what? She'd been gone four or five hours, easily.

The quiet house meant Dustin was probably asleep, though Vivacia's truck was still in the driveway. Molly stepped onto the front porch, moving gingerly so as not to make any noise—though as soon as she planted her foot, the floorboard complained mightily. *Skreeeaaaaaaaaaaaaaaaeeeeek.*

A sharp light struck her in the eye, and Molly nearly fell off the porch, swatting at the beam as if it were a bee.

The light moved away, and there was Vivacia, sitting in the dark, the flashlight on her phone lit up. "Have a nice walk?" the woman asked.

Molly swallowed hard and tried to keep her cool. "Fireflies were pretty. Pretty, pretty fireflies." She cleared her throat. "Yup."

"You seem scared. Rattled."

"Of course I'm rattled. You literally just, you know—" Molly gestured as if Vivacia were a ghost or monster jumping out from a dark closet. "I didn't see you sitting there."

"Where'd you go?"

"Around. Mommy and Daddy were fighting, so."

Vivacia leaned forward, a sharpness in her voice. "I'm not Mommy, and he's not—" She paused a moment, as if to consider whether to say more. "You know, your mother was a saint."

"Oh yeah. Polly Ashe, Patron Saint of Abandoning Children."

"She didn't abandon you. You had a father. You went with him."

"Leaving me with Steven Grim was worse than abandoning me. I'd have been better off in a cave with a couple of—" She was about to say *wolves*, but then fresh fear lanced through her. "Grizzly bears."

"That's a childish opinion from a girl who knows nothing. But I knew her well. We were close. And she was a noble lady." Vivacia's voice darkened. "So. You told Dustin you weren't taking my offer."

"Funny how he didn't seem to know about it."

"He's young. He needs me around to put order to chaos, to straighten the scribbled line. He trusts me enough to do things without his oversight."

"Not how it seemed to me. Maybe he *doesn't* need you around. Maybe soon he'll be the boss and you'll be out on your butt. Maybe *you're* the one hiding things around here." She filed that notion in the back of her mind. Dustin certainly hadn't accepted her and was just as likely trying to push her away. But maybe, *maybe* it was Vivacia really running this show. Maybe Vivacia was her true foe.

What does she know about the forest, the wall, the wolves?

Vivacia stood. She seemed taller than usual. Her shadow loomed, even in the darkness of night. "You're pushing your luck, little kid."

"You push me, I push back."

"Where were you?"

"What are you hiding that you're afraid I might've found?"

The other woman harrumphed quietly, gave no answer, and then finally moved aside to let Molly pass.

And pass, Molly did, chased by the memory of door-wolves, and with them, resurfaced anger and sadness over a mother who hadn't wanted her.

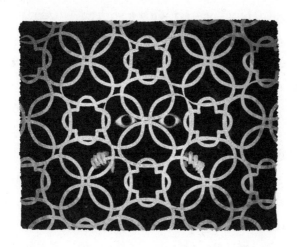

14. the boy who lived in the wallpaper

IT TOOK MOLLY TWO DAYS TO CALL GORDO. PART OF IT WAS THAT SHE didn't want Vivacia listening at the door, and the other part was...well, honestly, what was she going to say? "Oh, hey, Uncle Gordo, I found an impossible forest larger on the inside than the outside, like the Doctor's TARDIS, and there was a forever wall, and a big locked door, and two wolves-that-were-not-wolves who talked in my head and then tried to eat me."

She had to trim that down a little bit. Do a little *editing*.

She finally called him around midnight on the

third day. He answered with a snort. "Wuzza," he said. "Whuh."

"You asleep?"

He grunted. "Not anymore." Another grunt, like he was a pig rooting for an apple in the mud. "You find something?"

"I did."

"You went out there." He sounded awake now, for sure.

"I did."

"Well…?"

"I found a…wall. And a door. A big door, to be honest."

"What was inside?" She had a moment of, *he doesn't sound surprised.*

"I dunno. It was locked."

"Another lock. Another key."

"Five keys," she clarified. "I mean, it had five keyholes, so, yeah, I assume five keys."

"Hnnh. Keep snooping. Find the keys. We gotta start getting in these doors, girlie."

"By *we* you mean *me*—and don't call me girlie. It's dismissive and creepy."

"All right, all right, settle down. Yes, *young woman,* I mean you, because you're the boots on the ground.

Think of me as your commander. Directing your movements, giving you missions."

"Ugh."

"What?"

"Your military metaphor is gross and weird."

"Dismissive and creepy. Gross and weird. I'm beginning to think you don't like me very much, Molly."

I don't, she thought—but in a rare bit of prudence, did not say. Instead, she cut the conversation short: "I gotta go. Night, Unc."

"Snoop. Around."

"I know. I know. Good night."

"Find the key."

"Good! Night!"

She ended the call.

Ugh. What a jerk.

After that, she tried to sleep.

Key word: *tried.*

For the last couple of days, she'd found it unsurprisingly hard to fall asleep. She couldn't get comfortable, turning over and over and over like a log underneath a waterfall. Every time she felt herself drifting off...

She jolted awake again, sure that a pair of jaws was about to snap her up, chew her to pieces, and swallow her remains.

By the third time this happened, she sat up in bed, soaked in sweat. The summer night was mild, but she felt suddenly basted—humid in her own anxiety, pickle-brined in her own fear. The bed squeaked and complained as she sat up straighter, trying to calm her racing heart.

Which might have worked, except the hairs on the back of her neck unexpectedly began to tingle. They rose to attention. The hairs on her arms did the same.

The sensation swept over her with the certainty that she was being...

Watched.

"You better not be in here trying to scare me, *Vivacia*," Molly said with more confidence than she felt.

Dead ahead of her, she heard a scuttling. And a whisper of rustled paper, like how a gentle breeze or a ceiling fan might stir the page of a book or slide a piece of paper across a desk. The sound moved not left to right, but rather, down to up. As if something were...

Climbing.

Like a spider.

If a spider were the size of a Labrador retriever.

Quickly, Molly fumbled for her phone, charging by the nightstand, and flicked on its meager flashlight.

A circle of gray light shone ahead, illuminating

the—what was the design on the wallpaper called again? *Tessellated quatrefoil.* The interlocking pattern, like an elegant chain-link fence made of flowers and their petals. It was really quite hypnotizing—

Her gaze stopped short.

Two eyes were staring back at her.

Two very *human* eyes. Each contained in a separate quatrefoil flower.

They blinked and then were gone.

Molly gasped and chucked her phone down, stretching to turn on the lamp on the other side of the bed—

She heard more scuttling. Hollow thumps of several footsteps climbing the wall, going up toward the ceiling, then back down the wall on her right—

There. Her finger pinched the lamp knob and turned.

Pale golden light filled the room. Her own stare tracked the wallpaper, looking again for the two eyes watching her from within the pattern.

She didn't see them.

But, to her right, she saw fingers. And toes. Both gripping the quatrefoils. It looked like someone climbing the pattern on the far side of the wallpaper, from a room or world she couldn't see.

And then the fingers and toes retracted back into the wall and were gone. As if they never existed.

It's gone, she thought to herself. *It's gone. Whatever it was—it's gone now.*

A whisper directly behind her: "Don't scream."

She, of course, tried to scream.

A cold and clammy hand clapped over her mouth. It felt like earthworms and late-winter mud stuffed into a skin mitt.

"Mffffttt!" she said behind that hand.

When the whispered voice came again, it brought with it the smell of mold and mustiness and rain-on-an-asphalt-road:

"You're not looking for five keys."

"Whhmwwt?" she tried to ask.

"You won't scream, will you?"

She offered a trembling thumbs-up. Though she assumed that could be taken as *Yes, I intend to scream,* she hoped it was interpreted as *Nope, no screaming here, no sir.*

The hand peeled away, leaving her lips tasting like gravestones.

Politely, quietly, she asked: "May I turn around?"

A pause.

"You may."

Molly turned around.

And there, hiding in the wallpaper, was a face. A boy's face—her age and, quite plainly, not very alive.

His white eyes were shot through with dark veins. His face was a sickly bluish-green, sort of the opposite of a blush of life—more like, a bloom of death. Like the color of a chicken cutlet, had it been soaking in a rain puddle for weeks. The boy's lips were the rheumy gray of a thundercloud. He pressed a gray finger to them before his hand retracted back into the wall.

"Are you a ghost?" she asked, her eyes as big as moons, her pulse fluttering in her neck like the wings of a trapped sparrow.

"I suppose," he whispered glumly.

"Okay. That's…nice. Wait. No. That's not nice. Is it nice?" She bit her lip. "I'm sorry, I don't know what to say and I'm very frightened right now."

"You've no need to be."

"Oh. Uh. Good." She wiped away cold sweat. "You said something about keys?"

"Not keys. *Key*. The Fivefold Key."

"I don't understand."

The spectral boy came closer. "I heard you speaking to the man you call uncle. You said there were five locks for five keys on the door in the woods, but it is only one key—a master key with five prongs—that unlocks that door."

One key. Not five. That made it easier, at least, to know what she was searching for.

"Uh...thank you for the information?"

"I can help you."

"O...kay."

"I can get you the key."

Now Molly's heart really leaped in her chest, like a rat barely escaping a trap. "You can?"

"I can. For a price."

Molly knew this was a bad idea. Surely, *surely,* it was inadvisable to make deals with ghosts. Ghosts, which she did not believe in. *Just like you don't believe in creepy talking wolves, huh, Molly?* she asked herself. Regardless, a decision was now before her:

Trust the ghost? Make a deal? Get the key?

She had to be all in. She had to get answers. Curiosity and stubbornness formed a one-two punch.

"Name your price," she told the dead boy.

And the dead boy did.

15. the dead boy's price, and also, breakfast

BREAKFAST FOR DUSTIN WAS THIS:

A glass of POG juice, which he explained was passion fruit, orange, and guava juices mixed. ("Hard to get here," he explained to Molly, without prompting. Then, sniffing with pride, he said, "Yes, it's a Hawaii thing.")

Then: two soft-boiled eggs over gently, meticulously buttered many-grain toast—toast that looked so crunchy Molly half-imagined that before buttering it he'd rolled it in birdseed and maybe some driveway gravel.

And finally: A strawberry sliced into paper-thin slices, fanned out on the plate like a lush, crimson flower.

Her plate, however, was empty.

"So this is the new trick."

"I don't know what you mean," he said, clearly lying.

"I don't eat with you a couple times and you get rid of my food, huh?" After the forest and the door-wolves, Molly had kept a low profile, sneaking snacks from the kitchen and avoiding Dustin and Vivacia. She couldn't trust anyone or anything in this whole freaky house. But after a run-in with a ghost in her bedroom, and eating only dehydrated fruit and granola six meals in a row, she'd decided to brave an appearance, if only to see what her brother would say.

"I hadn't noticed," Dustin replied stiffly.

Molly slapped the table. "Oh, I get it now. Viv told you not to feed me. Right? Like, just because I have a room here doesn't mean I'm entitled to being fed, or something."

He hesitated. "Room, not board, is how she put it."

"You just do what she says, huh."

"She is wiser than I by a good many years. And she worked here with Mother. Our mother."

"*Your* mother."

"If she's just my mother, then why are you here?"

She sneered. "Touché."

He thrust a finger into the air. "An interesting thing—the word *touché* is meant to indicate a hit in fencing or sword-fighting, which is why we also say it when we have lost an argument or have been, ah, *dinged* on a rhetorical point. The word, you see, means *touched,* as in, the blade—or your argument!—struck me, but curiously, it's also the surname of a local family that—"

"Yeah, I don't care." She stood up. "I'm going to cook myself some eggs."

"They're not your eggs to use."

With that, Molly marched to the end of the table and put her face perpendicular to his. Firmly, she said, "No, but you're not going to stop me. And I figure the courts—when this goes to court—will frown on your trying to *starve* your poor little *sister,* who can't take care of herself."

He was nervous now. She could hear it in his voice—a tremor there. "You said it yourself. You're emancipated."

"Just like I'm going to *emancipate* some eggs into a pan and then further *emancipate* them into my hungry tummy."

And she *was* hungry, too. It wasn't just watching him work through his weirdo breakfast—even though Dustin ate like a persnickety woodpecker, erratically poking and pecking at his meal with a fork. It was everything that had happened so far: the offer, the chase, the ghost boy in the wallpaper. It was terrifying and had soured her stomach at the time. But now that the sourness had gone out to sea, it had left her *famished*. As such, she opted for pulling three eggs from the fridge—no, four! *All your eggs are mine, mine, I say, miiiiine!*

She found a bowl and gave them a rough scramble.

This was not her first time at a stove. Steve-o-Steve-a-roonie-Stevie Grim could barely take care of himself. So Molly learned to cook in the microwave, because that was easy and a hot stove was scary. But over time she'd adapted, moving to the stovetop and then eventually the oven. She was no five-star chef, but she could follow a recipe.

"The key to a nice scramble is to move it around a lot," she called from the kitchen. "You want small curds. Wet, not too dry."

"I see," Dustin said, making her jump a little. She hadn't realized he'd followed her from the dining room. "I like cooking, too. I soft-boiled my eggs myself."

"They looked tasty," she said, letting loose the compliment without thinking.

"Thank you." He craned his neck to see what she was doing. "And your scrambled eggs look particularly delicious. Usually I'm not a fan of the, ah, *texture*, but those…"

To that, she said nothing. She plated the eggs and asked: "Salt?"

"There's a small cellar by the lazy Susan."

Sure enough, she found a black ceramic saltcellar back in the dining room. It had good salt, too: big fat flakes. A quick, crunchy pinch over her eggs and she sat.

"That's just Maldon, but there's a salt I'd like to get called Alaea," Dustin said. "It's a red Hawaiian sea salt that comes from a volcanic clay rich with iron oxide and—"

"I have a message for you," Molly said, interrupting him. A spike of guilt struck her as soon as she said it. *We were talking about cooking,* she thought. She liked cooking. He liked cooking. *You don't have to do this right now.* But if she didn't, would she make herself later?

His fingers danced in the air nervously. "From the lawyer? Er. Our uncle?"

"No."

"Then…who?"

"From the boy in the wallpaper."

Dustin's fingers closed like the petals of a shy flower. His lips searched for words they could not find until finally they found a stuttered denial: "I d-don't know what you mean."

"Really? No idea?"

"Truly."

But he did. She could see it flash in his eyes like light off a nickel. "Well, then let's pretend I've lost my mind when I tell you I met a boy last night, and he was hiding in the wallpaper. He seemed pretty dead, and when I asked him point-blank about it, he said, yup, yeah, totally a ghost."

"That's—" Dustin stared down into the volcanic yellow slurry of his remaining broken-yolk egg. "That's quite the break with reality you're having. I don't know that a court will find *this* trustworthy."

Molly kept going, ignoring that Dustin didn't just look worried, but…what? *Hurt?* "Ghost Boy—I don't know his name, he didn't say and I forgot to ask, what with my being all shocked that ghosts are real—said to pass along a message to you, and so I'm doing that. He said—"

"I don't need to hear this."

"He *said*, he misses your talks."

Blink, blink. "What?"

"That's it. That's the message. Ghost Boy misses your talks."

For a moment, Molly was certain her brother was going to deny, deny, deny. He'd wave it off, stammer some half-baked lie, and then hurry away. And that is ultimately what happened.

But before that, Dustin's eyes grew wet. They brimmed nearly to spilling until he finally blinked the tears away and turned back to his breakfast. "Well. I don't—I don't know what to make of, ah, of all that. It's clearly just a mad fantasy."

Hastily, he shoved his plate forward and stood up.

"Do you, uh, have a message to relay back?" Molly asked, feeling uncomfortable with the reaction she'd caused. She expected shock, not... *this*.

"No, I do not. Because ghosts are not real. I am an expert in death and the dead, and ghosts are but a folkloric representation of our grief, a way to grapple with the loss of loved ones by believing they are somewhere still upon this plane of existence, watching over us, allowing death to not truly be the end."

"Cool," Molly said. "You practice that speech in the mirror or what?"

Dustin scowled and stormed away, half his breakfast uneaten. Molly was unsure how to feel. Part of her felt triumphant—after all, he was rattled, and that made her victorious. But she also knew she'd struck a vein, and that didn't make her feel very good at all.

Whatever. Molly grabbed Dustin's remaining POG

drink, guzzled that down, and ate what remained of his food, too. Her mission was accomplished, her hunger sated.

The day passed, and Molly and Dustin seemed to circle each other through the house—she'd catch him fake-polishing a table, he'd catch her standing outside the locked pocket doors of the funeral parlor conjuring the very *posture* of innocence.

She skipped lunch, and at dinnertime looked up a local pizza joint and had them deliver a large cheese, plus pineapple and ham. (She did not know if she was being somehow cruel or somehow kind to make it a Hawaiian pizza.)

It came. It was fine. She made a mess and didn't clean it up. And later she caught Dustin standing in the kitchen, a slice delicately cut by the guillotine of his flat, perfect teeth. His eyes bugged out and he said, after chewing and dabbing his cheeks with a napkin, "I assume I can have this."

She shrugged. "Coulda asked first."

"I could posit the same of you."

"Shouldn't have to ask for what's owed to me."

"The pizza is in my house, and so I am free to it."

She crossed her arms. "Is it your house? Or is it Viv's? And hey—aren't you a vegetarian?"

"Sometimes I fall off the wagon," he said, and hurriedly finished his pizza and shuffled off.

Victory, she thought, ignoring the pit in her stomach.

Night fell like a vial of ink knocked off a high shelf. She trailed Dustin as he readied himself for bed—a meticulous ritual seemed at play here. Toothbrushing and pick-flossing and lots of creams and such. He pasted some kind of beige half moons under his eyes and one on his chin. As she watched him from the bathroom door, he said, "I have routines. Don't you have routines?"

"Not many. Not before bed."

"And yet you're some kind of...costumer."

"Cosplayer. But costumer eventually. And when I'm kitting up, yeah, I have rituals. But bedtime is, like, a quick toothbrush and it's snooze city."

"As you get older, you'll adopt more rituals. We must if we are to dissuade the depredations of age."

"Deprewhat? I don't know what you just said."

He sighed, obviously frustrated. "I just mean, we get older, but I try not to...show it."

"You're eighteen, dude."

"Yes. And my age is already...accelerating." Worry

crossed his face. "A fast downhill ride toward the grave."

"Dude. You're *eighteen*. You're still a kid!"

"Hardly," he said. "I am an adult in the eyes of the state, and responsibility has been thrust upon me. Great responsibility. *Dire*. And further, I know what waits for me at the end of…everything."

"Oh my god, bro, you're having a midlife crisis in your teens. Honestly it's a little depressing."

He made a nervous, frittery gesture with his hand. "Perils of working in this industry, I suppose. Anyway. To bed, I go."

And then he pulled down the attic steps.

"Wait. That's your bedroom?"

"Up there, yes."

"You sleep in the attic." She felt like an idiot. Of course she'd never seen his bedroom. Where did she think he slept? In the closet, like some kind of dorky vampire?

Wait, if ghosts are real, are vampires?

No, no, of course not, that was far too silly.

Dustin sighed and looked over his own shoulder, resting his chin on his collarbone. "Mother gave me the attic as my bedroom when I was eleven, maybe twelve. Just to give me my own space. A room of one's own, to quote Virginia Woolf."

Molly froze. "Wolf?" The image of a gaping, unhinged jaw jumped to her mind.

"Yes. Woolf. You don't know her work?"

"Uh. No."

"Your loss. Good night."

And with that, he ascended the ladder—she saw now that the door covering that space had already been unlocked. She'd missed his doing that and cursed herself for having lost a step, especially to him. He pulled the ladder up behind him and closed the door in the ceiling.

She waited a few beats just to make sure he wasn't coming back.

Then she ducked into her room and said to the ghost in the wall:

"I did it. I did what you asked. Now give me what's mine."

16. a deal is a deal is a deal

SHE WAITED. NOTHING. SHE WAITED SOME MORE. *STILL* NOTHING.

"I said I—"

A shadow squirmed underneath the pattern of the wallpaper. Like an eel swimming in mud-stirred waters. A chill swept over Molly as the whispered response came from nowhere and everywhere. It was as if someone had walked over her grave when the boy spoke.

"I know," the ghost voice said. "I heard."

"So you also heard Dustin's response," she said.

The boy's gray sallow face pushed up out of the wallpaper. His shoulders, too—bony underneath threadbare ghost clothes. With evident sadness, he said, "Yes. It's what I expected, I guess."

"What's the deal anyway?"

"I don't understand your question."

"I mean, what's the sitch—uhh, situation—between you two?"

A moment of pause. "We used to speak and we no longer do. For reasons."

"Such as?"

"Reasons due to rules. He does not wish to break rules. I, as someone unliving, am no longer so fond of rules."

Molly took a deep breath. "Okay. Whatever. That's your business, then. My business is—"

"The Fivefold Key."

"Yes." She checked herself on mak'ng a demand—lest the ghost decide not to uphold his end of the bargain. "May I have it, as per our agreement, Young Mister Ghost Lad?"

"I have a name." That said with some petulance.

"Oh? You never offered it."

"And you never asked."

"I thought you might like to keep your privacy."

An echoing, unearthly sigh emanated from the boy. "I'm afraid the dead do not get to keep much at all.

But I can keep my name for as long as people remember it, and I hope if I tell it to you, you will choose to remember."

"Then by all means, tell me."

"My name is Lancaster Bauman Junior."

"That's quite the mouthful."

"My mouth contains only ashes."

"Oh." She made a sour-lemon face. "That's rough, buddy. Can I call you Lank? Or Lanky or—"

"My mother called me Link, sometimes."

"Like from *Legend of Zelda*."

"Zelda Fitzgerald was indeed quite the legend."

"Uhh. What? Who?" Molly waved her hands. "Never mind. Link, may I have my key now?"

A hesitation. The wallpaper seemed to ripple, as if it were pond water stirred. "You are allowed the Fivefold Key. It is yours to use, as per the Old Promises, as per the Blooded Ways."

She wrinkled her brow. "Cool. Is it going to just appear orrrrr—"

The boy's face disappeared.

And was replaced by a hand, like the Lady of the Lake thrusting the sword Excalibur out of the water— except this was the gray moist hand of a dead boy emerging from a wall of hypnotic wallpaper. And what he held was no sword, but rather, the strangest-looking key.

It was not one key, but five grafted together—all iron, each forming a prong and fixed at their base together with one common handle. A handle that had an iron loop on it, as if to connect it to a ring or hang it on a hook.

It was very large for a key.

Molly got up onto the bed and wobbled over to where the key had emerged. Gently, she took it. The key felt heavy in her hand; she nearly dropped it.

"Thanks," she said.

The ghost boy gave her a little wave before the hand sank back into the wallpaper, disappearing behind the pattern.

"I have the key," Molly said into the phone. She said it quietly, almost a hiss-whisper. (*A hissper?* she wondered.)

"Which key?" Gordo asked.

Molly paced the space at the foot of the bed. "The one for the forest. For the gate in the wall."

"The Fivefold Key," he said.

"Yeah."

"You scored big-time, kiddo. Good job. I'm proud of you."

A weird, warm glow filled her. What was this feeling? Pride? Satisfaction? Something-something family? She tried to shake it off.

"Thanks" was all she said.

"How'd you get it?"

"I…" *Made a deal with a ghost who lives in my room's wallpaper.* "I snuck into Dustin's room and stole it."

"Shows how smart you are—and how dumb he is."

"Well, I don't know that he's dumb. I just—"

"He's dumb. Just like your father was dumb. They don't see our potential, Moll. They don't see who we are." He paused for a moment—was he breathing heavily? Was he angry? "I'll be over in an hour. Less than that, probably."

Molly hesitated. "You'll be where? Here? Why?"

"We're gonna open the gate."

"Now? Tonight? But the wolves—"

"Wolves?"

Oops. Never told him about those. "There are… ahh, I dunno, big dogs in the woods." She knew they weren't dogs. And they might not have even been wolves. They were something else. *Monsters*, she thought. But dared not say it aloud.

"I'll bring a bat," Gordo scoffed. "Maybe some pepper spray or bear mace or whatever."

"You have bear mace?"

"No. But Walmart probably carries it."

"There are no bears in Pennsylvania."

"There are totally bears in Pennsylvania."

"Ugh, whatever. I don't think I wanna do this tonight, Uncle Gordo."

On the other end, she heard him sigh. When he spoke, it was soft, almost earnest: "Listen, kiddo. I know this is hard. But it's almost over. I figure that key is going to show us something real interesting. Give us the leverage we need. We're *this* close to the finish line. But that means we gotta push just a little harder. Go the distance. Okay?"

"...okay."

"You sure?"

"I'm sure. Come on over. Dustin is asleep. Vivacia isn't here." She nodded, realizing Gordo was right. No matter how much she might have wanted Dustin to like her, to bring her into his secrets, it wasn't going to happen. Look what he'd done to poor Link—dropped him the minute it interfered with the precious family business. That meant they'd have to go out there. Back into the woods. She shuddered at the thought.

But she could do it. Well, no, *she* couldn't do it—but in the right costume, she could be someone else. Hina Harumi, Han Solo, Morrigan. Anybody but herself. A hero. Not a zero.

"Now's the time," she said.

"Now's the time," he echoed, and the note of excitement in his voice was impossible to ignore. "See you soon, kiddo. Real soon."

17. gordo the destroyer

IN DARKNESS, MOLLY AND HER UNCLE TROMPED THROUGH THE MEADOW—
or, he tromped, and she followed in his wake, this time
in a hastily assembled elf ranger outfit. With no bow,
of course. No arrows. No quiver. Ugh, so many of her
costumes felt cheap and unfinished. *When we get the
money, I'm gonna go ham on buying gear,* she decided.
School, yes. But gear? Also yes.

It was hard keeping up with Gordo. He moved with
surprising speed and determination, though, like a
man on a mission.

It occurred to Molly that she had been maybe a
little overly judgmental of Uncle Gordo. Part of it was

that her father was a butt, and Gordo was her father's brother, so clearly he was a butt, too. (Though sometimes she wondered, if they sucked super bad by dint of their family heritage, did *she* also suck? Was she as terrible as they were? That saying about how apples didn't fall far from their tree made her worry.) Sure, Gordo was an ill-kept man in a cheap brown suit soggy with gross cologne, his face on bus depots and park benches and local YouTube commercials asking you if *you've* been the victim of a bad rash or a zoo-animal attack or some kind of wicker-furniture tragedy. Everything about him seemed shoddy and lazily put together. But— here he was, heading into the forest with her. Baseball bat in hand.

He'd gotten them this far.

She was maybe starting to even—

(Could it be?)

Like him.

Ew.

He seemed to really have it in for her father, and she understood why. Steve-a-roonie probably underestimated Gordo, just as Dustin was underestimating her.

Maybe Gordo was the family she really needed all along.

"What do you think is in there?" she asked.

"In where? The woods?"

"Beyond the door. Beyond the wall." *Inside Moth-stead*, she thought.

He twirled the bat. "I don't know, Moll. My guess is a cemetery."

"A cemetery?"

The meadow grasses whispered against his corduroy pants. "Uh-huh. Like I told you the other day, they got a license for burial plots: a bona fide burial ground. But there isn't one at the house. And that tells me it could be out here. Behind that wall you told me about."

Ahead, in the moonlight, the copse of trees loomed.

(Corpse of trees.)

"Why hide that, though?" she asked. "I mean, why hide a graveyard?"

"Means it's a real special graveyard, one they don't want anyone to find." He turned toward her, the moon giving his face a pale glow. "That's why we have to get in there."

Molly nodded.

And soon, they stood at the edge of the trees. The forest was so dark it looked solid, like you could put your hand flat against it.

"Looks a little thick," Gordo said. "There a path or something?"

She swallowed hard. "This is where it gets weird."

"It's already pretty weird, kid."

"Just…wait. Turn on your flashlight."

They'd kept the light off up to this point—not wanting to draw attention from the house. Now Gordo pulled out a good-sized Maglite flashlight and clicked it on.

Molly saw her shadow framed by the forest.

She took a deep breath and then stepped forward. For a moment, she feared nothing would happen, but as she took the second step, she once more felt woozy as the forest began to open itself up—corkscrews of thorny vines recoiling into the dark, brush and twig crackling as a path formed ahead of them.

"See?" she said.

"That forest just opened up for you."

"I know. You still wanna go in?"

He extended his hand. "Lead the way. It seems to like you."

Not if the wolves have anything to say about it, she thought.

"Turn off the light," she said.

"Why?"

Because that's how they'll see us, she thought.

"Just do it."

He shrugged and did.

And with that, Molly stepped into the dark.

All around, the forest seemed to swallow them up, a hungry mouth. The only light came from spears of moonsilver, scattered like the remnants of a celestial battle. Her eyes flitted nervously to the margins, left and right, back and forth, waiting to see if the wolves were lurking out there in the black.

So far, so good.

"Pick up the pace a little, eh?" Gordo said from behind.

"I don't want to trip on a...root or something." *Or be eaten by psychic wolf-things.* The thought suddenly occurred to her that she had no idea where she was going. Last time, she hadn't had a plan—she'd simply wandered into the woods and found the wall. Would that happen again? Already time had begun to feel slippery. She started to get that out-of-sync out-of-sortsness she'd felt before. Half in a dream. Half out of one.

Onward they stepped, the trees seeming to form arches over them, like the arms of dancing ballerinas. Molly was now quite dizzy and lost, and she was just about to turn around and ask Gordo if he was experiencing the same thing, if he was lost and dizzy and feeling like time was a slipped gear in a bad transmission, and if he'd like to get the heck out of these woods as fast as possible—

But before she could say anything, she saw the wall rise up before them. A stone barrier, banded by moonlight. She could make out the shape of the jagged, toothy stones at the top, and in the dark, her sense that this was a fortification only deepened.

"The door," Gordo said, pushing past her.

"Hey," she objected—but he was right. The door was right there ahead of them, illuminated by a single patch of pale light. Gordo did not bother gazing up at the name on the stone or the image beneath it.

The key felt suddenly heavy in Molly's pocket.

Her uncle traced his hand along the two hand-prints sitting dead center. Then he brushed his fingers against the underside of the lock and passed the pads of his thumbs along each of the five keyholes.

"This is what your father was hiding from us," he said. "He was a coddled, weak child and turned into a fool of a man. But I am no fool."

"Uhh. Okay?"

"Come here," he said, waving her forward. "Use the Fivefold Key. Five locks, one key. It's time."

Time, she wondered, *for what?*

Time, of course, to open this door. To see what Dustin was hiding. To get her due, to earn her inheritance. Right?

She fished around in her pocket for the key. It was cold, like ice. Gordo's eyes shone with catchlight as he watched her bring it out. A big grin split his face. Toothy. *Too many teeth,* she thought. Just a trick of the light, surely.

But then a little snippet of conversation replayed in her mind—

"I have the key," she said.

"Which key?"

"The one for the forest. For the gate in the wall."

"The Fivefold Key," he said.

Molly froze.

"How did you know?" she asked, stepping back.

His eyes narrowed to reptilian slits. "What?"

"How did you know it had a name: the Fivefold Key? I...I didn't tell you that name."

"You must've. You let it slip, certainly. I didn't invent the name."

"Your voice," she said, almost breathless with confusion and fear. It was Gordo's voice—but his accent, the one that hovered somewhere between a person from Philly, New York, and New Jersey, seemed gone. Now it was clipped. *Crisp*, like a bite into a sharp, tart apple. "I don't..."

Molly took another step back.

What's happening?

"Unlock the door, girl."

"No."

"This is it. This is our time. This is what we've been wanting, isn't it?"

"I...won't. What are you? *Who* are you?"

"Bah!" Gordo's arm lashed out. Normally short and stumpy, it now seemed almost freakishly long. His hand, firm and viselike, gripped her wrist. She cried out as he slammed her into the door. Gordo spun her toward the wall, grabbing the hand with the key in it. "Failure to commit when it really matters? I should have expected as much from the child of Steven. A loser father with a loser daughter." A flash of green lightning sparked in his eye. "Put. The. Key. In. The. Lock."

Molly tried to drop the key, but his hand clamped around hers, trapping it in her grip.

"Now!"

Grunting, she kicked backward with her heel.

It caught Gordo in the knee. The bone crackled and he *oof*ed, doubling over—and his grip on her hand slackened just enough for her to wriggle free.

Molly staggered away, key held tight. But she had nowhere to go. Spinning around, she pressed her back against the door as Gordo wheeled on her anew. His face, now out of the moonlight, still seemed to have a *glow* even as it stretched wider and wider in a rictus of dueling pain and rage. His mouth seemed to split his whole head like a human version of Pac-Man, and his eyes flickered with firelight. Then a seam formed down the middle of his face—like a stitch coming undone as you pulled the leg of a stuffed bear too hard and too far from its body. The skin began to *split*, and Molly screamed as a second face was revealed underneath.

This face was raw and red like a fresh-squeezed blister. The eyes were yellow, the mouth had lips fringed with squirming fibers and gums layered with row after row of needle teeth, like a fence pressed against a fence pressed against a fence. *Like shark teeth, but somehow worse,* she realized. His nose was gone—all that waited in the center of his face were two fleshy, gill-like slits.

She tried to push past him, kicking and swatting, but it was no use. He grew larger and larger, swelling up. His suit jacket split with a wretched *riiiiip.*

Molly screamed for help.

And then, for a moment, all went quiet. Behind her, she heard the rustle of leaves. The Gordomonster heard it, too, turning his raw red face toward the sound.

There, two wolves emerged. The world rolled under a prismatic shimmer, and they became the ones she had seen from before: not wolves, but door-wolves made of thorn and dream.

I SEE WE HAVE GUESTS, DREGIL, the dream-wolf said.

TRESPASSERS, YOU MEAN, the thorn-wolf answered.

They snarled as one. And as one, they leaped.

18. protectors of mothstead

AS THE DOOR-WOLVES LEAPED IN A GREAT ARC—TOO GREAT, FOR THE height and distance were impossible, though she was realizing she needed to *seriously* recalibrate her expectations of what the heck was possible—Molly knew she was dead. She'd escaped the wolves once, but this time, the creature she'd mistakenly thought of as her very human uncle Gordo held her fast. She braced for the impact of beasts crashing into her.

The impact came, but *not* against her. She was rocked only because Gordo was—the two wolves slammed into him, clambering upon his bent back and now-massive shoulders as if they'd just jumped onto a boulder. Lac, the dream-wolf, sank her teeth into the roiling meat at the back of Gordo's neck while Dregil tore at his legs. Gordo strained and rippled more as the shreds of his suit jacket fell away—his shirt, too, revealing that the zit-red flesh of his new face was everywhere else on his body. She caught a glimpse of something dangling against his skin:

A necklace with an odd, misshapen stone hanging from it.

He clutched at it protectively.

Molly had no time to worry about his choices in jewelry, so she gritted her teeth and kicked and punched at him, trying to wrench herself from his grasp.

Her hand started to slip from his grip—

A half inch—

Then another inch—

Almost…got it…

Gordo's head craned back on his shoulders. His spine crackled as his neck elongated, and his jaw opened toward the patch of open sky above. In a gargle of rage, he began disgorging a shower of something wet and wriggling into the air—

Centipedes, Molly realized as they splashed down on her, their legs tickling. She shook them off like a dog ridding itself of fleas.

But she was not their target.

The rain of many-legged things fell upon the wolves, and even in the spare moonlight, she could see their fur rippling with the intrusion. The wolves yelped and snapped at their own coats, and Gordo used this to his advantage. He arched his arm back—an arm that now seemed to have far more joints than just the one human elbow—and grabbed each wolf, one at a time, flinging them into the dark. Dregil struck a tree with a heavy thud; Lac tumbled into the understory with a crashing and snapping of branches.

"*Now*," Gordo said, his voice somehow both a boom of thunder and a hissing whisper like a snake in her ear. "Let us *finish* this."

"No!" Molly shrieked.

He yanked her forward. She held her ground. Her arm felt like it was coming out of its socket. Gordo smashed the key against the lock, though it did not go in—Molly still gave fight, thrashing and twisting in his grip. The one key rattled against its five slots, clicking and clacking as Gordo roared with rage—

And then—

He twisted her wrist sharply—

Pain shot through to her elbow, her arm going limp—

The key pressed into the five locks.

One more twist, and it turned. And with a great

unmooring, the lock mechanism clicked and whirred. The bar banding the gate slid to the other side. And the door drifted open with a mewling *creak*.

And for Molly, the world went end over end.

Her ears rang. Her head swam. Her vision went in and out, in and out, with a sound that kind of went *wob wob wobbbbb.* Molly sat up, wincing in pain as fresh misery shot down her arm like a whip of lightning.

Looking up, with darkness threatening to swallow her vision, she saw that the gate in the wall still hung wide open but had begun to close as Gordo gently stepped through. Once again he appeared man-shaped, in an untorn suit, hands behind his back like he was going for a merry stroll in an English garden, pip-pip. He had his chin lifted high. He gave a little shudder— one of joy, delight even, not revulsion, not pain—

And then the gate swung shut behind him with a dooming *boom.*

The lock reengaged with a *click.*

A few moments passed.

And then—

WHOOM.

The ground shook as if a meteor had struck. Molly's teeth clacked against one another and she felt herself *lift* off the ground. She could feel the wave of motion ride the earth, like the first ripple after a rock strikes a puddle. Except this was a big rock in a little puddle. She came back down hard on her tailbone. Again her teeth bit—this time around her tongue, *ow ow ow.*

Up above her, the trees shook and swayed, as if in the winds of a storm—but Molly felt no wind, none at all. The leaves shushed and whished back and forth, and the trees began shaking them off. Black shapes, not green, fluttered down through the brightening moonlight. So many shadows around her, only leaves, but it seemed like blackbirds flitting this way and that.

Molly stumbled over to the gate and tried to open it. She didn't want to follow him, and fear nearly stayed her hand, but she had to know: What was in there? Where was he going?

It wouldn't budge, not an inch. She reached for the lock—

But the key was not in it.

She muttered a curse under her breath, turning to look for her allies, but neither of the door-wolves was here. *No one* was here. Now the trees had shaken themselves of their leaves; the forest lay bare before her, every branch like a skeletal hand reaching to pull the moon out of the night sky.

So Molly did all she could do: She ran through the

forest, underneath the leafless trees, through the dead underbrush. She pushed through the pain, bolting across the meadow—which seemed unaffected by the events that had just occurred—and toward the house.

And all the while, one thought ran laps through her mind:

What have I done?

Dizzy and queasy, Molly hurried through the front door, only to almost collide with Dustin—who was himself hurrying down the stairs. Her brother looked her up and down.

"What is it?" he asked, hurried and worried.

"Dustin, I'm sorry," she said, her voice brittle like a crack in glass slowly spreading.

Her brother, looking frightened and confused, asked her the question that she'd been asking herself over and over and over again:

"Molly, what did you do?"

19. what molly did

THEY STOOD IN THE MOONLIT DARK, UNDER THE BARE-BONED TREES, IN front of the closed gate. Or, rather, Dustin stood in front of it—stock-still, centered to the door itself, arms at his sides, just *staring*. Molly, for her part, paced back and forth, cradling her injured arm. As she did, she babbled everything that had happened: She'd found the door a few nights before, she'd made a deal for the key, she'd told Gordo, Gordo had come with her to the wall and the gate, he'd tried to get her to open the door but she'd known something was wrong, then he'd started to *transform* into some kind of *monster*....

"And then all this happened," she said, the words

coming a mile a minute. "The big boom. The trees losing their leaves. I...I don't know what this place is, or what I did, or what Gordo wanted, or what is happening at all."

Dustin's shoulders rose and fell with frustration, anger, anxiety, or some combination of all three. "Oh, by the gods. Beautiful Mothstead. Why?"

"What is this place, Dustin?"

"It's a cemetery. A place of the dead."

"A graveyard."

"Technically, a graveyard is connected to a church. But yes, a cemetery. But also much more than that." He paused. "Or, it was, anyway."

Then he turned tail and brushed past her. He gave her no look. Instead, Dustin stared ahead as he walked quickly beneath the skeletal branches, his head forward, his chin down, his gaze dark and resolute.

"Wait up," she called. *Please.* But he didn't.

Molly sat, alone, outside the pocket doors. Dustin had pulled a chair from the dining room, carefully but forcefully placed it against the wall, and told her to sit there.

For once, she knew enough not to object.

Part of it was knowing she'd really screwed up. She

wasn't exactly sure *how* she'd screwed up, but she knew she had. The other part was shock and trauma. She sat there, shivering, her arm hanging limp. It wasn't broken—she could move it, but not without pain. Her elf ranger costume hung in tatters, slashed and shredded.

When Dustin had gone through the pocket doors to the funeral parlor, so had Vivacia. Dustin had called her as they walked back toward the house, and she'd come quickly. (Molly realized now that the woman must live nearby.)

Just like Dustin, Vivacia had given her no look, no acknowledgment at all. Molly was but a bug to this woman, and not even the kind of bug that got in your face, or ran across your feet—a bug that demanded to be witnessed. No, she was a mere gnat. Or smaller! An example of microbial life.

The pocket doors had slammed, leaving Molly alone, sitting outside the parlor with her thoughts.

Thoughts that chased thoughts. Nightmare visions of Gordo's face splitting open, of his zit-red flesh, of his throwing the two wolves as if they were nothing more than chihuahuas nibbling at his neck. She tried to process it and could barely hold it all in her mind. Even after seeing a ghost boy hiding in wallpaper, and two door-wolves who spoke in her head, Uncle Gordo's transformation was somehow...extra impossible.

Molly wondered if she was having a break with reality, as Dustin had said about her at breakfast....

Or maybe reality was having a break with her.

But even through all that, the greatest shock was that the man she thought—or hoped—she could trust, she could not. He had betrayed her. And maybe wasn't even human to begin with? (She didn't understand how any of this worked.) The one family member she thought she could put some faith in—not Dustin, of course, because he had rejected her right out of the gate—had broken the back of that faith.

Figures. First, Mom, then Dad, now Gordo.

Wait. Did that mean her father was also inhuman?

Wait.

Did that also mean *she* wasn't human?

She patted herself down. She *felt* human. No horns. No rows of teeth behind her regular teeth. *Whew.*

But was it really a *whew*, or was a small part of her hoping that maybe, *just maybe*, she was a secret monster? *I would be so awesome at that*, she thought. And those wolves had said something about her being "Blooded." Come to think of it, hadn't Ghost Boy Link also mentioned something along those lines?

The pocket doors slid open with a rattle.

There stood Vivacia, one hand on the edge of each door, watching Molly with her fingers in her own mouth, checking for demon teeth. The woman's lips were pursed, and she had a dour look. Dustin stood behind her, staring off at nothing.

"Molly," Vivacia said. "Can you come in here?"

"I…" She didn't know what to say. She didn't want to go. But still she stood and went through the pocket doors, awaiting dire consequences.

The mundanity and dusty dullness of the funeral parlor felt extra off-kilter given how *weird* everything else was: The room stood in stark contrast to the unreal wolves and the mysterious cemetery and the monstrous uncle. Vivacia stood at the front, Dustin in the corner, staring at his feet. The woman asked Molly to sit in the first row of chairs.

Molly gulped but did as suggested. "I—" she began.

"I'm…sorry," Vivacia interrupted.

"Yes. I'm sorry, that's it, those are the words—I am sorry, I really am—"

"No, you're missing the point," Vivacia said. "*I'm* apologizing. To you." It sounded like it was difficult for Vivacia to say, but there it was. An apology.

Molly blinked. "Wh— Uh. What?"

"I'm apologizing to you. This is our fault. *My* fault. Because you came into our lives and we immediately treated you like an enemy. Me, more than Dustin, and in fact, it was I who helped…steer him toward seeing you as a foe and not what you are: family. For better or for worse. And further, you are a young girl, *his little sister*, Pollyanna's daughter, and we should not have expected your judgment to be pristine in these, or any, matters."

"Hey!" Molly protested.

Vivacia said, "It is perhaps imprudent to object during someone's apology, Molly."

"Oh. Uh. Sorry."

"We were standoffish and unkind to you, and by pushing you away, you pushed back against us harder. That only heightened your curiosity around the mysteries we hoped would remain…well, mysteries. And now, here we are." Vivacia looked pained, as if all that hadn't been easy to say.

Molly took a deep breath, and then the words came tumbling out like a clatter of toys from an upended toy bin. "I don't know what happened I didn't mean to do it and I know you say it's your fault but I got suckered in by Gordo *stupid Gordo* and *god* even in the beginning I was so *so* mad that Dustin got to have a mom who didn't suck and I got stuck with that butthole Steve— *Steve!*—and—" She gasped. "Was Dad a monster? Am I? Are you? AHHHH."

"Breathe, Molly," Vivacia said, smiling stiffly, her

head atilt. She looked to Dustin. "You have anything to...add?" The woman made a face like she was egging him on. Her eyes said, unspoken, *like we talked about?*

He again cleared his throat and then made a pained face, as if the words just wouldn't come out.

"I can't," he said suddenly. "I can't apologize. You have done an awful thing, Molly. You've broken something *vital*, and to fix it—I don't even know if it *can* be fixed, or what will happen now."

Fresh tears rose to Molly's eyes. There was half a moment where she wanted to return fire, but it passed fast, the spark hissing out, drowned by those tears. She said, "Okay, you know, maybe Vivacia is right, maybe you could've been nicer to me. But I could've...been nicer, too, and I stormed in here and I made demands, like some stupid little sister knocking over her brother's LEGO set. So, I'm sorry. Okay? Just let me help fix this. Tell me what to do. Tell me *what's happening* and I'll fix it all. Somehow. I don't know but please *please* let me fix it—"

He just looked again at his feet.

"For that," Vivacia said, "we would have to tell you the truth of this place. Are you all right with that? I'm talking to the both of you."

Dustin crossed his arms. "I suppose if we have to."

"I'd...like to know," Molly said.

Vivacia said, "Dustin? You should do the honors."

For a time, he stood there staring through his feet, through the floor. Then he closed his eyes, and he told Molly the truth.

part two

MOLLY AND THE MONSTROUS INHERITANCE

20. everything is getting bdaahhfffgggh

"THIS PLACE," DUSTIN SAID, "BESIDES BEING OUR HOME, IS A SOLEMNITIES parlor and final resting place for the nonstandard citizens of the Northeast Celestial Protectorate, which, in turn, is part of the Larger Consanguinity of North America, and *that*, in turn, is one of the seven Consanguinities of the Greater Supernal Dominion. We provide bereavement care and burial rites tailored to some of our most unusual and hidden members of society."

Molly blinked. "You just said a buncha words but I don't know that you actually"—she narrowed her gaze—"*told* me anything."

"We're a funeral home for monsters," Vivacia said.

"*Viv!*" Dustin said, scandalized.

"Fine. The *supernatural*," the woman corrected. To Molly, in a lower voice, she said: "*Monster* is a bit of a no-no word. We prefer not to use it, and they certainly prefer us not to use it. But we need common ground here, and I hope it helps you to understand."

"Monsters," Molly said, repeating the no-no word.

"The supernatural," Viv corrected again.

"The *nonstandard citizens*," Dustin said sharply. He put out his hands as if to steady Molly against the onslaught of surprising information. "The mythical, folkloric beings you think of as vampires, or shape-changers, or sorcerers—"

"Not to mention the Goodly Neighbors, or the various uncategorized cryptids or fiends—"

"And specters, demons, devils, wights, ghouls, mummies, imps, horsefolk, hobs, gobs, two-heads—"

"Three-heads," Vivacia added with a dark chirp.

"Shades, blades, sea-goats, the possessed, the wisp-chosen, the Galateans, revenants, half-geists, succubuses, incubuses, snallygasters, gallycasters, chitterings, glitterings, witches, warlocks, dryads, nymphs, sylphs, the Hivetenders, the Maledicted—"

Vivacia: "Oh, the poor Maledicted."

"The—"

Molly jumped in. "Stopstopstopstop*stop*."

They both looked at her.

"This is a lot," she said. "*A lot* a lot. Very, very extra."

"Sorry," Dustin answered.

"You know, I haven't eaten in a while," Molly said idly.

"Well," Vivacia responded, "we should get you—"

"Or had anything to drink. Not even water."

"We can get that, too—"

"Or sleep. I'm tired. I'm suddenly very tired. Everything is getting—" She was going to finish on the word *dark*, or maybe *black*, it was hard to say. Literally. Because the word came out a kind of gabbled gush of sounds, *Everything is getting bdaahhfffgggh*, and the next thing she knew, a bottomless well of hungry shadow drew her down and swallowed her right up, gobble and gulp.

21. wakey wakey

MOLLY LURCHED UPRIGHT IN BED.

Through the split in her curtains, a thin, searing beam of sunshine shone like the light of a cutting torch. For a moment, she thought: *It was all just a stupid dream*. She must've eaten something weird (eggs always gave her strange dreams) for her brain to conjure up wallpaper ghosts, magic wolves, a monster uncle. But then, as she moved, pain filled her up like air inflating a balloon. She hurt. Her arm hurt. Her hand hurt. Her *ribs* hurt.

Wincing, she swung her legs over the edge of the mattress.

The pain that radiated throughout told her it was no dream at all.

Well, poop.

Weakly, she called for Dustin. Then Vivacia. But no one answered. A faint chord of fear struck inside her. *Something has happened,* she thought. Whatever it was that Gordo wanted with the cemetery—a cemetery for monsters, she reminded herself—he had gotten it, she feared, and that meant he was back here at the house. It would be no big thing for him to kill Dustin or Vivacia, would it? He was truly a fiend. An impossible, brutish lobster-red fiend.

Panic tightened around her like a corset. Molly gently stepped to the floor, hobbled out to the hall, then down the stairs, calling Dustin's name the whole time—

The basement door. It was open. Not all the way— but enough so she could see light coming through it, faintly. The locks—including the buzzy, old-fashioned padlock—had been undone.

Molly crept to the door and drew it fully open. It creaked as it yawned wide. Down below her waited a series of dusty cellar steps—wooden, crooked, like a mouth of bad teeth—and walls of craggy stone. Spiderwebs hung above. Long-legged cellar spiders hung in the silk, pirouetting in midair like arachnid ballerinas.

Her mouth, suddenly dry, didn't work as well as she

wanted it to when she called her brother's name again: It came out as creaky as the door. "Dustin?" *Please be okay please be okay.*

Moments passed.

And then from somewhere in the depths: "Down here."

It was his voice. Molly breathed a sigh of relief (which hurt her ribs). Gingerly, she descended into the cellar—only realizing halfway down that, given how the door was locked before, she was about to get a peek into another of the secret places. The parlor was a real bust, but who knew what lurked below the house?

Turns out, a library.

And a laboratory.

A…libroratory? (A libroratory!)

The cellar seemed to run the length of the house and then some. The floor was slate stone tile. The walls were covered in old wooden shelves bolted to the rock, and in the center of the room: a broad metal table, upon which were various accoutrements of a mad scientist's laboratory (beakers, tins, little ceramic cellars, jars of odd and unearthly reagents), and below which hung several metal drawers, each with a label on it (that she couldn't quite read). Dustin stood at this table, a massive book splayed out in front of him—with several other books piled up to its side. He hunched over it.

Same clothes as last night. When he finally looked at her, his eyes seemed in pits, encircled by shadow.

"You didn't sleep," she said.

"How could I?" came his clipped answer.

"You probably need sleep." *I definitely did.* Her stomach also reminded her what else she needed: food and water.

"What I *need* is to have this nightmare be over with."

She crept closer and swallowed hard. "How bad is it?"

"How bad? How bad. *How bad.* Well." He closed the book with a mighty *fwomp* of the pages. A dust cloud kicked up. He turned toward her with a piercing stare. "As I said, it's a *nightmare.* Some kind of…monster is loose in our cemetery. I don't know why our so-called *uncle* wanted entry, but he's in there now, and the damage he can do is incalculable."

"What…kind of damage?"

Dustin pinched the brow of his nose as if he were speaking to a simpleton. It stung but Molly tried not to show it. "What you need to understand is that the cemetery is not a one-size-fits-all solution for the passed-on. The denizens of the supernatural do not all want a simple burial plot. They have particular *needs.* Some require certain kinds of crypts, others must be buried by a kind of tree, another still might demand a particular set of *memento mori* be buried with them. And, just as they lived a magical life, they often confer upon the world a magical *death*—their passing has resonance. The objects they are buried with have power. Sometimes certain kinds of mushrooms or plants grow up at their gravesides, and those have power, too. This kind of cemetery gathers a great deal of magical energy—mostly death energy—you see, unparalleled except by other such burial sites. An opportunistic monster might be able to use that energy for terrible purposes. And—" His tone softened. "Even if all of that weren't true, our burial ground is a sacred place for many. They get so few spaces that are truly their own. They can be assured that their friends and family and other loved ones are given whatever peace they are afforded, and a place to rest, and a place to come and visit with them safely."

"Visit with them," she said, rolling that thought around her mind. "Wait, doesn't that mean *they* have keys?"

Dustin sighed. "I'm afraid not. We're the keepers of the cemetery—in particular, who may come, and who may not. The Fivefold Key is our way to protect it, to make sure someone doesn't use the resting place for ill intent. Besides," he added, "the supernatural denizens sometimes exist in a, um, let's call it a *tenuous balance*. Their alliances are less alliances and more carefully avoided blood grudges and hoary vengeances. We can't have them all in there at the same time. That key was our one way in."

"You had just one key?"

"Yes."

"And…it was just…unprotected? I'm not trying to absolve myself of blame here, dude, but if it was that important…"

"It was in a mystically locked safe in my room in the attic." Dustin's eyes widened. "Come to think of it, you never told us how *you* got it."

"I…didn't. I mean…somebody, uh, got it for me?"

"The safe does not exist entirely in this plane of reality. It straddles this reality and the spectral realm of the restless dead! Who could possibly—" It was then he realized. He again pinched the bridge of his nose. "*Lancaster*. Of course."

"The ghost boy in the wallpaper. Yeah. What's the, ahh, deal with you two?"

Dustin flinched. "*That* is a topic for another time. For now"—his nostrils flared—"we need to find a solution. We must find a way *in*."

"Maybe we climb over? Or dig under—"

"No. The cemetery is magically sealed. Try to climb

over, the stones will rend your hands to ribbons. Try to climb under and the wall goes deeper than you could ever dig. But one thing is clear: We must find a way in. We need to remove Gordo—"

"Gorgoch."

Vivacia's voice traveled down from the top of the cellar stairs. The woman came down and the contrast of the spiderwebs and the rock walls and the dusty-musty steps only served to highlight her elegance. This was not a place she often entered, Molly realized. To Vivacia's credit, though, it didn't seem to bother her to be around all this dust and must. (Unsurprising, given the beater truck she drove.) She stood tall and crisp in a sharp-angled navy dress, her chin up, her eyes down.

"Gesundheit," Molly said, as if the woman had just sneezed.

"Who or what is a Gorgoch?" Dustin asked, ignoring the joke.

Vivacia said, "Your Uncle Gordo is actually Gorgoch. His true, chosen name." She took a deep breath and then said: "He is a defalcator."

A defalcator.

"He…poops on stuff?" Molly asked.

"No," Dustin corrected, making a face like a crumpled napkin. "What? That's a *defecator.* This is a *de*-fal-*cator,* one who becomes a sorcerer by stealing magic

from other magical beings. Some call them robber flies." To Vivacia he asked: "Are you sure about this, Viv? Really, really sure?"

"I had agents, people I trust, investigate his home. It was clean, but they found a second location: a storage unit off I-80, and inside, they found, well." Vivacia scowled. "Heretic tomes. Old scrolls. Ancient relics."

Was this the same storage place where Molly kept some of her stuff? How close had she been to finding out Gordo had been...messing with unholy forces? "What kind of relics?"

"Supernatural ones," Viv said. "Old troll bones, canopic jars, dried gremlin organs, and the like. All broken or damaged—I suspect that's where he was getting his magic from. Draining them dry and drinking it up. In some cases, even eating them. Quite a few had...chunks taken out of them. Bite marks."

"Wait." Molly crossed her arms. "Magic? You're saying Uncle Gordo—er, Gorgoch—is some kind of wizard? I thought he was a monster. I thought we might *all* be monsters—"

Dustin clarified: "He had no magic of his own to start with. He was like you or me. But defalcators find a way to take it. Rituals and the like. He can only manifest magic by stealing it—and, to clarify, wizards usually prefer the title 'sorcerer.'"

"So, like Gandalf."

"No. What? Not Gandalf. Gandalf was a wizard."

"Doctor Strange, then? He was a sorcerer."

Dustin said: "Not like any of that! None of that is real!"

But Vivacia said, "*Well*. It's a little like that. Definitely more Stephen Strange than Gandalf. Occasionally a bit Willow Rosenberg, or even Neo from *The Matrix*."

It was then that Molly thought that maybe she and Vivacia could get along after all.

"Gordo—Gorgoch—didn't look like any of those, though."

"No," Dustin said. "Some don't choose to participate in the culture of it or the trappings. And he clearly wished to remain hidden. Robber flies often do, for they are anathema—illegal, in sorcererspeak. Not illegal as in stealing a candy bar, either. But illegal as in one of the highest sins. The only sin higher is if one pilfers magic not merely by stealing it, but rather, by killing— and, ah, *eating*—a magical being."

"Like, *eating* eating? Cannibalism?"

"Of a sort," Vivacia said. "Those who eat the living and the dead, they become Devourers. The worst of sorcerous fiends. We do not believe Gorgoch has become one yet—but his journals, his spellbooks, they were rage-filled things. Full of jealousy against his brother, Steven, and desirous to become more than a mere defalcator—to become a true Devourer."

"Which is why he wanted in to the cemetery," Dustin said. "Of course. He wants the death energy. He wants…to feed."

Molly's head was spinning again. *I really, really need to eat something.* But she had to make sure she understood the timeline. "So you're telling me that this guy who found me after our dad died is an evil sorcerer and was planning the whole time to bring me here so I could use the key he needed to get into your magical cemetery?"

"That seems to be the case," Vivacia confirmed. "And he *is* your uncle, but my agents informed me that he was long estranged from your mother and father, which is probably why you'd never heard of him until after Steven Grim's death."

Well. Okay then.

Dustin looked up momentarily from the table he'd been staring at and met Molly's eyes, almost looking a little sorry for her.

Forget it, bro. Now was not the time to deal with the gut-punch of meaning *nothing* to yet another family member she'd thought she could trust. "So what do we do?" Molly asked.

"Tonight," Viv said, "we have a parley with the Five Watchers. They will help us see the way forward."

"We hope," Dustin clarified.

"Yes. Hope is all we have right now. Because if Gorgoch becomes a true Devourer in such a place of power? The world will tremble against him, and he may become truly unstoppable."

22. fairies and foxfolk and florgs, oh my

EVENING CAME.

Molly finally ate—just a sandwich, for she was still rattled, which left her stomach unsettled. And she had water, too, which tasted far more precious than she remembered water to be. Her arm, though it still ached, seemed to be feeling better—thankfully, nothing appeared to be broken.

Dustin paced on the front porch of the house. Molly sat perfectly still while Vivacia tried to calm him. "It'll be fine."

He blanched, going green with woe. "I'm not looking forward to this parley, you know."

Earlier, Viv had explained that the Watchers were a council of five, chosen by the denizens of the region to represent, in her words, "fair and equal access to the cemetery," and to deal with any trespassing. And a *parley* was just oldspeak for a talk, a meeting, a gathering of words.

"What kind of, um"—she almost said *monsters*—"nonstandard citizens or whatever you call them are these Watchers?"

"The five are: Marsha Skullcap, of the Goodly Neighbors; Ember Felix, or sometimes Felix Ember, of the Foxfolk; Gabriel Valverde, sorcerer of the Nine Kitchens; Florg, of the Hob; and Dave Peterson, the vampire."

Molly made a face. "Dave…Peterson?"

Dustin nodded, continuing to pace. "Dave Peterson."

A period of silence stretched out among the three like chewing gum.

"Dave Peterson, the *vampire*," Molly confirmed again, just to be sure she'd heard that right.

"Yes, that's it," Dustin said, his tone clipped like a fingernail cut down to the cuticle. "Vampires are people, too. That's the point, Molly; that's very much the point."

Viv went on: "Gabriel is a mage of sorts. Thinks he's a hip, cool guy but is actually more a rules guy. He's a traditionalist without believing he's a traditionalist. Ember is very much the trickster you'd expect from the Foxfolk, but don't let that fool you—she can be quite serious when the fate of her kind is on the line. Marsha's lovely, if a bit…" She looked to Dustin for help.

"Awkward?" he tried.

"Enthusiastic," Viv said. "Dave is quiet and polite—"

"Dave, the *vampire*," Molly said.

"Yes." Viv seemed to be getting a bit irritated now. "And Florg is…" Another look to Dustin. "Well… Florg."

"Yes. Florg is Florg," Dustin agreed.

"Makes total sense. And the point of this meeting is?" Molly asked.

Viv said, "To determine the course of action. Both to figure out what Gorgoch wants and to help us get back into the cemetery."

"Certainly there are…protocols," Dustin piped up. "Mother had some plan for this kind of thing, didn't she, Viv?"

The woman was silent, though. Which answered the question. Instead, she said, "I'm going to the barn. They'll be here soon. I need to make sure all is prepared."

And with that, she left Molly alone with Dustin.

"So," she said, watching him pace. "I want to go."

"Then go. Wherever your home is, go. You've done your damage." In those words, she detected no anger—just a kind of resignation. But he'd also misunderstood her.

"No, I mean, I want to go to the parley."

"No," Dustin said.

"But—"

The cords of his neck stood out like piano wires as he again said, this time with greater tension: "*No*. This is your fault. Viv may have apologized for the way we treated you but that doesn't mean I have to forgive you. You mucked about with something you don't understand. As has been pointed out, you're still a…child."

"So are you," Molly said.

"I'm not a child!"

"You're not exactly an old man, either." Under her breath she added: "Even though you kinda act like one." But before he could protest further, she stood up and cut him off: "You're right. I'm just a kid. And I screwed up. But like it or not, I'm your sister, this is the family business, and…well, I'm in it now. *All the way.* Lemme help."

His eyes scanned the darkness. Finally, he relented: "*Fine.* You can go to the parley. But you will be quiet. You're there to listen and to learn. Only!"

"Only," Molly said.

"Only."

"Be quiet. Listen and learn. Got it."

She could do that. (Couldn't she?)

Nighttime in the barn.

Molly had—reluctantly! as commanded!—found a seat in the corner. A dusty, hay-strewn corner. From there, she could see a long wooden table in the center of the barn with seven mismatched chairs. Hanging above the table: a series of seven Edison bulbs, glowing with umber light. ("No candles," Vivacia said to Molly quietly, "as the denizens of the celestial do not care much for *fire*." Molly knew it was not the time to ask, but she put a pin in that phrase: *denizens of the celestial.*) For her part, she chose a particular outfit: a hastily thrown together cosplay of Lady Aven Valus, vampire falconer from L.L. Morgenschwab's young adult novel, *Into the Crimson Gloaming.* Red high-collar jacket, lots of makeup, hair in a crown of braids, and on her left wrist, a falconer's glove. (Okay, not really a falconer's glove. Lady Aven's glove was brown leather with cool buckles and stuff, and this one was white, as she'd borrowed it from a Hina Harumi outfit.)

She was about to stand up and get a full gander

of what was on the long table in the center of the room when the first guest came in—a tall woman with gawky, reedy limbs, hair a tangled scribble all around her head. In that black tangle, Molly spied bits of leaf and twig, maybe even a few berries? She immediately began to imagine how she would cosplay this woman, what archetypes would go into summing up her character in an outfit. Chaos librarian meets park ranger? With a little crazy cat lady for good measure?

Dustin and Vivacia moved to greet the woman, but they weren't fast enough. The lady was in the barn only half a moment before she whirled to face the corner, staring through bug-eyed spectacles perched upon her gull's beak nose. Her whole body jumped like a Tasered rat when she saw Molly.

"Who the foxglove is *that*?" She spun to face Dustin, pointing not a finger so much as a wildly gesticulating hand in Molly's direction. "We are invaded! Interloped! Trespassed upon!"

"Marsha," Dustin said, clearly trying to evoke *calm*, "I assure you—"

Marsha wheeled again toward Molly, her arms stiff and her fingers splayed out. Then her eyes went different colors—one a cloud of dark purple, like from a popped grape, and the other a bright lime green, like the color of a smoothie that was too healthy to taste good. Around her, the air seemed to *thicken*, and a strange frequency arose in Molly's ears. Her skin prickled; her hairs stood in panic and something more.

"No!" Molly said.

"The shadow speaks!" Marsha shrieked, recoiling.

Dustin gently put his hands atop her wrists and eased the woman's arms down. "That's...that's my sister."

Marsha blinked. Three blinks in, her eyes lost their mad gush of color and returned to their standard brown. "Your sister?"

"Her name is Molly."

"I'm learning the ropes," Molly said, gulping.

"Oh. Oh. Hah." Marsha gave a goofy smile and pushed the glasses back up to the top of her nose. The air thinned anew. "Oops!"

"Oops," Molly echoed. "Ha, uhh, ha."

Marsha leaned in, offering a long-fingered hand. Molly took it with some hesitation. As they shook—a bit too aggressively for Molly's tastes—the woman said, almost in a singsongy voice: "I'm Marsha Skullcap of the Goodly Neighbors. The Fair Folk? The Friendly Ancestors? Heard of us? That's okay! We have time to get acquainted." Then she laughed: a goofy guffaw. Teeth out, mouth wide. Kind of a *haw haw har har* laugh.

"Sounds...good?" Molly said.

Then Marsha returned her attention to Dustin and Viv. With an awkward flourish of her arms, she said, "So what's the scoop? The deal? The sitch? Been a while since a parley. I think the last one was when the Trog was rampaging around—" On this she once more whirled to face Molly. "A Trog, little sister, is a vicious thing, kind of a...leathery blob with a hundred mouths and a thousand teeth? Though quite sweet when they're *babies*—"

Viv interjected. "We'll wait for the others to arrive before we get into it. Would you care for a refreshment?" She produced a tall glass of something bright red. "Watermelon agua fresca?"

Marsha beamed as she seized it, taking a noisy sip. "You take *such* good care of us."

As if on cue, another Watcher entered the barn. This one was a man with brown, almost bronze skin—his round face sported a sharp-angled black beard, thick as steel wool. A concert T-shirt (*Storg & Japertha, Live in Oslo 2003*) strained over his round belly. He had his hands stuffed in the pockets of a pair of dark chef pants, like he was one of those Food Network personalities in his off-hours. When he entered, he did so affably, with an easy lean so that his feet were forward but his shoulders were back.

"Hello, hello," he said, his voice with a cool-dude affect. "Dustin, Viv. Marsha, good to see you, been a while." Then to Molly, who had since come out of her corner. "I...don't know you. Dusty, who is this?" But he didn't wait for Dustin's answer and, instead, kept on. "I'm Gabriel Valverde," he said to Molly. "And you're—"

He narrowed his eyes and from his pocket pulled a pinch of something that he drizzled across the open air. *Salt*, Molly realized. Flaky sea salt. It scattered on the barn floor, and for a moment, the man stared at it—almost *through* it—as it fell. "Ah. There it is. You're Molly, his sister. A Grim. Not an Ashe."

She gaped. "How'd you—"

"He's a sorcerer," Vivacia said with ill-concealed irritation.

"I like to think of myself as a *culinary wizard*," Gabriel said, a twinkle in his dark eyes. "At least, that's what my latest review called me."

Dustin smiled stiffly. "Mr. Valverde is the chef and owner of a local farm-to-table restaurant—"

"More of a *food boutique*. Your brother never takes me up on it, but you can always get a meal there on me."

"I prefer not to *intermingle* with the, ahh, clients—"

"Ah yes, the Old Ways," Gabriel said. "I respect that."

"We must respect the Old Ways!" Marsha chimed in.

From the doorway, a raucous cackle of laughter followed by a sharp-tongued voice with a Celtic lilt: "Oh heavens to hell and back, are we talking about the Old Ways versus the New Ways again?" The voice came from a bony, ropy woman in a loose-fitting ragamuffin's coat. Her hair was a short, chaotic shock of red sticking up at all angles—the chaos was artful, though, like this woman worked very hard to make it look that way. Unlike Marsha's mess of hair, which looked like she rolled out of bed looking that way and then ran through a bramble, and maybe through a wind tunnel. And now Molly realized that the hair was less red and more the copper color of a fox's coat. And that was how she'd cosplay this Watcher—like a gender-flipped Gambit from the X-Men. But more decidedly *Irish*. The woman continued: "The ways are the ways, away and away, who cares about old or new. We just do what we do and have fun doing it."

"Ember Felix." Gabriel and Marsha said in unison. But the way they said it was quite different. Marsha sounded excited, or at least excitable. More: "Ember!" And Gabriel was more glum, like there was an unspoken *Oh, it's you* hiding after the "Felix." Dustin and Vivacia's faces were carefully neutral.

But Ember wasn't alone. Next to her was a—

Well, a shimmer. Like heat haze off a hot road. Like

the Predator. It moved in a person shape, but a *huge* person shape—twice the size of a normal human being.

Was anyone else seeing this?

"**I AM FLORG**," boomed the shimmer. "**FLORG OF THE HOB. FLORG'S FORM IS CHAOS INCARNATE, AND TO GAZE UPON IT IS TO INVITE MADNESS, A FRACTURE OF THE MIND SO DEEP THAT WHO KNOWS WHAT WOULD ENTER THE CHASM—OR WORSE, WHAT WOULD COME OUT OF IT. FLORG'S CORPOREAL APPEARANCE IS TOO HORRIFYING TO COMPRE—HHEEEY, ARE THOSE CHEEZ-ITS?**"

On the table, Vivacia was, indeed, putting out a bowl of the crackers.

"I know you like them," she said.

The shimmer shimmied its way over to the table and began delicately eating one cracker after the next. It crunched and munched quite diligently. The cracker would float in the air, buoyed by the shining air, and then would disappear into nothing. The rest of the group went back to murmuring among themselves, but Molly couldn't look away—she was fascinated.

And then the faint scuff of a heel caused them all to turn slowly to see:

A middling, nondescript white guy in a pair of khakis and a blue button-down shirt. His hair was... brown? Blond? Did it even matter? It was hard to really pin any kind of description on him except, *Picture an accountant, any accountant,* and voila, there he was.

Instantly, Molly knew: This was Dave Peterson, the vampire.

"Hey, everybody," he said cheerfully.

In unison, a vaguely uninterested, "Hey, Dave."

(Though from Florg, it was: "**HEY, DAVE.**" That plus an aerosolized mist of cheese-cracker dust.)

Ember Felix cackled again and said, "All righty, then, mates. That's all of us. Let's ride this pony until it dies! Pitter-patter, everyone."

Her way, apparently, of starting the meeting.

23. the parley, the choice, and the who did what in the graveyard?!

THEY ALL SAT WITH THEIR SNACKS AND BEVERAGES: FROM HER CORNER, Molly could see Florg with their crackers and Marsha with her watermelon agua fresca. Gabriel had brought his own "glacier water" and a little baggie of roasted Paraná pine nuts. Ember was given a hot tea by Vivacia but on the sly sipped from a flask when she thought no one was looking. And Dave, well, Dave had pulled out a glass of something that looked a little like the watermelon agua fresca, but was considerably darker and richer in its redness.

(He sipped it from a bendy straw.)

It was a bit like herding cats, Molly saw: As soon as they sat, each of them tried to steer the conversation to what was happening in their respective corner of the world.

Gabriel noted that sorcerers were mostly loner types but that he'd heard the Society of the Hidden Light and the Travelers of the Interstices had put away their beef, and then he went on to ramble about the upcoming fall menu at his restaurant.

Ember said in a voice tinged with that Irish brogue, "Our dens and warrens are safe, we've peace with the Hivetenders, had a raucous drunken to-do with the Loops, nature continues to be red in tooth and claw." That, before adding, "Our only real and persistent problem is with you hairless spider monkeys, eh?" She cleared her throat. "By which I mean, you wee pesky humans."

Florg said little, only that, **"THE MYRIAD GUARD-POSTS MARKING THE WAYS BETWEEN WORLDS ARE KEPT, AND THE VIGIL OF THE HOB IS CARRIED."** Then, in a grumbling voice, **"THOUGH THE GOBLIN MAN PLAGUES US STILL."**

It was enough to make Molly wonder anew if she had taken a hard fall at some point and all this was a coma-fed delusion.

(Either way, she decided to keep quiet for the

moment, because though she wouldn't have said it out loud, she was kinda loving this?)

Marsha kinda blabber-stammered her way through an update about trods and circles, about the Queen-King and something called the Walkers Behind the Walls. She said it nervously in the way someone says *everything is fine!* but totally means the opposite.

After their updates, they dissolved into a gregarious din of talking to one another—a white noise roar of personal updates and jokes and gasps and laughs. Molly watched Vivacia and Dustin share increasingly uncomfortable looks, and from time to time Dustin tried to gain control of the parley—he'd clear his throat, or lean forward as if to focus attention on him, or actually start *speaking.* But none of it worked. The look of frustration on his face hardened into what Molly feared would become a permanent mask, so she decided to just skip all that. She was here to fix things, after all, and that meant helping her big bro.

She stood up and clapped her hands a bunch of times. *Clap clap clap clap.* Like a preschool teacher focusing attention. Maybe it even helped a little that she was dressed like a vampire falconer—a kindred spirit to those in front of her.

"Hello!" she said very loudly. "It's time to listen to Dustin now!"

Then she sat back down.

All went quiet. They looked at her, then at Dustin, where their gazes collectively settled like laser beams of pure heat. He looked *less* comfortable than he had before. Suddenly awkward. Sweating a little, too.

Which seemed strange to her. Hadn't he done this before? Shouldn't he be good at it? Their mother had died only the year before this one, but...certainly he'd had practice? He'd grown up in this world....

She gave him a nod of solidarity, like, *You got this, dude.* But he frowned disapprovingly at her in response. Then, clearing his throat, he spoke.

"There is a, ahh, there's a problem with the cemetery," he said.

The Five Watchers looked to one another. Ember said: "What *kind* of problem, Mr. Ashe? Hm? Grass gettin' a little overgrown?"

Gabriel chuckled. "Did some rowdy teens knock over a headstone? Maybe spray-paint something inappropriate on a tomb?"

"BETTER NOT BE GOBLINS," Florg said with a disruptive shiver. **"IF THE GOBLINS GOT OUT OF THEIR GOBLIN JAR, FLORG WILL BECOME FUELED BY RAGE."**

They did not, Molly realized, take this job—or her brother—seriously. That or they'd had such an easy time until now that nothing seemed like a big deal. And so she found herself erupting, without meaning to:

"It's a defibrillator!"

They all turned to her, confused.

"A...a defenestrator? No. Aaagh. *There's a pooper in the graveyard.*"

Wide eyes stared back in confusion and horror. Dustin noisily cleared his throat and said: "What my sister is trying to say is that the cemetery, *not* grave-yard, has been breached."

Marsha leaned forward and asked in a panicked whisper: "What does that mean, Dustin?" She suddenly recoiled. "A defalcator. The girl means a defalcator."

"Yes. The night prior, a defalcator—our uncle, Gordo—used the Fivefold Key to secure entry to the cemetery. He took the key in with him. I cannot say what he is doing, but...I assume it isn't good. He seemed to be jealous of our father, his brother, and there seemed to be some intent to become a, ahh, *Devourer.*"

"Well, then," Ember said, her voice cold. "A proper Devourer."

The shimmer that was Florg suddenly sprang out of their seat, knocking over the bowl of Cheez-Its. A pair of shining, flyswarm arms came down against the table, cracking it in half with a sound like a thunderclap.

Glasses fell, shattering. Florg bellowed, and then Molly watched as the two halves of the table—

Poof! Turned into a cloud of moths. Brown and white—the white of marshmallows, the brown of cocoa. The insects, eerily beautiful, swarmed upward, gathering in the eaves of the old barn, some surely caught in the webs up there. Food now for spiders.

Moths, Molly thought again. *Moths that were recently a table.*

"Oh my," said Dave Peterson.

Then came another wave of quiet. Most of the Watchers stood now at their chairs—except for Ember, who sat back, cool as a quart of ice cream.

"This is unacceptable," Gabriel said, his voice seething. "Our friends, our family, our cohorts, and our people are in that cemetery."

"Wouldn't have happened if Polly were still around," Ember said, clucking her tongue. "Shame, innit. Shame, shame, shame."

At this, Dustin's face turned bright red and Vivacia's eyes narrowed. Even Molly felt her hackles rise, not because she cared one fig about her mother but because this Ember person was twisting an emotional knife into Dustin's back.

"Oh, Aunt Copperleaf," Marsha moaned. "Tom Baneberry. Brother Beardtongue." She gasped. "The

Margined Calligrapher!" Marsha buried her face in her hands and wept.

Gabriel continued: "Those who have passed are bound to that place and to us by magic and bereavement, and, so help me, if by all the stars and the moons this *uncle* of yours disrupts the Fundament, you are in the deepest of—"

"I take full responsibility," Dustin said. "I was protector of the key and I failed to maintain the integrity of that protection. As such, the cemetery was violated and now we must—"

"It was *my* fault," Molly blurted out.

She didn't really *know* she was going to say that. But there Dustin was, taking the blame. Falling on the sword. Jumping on the grenade. And she just couldn't allow that. Which surprised her, because she still had that tickle in her belly that she didn't owe him squat, that he had something she didn't, and that if they'd just told her about all this from the get-go, nothing bad would have happened.

But also, Dustin and Vivacia were obviously protecting something delicate—and important—to these denizens, these *nonstandard citizens*. (*Celestial denizens*, she thought again. *Gotta ask what that is.*)

So it felt right. The sword was hers to fall on.

(But it sure hurt, just the same.)

The Watchers turned toward her again. Marsha, with her tear-slicked cheeks. Gabriel, with eyes of rage. Ember, with a kind of…mad curiosity. She couldn't see how Florg viewed her—only that the hulking shimmer-shape was rising and falling, as if with labored, angry breathing. Dave Peterson just looked upon her with a kind of…sadness. It might've even been sympathy.

"I did it," she said. "My father died and left me part of this place and I thought—" Already her voice was getting tacky with the threat of tears. "I thought I was owed something. I didn't know about you guys or the business or anything, and my uncle convinced me to help him get into the cemetery and…I didn't know what he was…"

"The key was my responsibility," Dustin said. "This still falls on me."

"But I stole it!" she objected. "Well. A ghost stole it. For me."

"And I let it be stolen! I was negligent in my duties—"

"*All right,*" Ember said, finally standing and waving her hands about. "We don't need you to compete in the Blame Game Olympics. Congrats, you both tied for the gold!" She clapped her hands sarcastically.

Gabriel cast his gaze to Vivacia. "Would you like to take some ownership of this, too, Viv?"

"I'll take my share of the blame," she said, making her choice. "I *am* the adult in the room."

She did not mean it to sting, but it hurt Molly just the same. And seeing Dustin's face—it stung him, too.

"There it is! The trifecta. The prize split three ways." Ember sat back down with a lazy slump, shaking her head.

"What's your plan?" Gabriel asked. "Hm, Dusty? I expect you don't have one and need us to fix it for you."

"That's why we invited you here," Vivacia said, cutting Dustin off. "You all have a stake in this, and as Watchers, you have a voice as well."

"FLORG WILL FIX THIS. FLORG WILL OPEN THE BOOK OF SPACE AND TIME AND TURN TO THE PAGE THAT TAKES FLORG TO THE CEMETERY. THIS UNCLE OF YOURS WILL EXPLODE IN A RAIN OF VISCERA AS FLORG NESTS WITHIN HIS RIB CAGE AND IS BORN ANEW A HUNDRED TIMES—"

"Florgie-pie," Ember said, "you know as well as I do the cemetery resists magical intrusion. No portals, no gateways, no hopping the fence, no going under the wall, no picking the lock. Not one wee bit of it."

"BAH," Florg said, their shimmering shoulders slumping.

Through her sniffles and sobs, Marsha said, "So what's the plan? What do we *do*?"

Dustin was quiet for a little while, then he answered:

"Each of you go to your people and try to figure out how to get back into the cemetery as quickly as possible. I'll keep consulting the old books. And once we know how to get in, we'll figure out how to stop Gorgoch from doing whatever it is that he's doing."

"Cool," Dave Peterson said.

But the way he said it was decidedly *not cool*. Not cool at all.

24. meadow talk

OVER THE NEXT FEW NIGHTS, THE WATCHERS, DUSTIN, AND VIVACIA buzzed to and fro, ramping up their research, suggesting plans, and other stuff that didn't really include Molly.

Which made Molly feel alone. And sad. And mad. And worst of all, *lost.* The other night in the barn, she'd felt like, okay, maybe she could help them fix this. Perhaps she had a role to play yet. It was, in a sense, like cosplay: She knew she wasn't really prepared to fight any of these fights, but that's how cosplay was. You put on the outfit of someone else—someone much cooler, someone way more capable—and then you played the role of superhero, or space pilot, or anime assassin princess. And if you got the outfit *just right*, and the attitude *just so*, you could almost believe it was real.

But she couldn't pretend her way out of this one.

It was only now that she understood that any hope she'd had of fixing what she'd broken was gone—what could she do? She was in over her head. So, in her Molly costume (T-shirt and jeans), she wandered out into the meadow and sat down in the dark, amid wildflowers whose blooms and blossoms had closed up for the night.

She tried not to cry. But she cried, anyway. A little bit.

A presence startled her, and she quickly wiped away tears.

"You're sitting amid all kinds of *really cool* flowers," Marsha said behind her. "I see swamp buttercups and some hairy beardtongue and star grass and—ooh, there's my namesake. Some skullcap. Little purple flowers. Not particularly showy, but I like them. Bonus medicinal value, if you care about that sort of thing."

Marsha plunked down next to her. It was a movement with little grace, but Molly appreciated that, feeling very ungraceful herself, with tear tracks on her face.

"How can you see all those flowers?" Molly asked. "It's dark out."

"I can see in the dark."

"Of course you can," Molly said dully. "You have special powers. Gifts. I have…" She sighed. "Nothing."

"You have your family."

"I don't have them. And they only have me because I shoved my way into their lives. And actually, it's just Dustin. I'm not related to Viv. I *am* related to Gordo, who turned out to be a monster." She winced. "Sorry. Not supposed to say that word."

Marsha sighed. "Well, if your uncle is truly aspiring to become a Devourer"—she lowered her voice—"then that word super-duper applies." She let out a weird little giggle.

They sat for a while, quiet. The wind swept across the dark meadow.

"So, like, I have questions," Molly said finally.

"And I have answers." Marsha pushed her glasses back up her nose. "Let's hope they match!"

"You're…I don't know what you are. The Goodly Neighbors. Are you like…fairies? Is that a thing? Is that a rude word? I don't want to use a slur or whatever."

Marsha laughed another of her goofy, knee-slapper snorts. "Aw, no, it's not a nasty word. It's a bit anti-quated but we don't hate it. *Fairy* comes from *fae* or *fey*. We've been called Fair Folk, changelings, the Hidden Ones. We're not demoted angels, nor are we demons. We don't like being called *elves* because we're not all elves." Her brow darkened. "And we definitely don't like *the wee folk*. Wee. Tiny. Also a word for pee. Did you know that? I think it's very rude to suggest we are small and related to urine."

Molly worked to stifle a laugh, but this only gave the forbidden laugh strength. A chortle karate-kicked its way past her lips, and her eyes went as wide as moons. "Sorry! Sorry. I just—you know. You said *pee.*"

Marsha shrugged. "Never apologize for a laugh. I never do! HaHA!"

Molly grinned. "So—okay, but the Goodly Neighbors, that's your preferred thing?"

"It is, because once—and still—we were known for being exactly that. The neighbors to humans. Next-door, one world over. And we made bargains with them, deals and pacts that had us helping them and them helping us." Marsha sighed. "A lot of the old pacts are forgotten, of course. And few humans really believe in us or our magic now—not to mention nearly all of us these days *are* humans, or started out that way." Molly looked up at this, questioning. "That's a story for another time. But I like to think our original intent and undertaking is the same: to make the world a better place. So we are truly the Goodliest Neighbors."

"Cool," Molly said. She didn't know what to *do* with that information—everything she'd learned had been oh-so-*extra*, but she filed it away. For now, she just liked that Marsha had trusted her enough to tell her anything.

Switching gears, Molly asked, "So how are you all gonna get into the cemetery?"

"Well," Marsha said, thrusting out a finger and pushing her glasses back up her nose, "I don't rightly know. We used to all be keepers of the keys to the necropolis, but that…changed. Due to a situation just like this one."

"Really?"

The story, as Marsha told Molly, was this:

Once upon a time, the Five Watchers each held an iron key to the cemetery door. This key allowed them to enter whenever they wanted, choosing who could and could not come with them; so, if a vampire wished to bring some of his vampire cohorts into the burial ground to pay their respects to a dead vampire pal (here Molly got confused about why vampires even *needed* burial plots), they could open the door and usher them in. Bereavement would occur. Sorrow was shared. They would pour a little blood on the curb for their lost blood buddies. The end. Right?

Not so much.

Marsha said, "The truth of our kind—our *kinds*, I guess—is that we're called monsters, but we're no more monstrous than regular people."

"But regular people can be monstrous, too."

"Bingo, kiddo." Marsha went on to say, "Monstrousness isn't because of who you are, but because of the choices you make."

She continued the story, explaining that cemeteries of this kind were rare and home to considerable magic. "Everything in such a supernatural place is *suffused* with energy—every bit of moss, every pebble, every moth. And the *bodies* of the celestial dead have even more energy in them—pooling like the juices from overripe fruit, fermented and strong.

"So it happened one day that four Watchers discovered that the fifth—a sorcerer named Margove—was collecting death energies for use in his spells. And when called on it, Margove said he only began this heretical act when *he* found out that the vampiric Watcher, Bettina Blackmoore, was sneaking in to drain the dead blood out of recently buried magicians. And *she* said she only did it because the shape-changer Watcher, a Loop (or werewolf) named Black Socks, was *devouring dead fairies* and then selling their wings to collectors. And on and on, until they all figured out that each of them was using the cemetery not just as a place to express sorrow but also as a place to personally enrich themselves."

And so, Marsha explained, it was decided:

"The Watchers would no longer have keys. All entries into the cemetery would be accompanied, if allowed, by a Keeper. Meaning, Keykeeper. The five keys were merged into one—literally forged together into the Fivefold Key—the door to this and all supernatural cemeteries was given a fitting lock, and each cemetery was looked after by a Keeper. That's how the supernatural solemnities industry came about, nearly two hundred years ago: Those who would guard the gate into the cemetery also became the curators of centuries', even millennia's worth of bereavement rites, rituals, and reagents for the celestial kin buried there. Keepers were no longer just the guards at the door but an integral part of the funerary and bereavement process for the supernatural."

Molly paused to think about her next question. It seemed as good a time as any to get this next answer. "I keep hearing that word—celestial. Does that mean, like, planets?"

"I don't want to get into the *weeds* on all this—even though I like weeds! A lot!—but all of us Watchers, all the supernatural inhabitants of this world, are connected via common ancestors. Beings who, depending on the story, were either blessed by the moon, the sun, the stars, the planets, *or* whose magic came from being able to channel the power of those faraway places."

"That sounds awesome." Molly moped. "Too bad I have nothing like it."

"Well…"

Hope flared anew inside Molly. "Well, what?"

"You are probably Blooded."

"Oh yeah! I wanted to ask about that. It sounds *awesome*. Tell me more, please, now."

Marsha smiled indulgently. "The Blooded are ones who have the blood of the celestials"—*Okay this is amazing I have magic in my blood holy cats*—"but who cannot do, well, *cool magic stuff* with it. You are the bridge between the normies and the supernaturals."

"Ugh!" Molly's excitement crashed back to earth as she stood up. "See? Even if I have magic, I can't do anything with it. It's just…in me. Like a lump. Like a recessive gene." Again her mind turned to Gordo—was he Blooded, too? *Was that why he went after others for their magic? Maybe he couldn't stand being a regular old nobody.*

"You're special, Molly. You're special because you're you."

"Ugh. Save me the therapy. I'm not special except in how spectacularly I messed all this up."

"We'll fix it."

"Really?"

Marsha laughed.

"Oh, I dunno. Probably not! I'm just trying to be encouraging." She gave Molly an awkward, overeager hug and then hurried off to help the others. Leaving Molly once again alone, in the dark, under the stars. Surrounded by flowers she could not see.

25. impostor syndrome

THROUGH THE NIGHT AND THE NEXT DAY THE OTHERS CAME AND WENT. Molly offered to help. She had eyes and hands, after all. But the Watchers seemed to act like she'd get in the way.

Because I would, she knew.

So she decided she'd help in her own way.

If only to make amends.

First, she went to Gordo's car—the Caddy was still parked in the driveway. It was locked, so she found a brick around the back of the house and put it through the driver-side window. The crash was louder than she expected—it made her flinch—and also considerably more dramatic. Most modern cars had safety glass, so the pane kinda *stuck together* even when broken. This? Did not do that. The Caddy's window smashed like a mirror falling off a wall, *ksshhh,* and she nearly peed herself when it happened.

Still, it let her unlock the door and poke around (carefully, so as not to cut herself). The car was covered in a lot of fast-food trash and receipts for the fast-food trash. Though one receipt, not for fast food at all, was curious:

Hiram's Occult Emporium.

On it was only one item: *Elk bezoar: $149.99.*

"What the heck is that?" she asked no one.

It seemed better, instead, to ask *someone,* so Molly reversed course out of the car (again careful around the glass) and tried to flag literally anybody down. Dustin was in the libroratory and hissed that he was busy reading. Viv was on the phone. Molly got tired of waiting, so she headed to the barn to see who was out there, but all she found was Dave Peterson, who sat in the dark with a black umbrella at his side and what looked to be another…bloodred milkshake in his hand, bendy straw in his mouth.

"Hi," she said.

"Oh! Hi," he said, dabbing his lip with the pad of his thumb. He looked down at the thumb with a flash of hungry eyes, and he licked a red drop off it. "We didn't formally meet the other night: I'm Dave Peterson."

"Yeah. Hi. Molly." She looked around. They were alone. A sudden thrum of fear plucked her strings. "Um."

"Oh, you're wondering if you're safe." He paused. "From me."

Blink, blink. "No, no, I mean—"

"Aw, it's okay. It's a common misconception that vampires are all voracious predators at worst, sociopathic manipulators at best."

"Vampires aren't like that?"

"Oh." He hesitated. "Some are."

She backed away.

"But I'm not," he said, a simple smile stuck to his face like a piece of gum. "I'm fine."

"I'd think that a sociopathic manipulator would not admit to being a sociopathic manipulator," Molly countered, trying to keep the tremble out of her voice. "Plus, you know, you're drinking blood."

"I am. It's bison blood, though. Does it bother you? I can put it away."

She gulped. "It's...frothy."

"I get it infused with nitrogen. Makes it a smoother, kinda *silky* mouthfeel. It was Gabriel's idea. He also hooked me up with a local bison guy. It's been great being a part of a community, finally."

"Are you not…part of your own…uh, community?"

He smiled again, but it looked like one of those smiles when you're trying not to look sad. "Oh, well, gosh, you know. I'm a bit on the outside of my people." He narrowed his eyes. "Which is why they gave me this job, because nobody wanted it." But again his face brightened. "Which is great! Really great. I've met some wonderful friends."

"Oh. Uh. Cool! Hey, so, like, do you know what a *bezoar* is?"

"A bezwhat now?"

"A bezoar."

"A bazaar?"

"Bezoar."

"Bee's oar?"

"So that's a no."

"Yeah, that's a no." He shrugged. "Sorry."

"Thanks, anyway."

"No problem. Hey, are you okay?"

"I'm okay," she lied.

"It's hard not knowing where you belong," Dave Peterson said. "It's maybe one of life's—or unlife's—most important quests."

"Why are you telling me that?"

"Just feels like it was a piece of advice I could pass along."

"Are you trying to manipulate me, sociopathically?"

"I'm not, but I guess I wouldn't tell you if I was."

"Right. Well. I'll see you later. Have a nice…time in the barn."

"Have a nice time finding out what a bee's oar is!"

She nodded and hurried out. It struck her that other than Marsha, that was one of the only pleasant interactions she'd had since coming to this place, albeit useless. Dave Peterson was a very nice vampire but he didn't seem particularly tapped in to any kind of actual magic shenanigans. She needed someone who would stop and talk to her.

Preferably someone who didn't belong.

But who?

Oh.

Oh.

"Hey, Wallpaper Boy!" Molly barked at the wall of her bedroom. She walked over to the *tessellated quatrefoils* and began pounding on them. *Whump whump whump.* "Come out of there! You and I need to talk!"

But no ghost emerged.

"Lancaster! Link! Ghost Boy! Wallpaper Lad!"

Still nothing.

Molly growled, then stood on the bed and reached to the tippy top of the room—where the wall met the ceiling. She got her fingernails under the barest lip of wallpaper and peeled a strip of it off. It tore away with a satisfying *rrrrrip*.

"Stop!"

That from across the room.

Molly spun, swatch of wallpaper in hand. Emerging from the wallpaper was Lancaster Bauman Jr.

"Lanky," she seethed.

"Hello," the ghost said in a small voice.

"You really borked me, buddy."

"I don't know what that means. I helped you. I helped!"

"You stole the key!"

"And gave it to you! You asked me—please remember."

Molly gritted her teeth. The ghost had a point. "Even still," she continued, "I didn't know what it did or what it meant. I didn't *know* that my uncle would use me to open the gate and do"—she flailed—"whatever it is he's doing!"

"He entered the cemetery?" the ghost boy said in a hushed whisper.

"He did."

"That explains why Dustin is so…agitated." The ghost boy buried his face in his spectral hands, his noncorporeal body racked with silent sobs.

"Yeah. Ready to tell me what the deal with you two is now?"

Lancaster sighed. "We were friends. Very close. We spoke long into the night, almost every night. He'd speak of the Hawaiian Islands in this way that made them sound like a fantastic land where we could get away from everything. But when his mother died… and he took on the role of Keeper…" Another silent hitching sob. "He took the job so seriously. He felt he could no longer fraternize with me. In case I…influenced his decisions or tried to get him to let me into the cemetery."

"You're a ghost. Can't you just…go in?"

"I can go many places, but I cannot go there. It's warded off from my kind. Keeps us out. And keeps the ghosts of that place *in*, too."

"Oh. Sorry."

The ghost shrugged. "I don't want to be in there. I just want my friend back. I hadn't had anyone to speak with in years—decades! His mother wouldn't speak to me, and Vivacia kept her distance, too. I told him I'd never try to influence him.…"

"Wait, how long have you been in this house?"

"Oh, I don't even know anymore. Time is strange to me, you see. It's like trying to catch rainwater. But I suppose it was at least a century ago. There was a fire. This house, it burned down. My mother and father got out, but I and my cat, Jerome, were not so lucky."

"Your mother and father...wow. Dude, I'm sorry." Suddenly, Molly snapped her fingers. "Whoa. Hold on. Did you know *my* father, too?"

"I recall him, yes."

Link was a ghost and had been here for a century or more. Did that mean he knew more about her family? The questions came pouring out. "Why did my mother and father separate? Was he mean to her? Was she mean to him? Did he just suck so bad? Or was she like...too prim and proper?" And then, the big question, the one that proved why question marks were shaped like hooks all along: "Why did Polly get rid of me?"

"They separated because of you."

"Wh...what?"

"They loved each other. They were quite moon-eyed, or at least seemed to be. Vivacia did not like him, of course, because he was...different from Polly, different from her family. But he worked here for a time. They had Dustin, and a few years later, you."

"And? So?"

"I don't know. I just know after that, they separated. Polly kept Dustin here, and Steve took you with him."

"So it was my fault. They…didn't want another kid, I guess. I was too much." But did that make sense? Steve couldn't handle her on his own. Certainly it'd be easier to handle two kids with a full set of parents. Something nagged at her. There had to be more.

"I'm sorry I can't help you. My own parents left me here," Link said. "I tried speaking to them as they poked through the ashes of their home, and it only scared them, and they ran away."

"Sorry."

The ghost sighed—the sound of wind through a broken bottle.

"Did you steal the key to get back at Dustin?" Molly asked. "For abandoning you the way your parents did?"

Lancaster offered a reluctant nod, then hid behind the wallpaper—slipping into the pattern like a piece of paper through a heating vent. She could still see his shape but not his features.

"Well, thanks for telling me all that," Molly said after a moment.

"You're mad at me."

"It's not your fault."

"You're still mad." The voice was now an unearthly, mournful echo.

"A *little* mad. But you can make it up to me," she said, remembering why she'd come at all. "You know what a bezoar is?"

"I do not."

Ah, poop.

"Thanks, anyway."

The ghost boy moaned and sank back into the wallpaper again. Molly sulked out of the room, unsure of where to go, or what to do now, or why her very existence was the thing that broke her parents apart.

26. back to the wall

MOLLY FINALLY GOOGLED "BEZOAR" AND LEARNED IT WAS A "MASS OF indigestible material" often found in the stomach or intestinal tract of animals or people.

Um, ew.

Other than that, the only idea she had for helping was the obvious one:

Go back to the gate.

She wandered away from the house and past the barn. This time, an orange tabby cat bounded through the grass in front of her, chasing—and failing to catch—a fleeing goldfinch. She didn't see where the cat went after that; it was as if it had disappeared entirely. The sun inched toward the horizon, casting everything in oranges and pinks.

Molly crept toward the forest once more.

Her reason for going into the woods wasn't particularly strategic. A little part of her thought, *Ah, I'll be able to go to the door and find a secret way inside, some hidden passage or gopher hole or Narnia cabinet.* But mostly it was her way of *going away.* Or maybe just getting *out* of the way.

As she stepped up to the forest, it did not open for her. The trees had gone still and lifeless, the ground a gray damp carpet of dead leaves. The thorn tangle was a brittle scribble, and though the vines did not shift to allow Molly past, it didn't take much to move them aside—or break them entirely. The foliage snapped like cheap candy.

Into the woods she went. Though before time had seemed strange, now it just seemed like, well, time. The normal flow of things. Which on the one hand was nice, to not feel so unmoored from reality. But it remained a firm reminder that something had broken—

Or is dying, she thought grimly.

Soon she found the wall, and along the wall she walked. It was cold to the touch. Bits of moss along its cracks and crevices had gone brown and crumbled to dust when her fingers barely touched it.

The door—or gate, or whatever you wanted to call it—loomed. Its wood was cold, too, but when she pressed her hand to it, it seemed to vibrate. It hummed in her elbows; it sang in her teeth. Not in a good way. It made her feel queasy. As if it were white noise poisoned by some other worse sound, a frequency of illness and despair.

She pulled her hand away and made a frustrated noise. "What are you doing in there?" she asked aloud—a question for Gordo, but one she didn't expect answered. Would he have to come out eventually? Was there food inside? Were the bodies food?! She shuddered at the thought.

Behind her, the brush crackled and snapped like little bird bones underfoot.

Molly whirled.

And there she found the two door-wolves. Each looked haggard and weak. They staggered with clumsy, woozy steps. Drool slicked their strange, panting muzzles. Dregil's thorns were bent and drooping. Lac's dreamy, phantasmagoric coat looked drab and gray.

CHILD, Dregil said.

THE BLOODED SISTER, Lac said.

They crept toward her, following a serpentine path, each crossing in front of the other. Molly backed up against the wall. "I...I'm sorry about what happened. I didn't know—"

YOU SHOULD BE SORRY, Lac said.

BUT IT IS TRUE THAT YOU DID NOT KNOW, Dregil added.

Each bared their teeth. Lips curled up.

"I want to help. I want to fix it."

They stopped in place. Both cocked their heads in the curious way dogs do when they're pondering something.

FIX IT? Dregil asked.

DO YOU THINK YOU ARE OF HARD ENOUGH MATERIAL? Lac challenged.

YOU FELL FOR THE INTERLOPER'S TRICKS.

YOU LET HIM ENTER.

YOU LET HIM *TAKE*.

"I am!" she blurted out. "I'll do anything. I just need to get in there. And I don't know how."

CHILD, HAS NO ONE TOLD YOU THAT THERE IS A WAY IN, ONLY FOR YOU? Lac asked.

NOT ONLY FOR HER, Dregil corrected.

AH, YES, NOT ONLY FOR HER. PERHAPS HE DOES NOT KNOW. PERHAPS HE IS AS UNAWARE AS SHE.

THE GIFT OF THE BLOODED. THE BOND BETWEEN SISTER AND BROTHER. TRUE FOR THEM AS IT IS FOR US.

YES, Lac said. AS IT IS FOR US.

"I don't know what you mean."

THEN LET US SHOW YOU, Lac snarled.

And together, the wolves leaped for her throat.

Molly didn't even have time to scream as Dregil's jaws snapped tight in the space just in front of her—inches from her neck. And Lac's mouth did the opposite: It opened, and from its maw emanated a whishing hiss of vapors that blurred the air. They swirled and colors ran. And in that mad miasma, a vision was shown to her:

The wall. The forest. Healthy and vibrant. It was overlaid across the leafless trees like a second image, a hologram or hallucination or some kind of *augmented reality app*, except she had no phone. Molly watched as two children, each glowing with a kind of inner light, traipsed up to the gate. One had hair a muddy blond, her braid like coffee with too much cream in it. The other, a boy, had hair as black as a rain-slicked raven. They held hands. They were talking, laughing, though what they were saying was unclear. They were not dressed as anyone would dress today, but rather, costumed as kids from the seventeenth or eighteenth century—billowy white linen, dark brown stockings, pockets not sewn into their trousers but rather, hung around their waists like little purses.

They tra-la-la'ed their way to the door. They looked at each other with wide, innocent eyes.

Then they put their hands on it. Her left. His right. Arms crossing, and thumbs facing in different directions. And they did it just over the handprints now emblazoned upon the gate.

But the thing was: Those handprints were not in the image Molly was seeing. They were present *now*—

But not *then*.

As the children pushed their hands against the door, it began to vibrate and glow, as their inner lights did. Then around their hands, the glow turned red, searing into the wood with curls of smoke rising.

With that, the door opened, and the two children— giggling—held hands and skipped inside without a care in the world.

The gate closed behind them.

And then the vision ended.

Molly gasped, pressing her back against the wall. The wolves, momentarily frozen in midair, dropped to the ground.

DO YOU SEE? Dregil asked, his broken, drooping thorn-hide rippling. YOU ARE THE BLOODED SISTER.

THE BLOODED BROTHER MUST JOIN YOU, Lac said, wisps of dream still drifting lazily from her muzzle—around her teeth and from her nostrils.

"The handprints," Molly said, swallowing hard. "They can let us both in. That's what you're telling me."

THERE ARE ALWAYS SIBLINGS. AND TOGETHER, THEY FORM A KEY.

She started to race off, to tell Dustin. But she turned

to ask the wolves, "Why are you telling me this? You…
wanted me gone before. And you were right. I was an
interloper."

BECAUSE NOW, Dregil began, though Lac finished:
THE DANGER IS FAR WORSE THAN YOU, LITTLE MOUSE. NOW RUN. GET YOUR
BROTHER. TIME IS NARROWING, LIKE THE PASSAGE BETWEEN TWO CRUSHING
ROCKS. *RUN!*

27. the passage between two crushing rocks

MOLLY RAN. HER FEET PUMPED AS HARD AS THEY COULD CARRY HER, through the eventide meadow, under the rising moon, toward the house. She threw open the front door and practically dove down the basement steps to Dustin's libroratory, skidding to a stop in front of him.

He gave her a startled, quizzical glance as he looked up from a massive book whose cover appeared to be mostly just strips of pale bark.

"Molly, if you don't mind—"

"I figured it out," she said, though she didn't say that exactly because the words *rushed out* of her like garbage from an overturned trash can. It sounded more like *Ahhfiggededout.*

Pant, pant, pant.

"What?" He seemed annoyed.

She tried again.

"I. Figured. It. Out."

He stared at her the way a dog stares at something it does not understand. "Figured…what out, exactly?"

"How to"—gulp, deep breath—"get into the cemetery."

Behind her, she heard footsteps coming down the stairs. It was Vivacia. Her hands were clasped behind her. "What did you say?" the woman asked.

"I said I figured out how to get in. How to open the door."

"What?" Dustin snapped. "Are we just going to break it down? Climb over it? I told you, those won't work—"

"The two handprints," she said, ignoring him. "We both need to put our hands there, at the same time. Thumbs facing apart. Because we're siblings. We're Blooded." She saw their dumbfounded faces. "*We're* the key!"

Hope bloomed on Viv's face. She and Dustin exchanged looks—he seemed warier than she. "Dustin, if this is true…"

"Yes. Perhaps. But we've never heard anything like this before. We'll need to gather the others—"

"We can go now!" Molly said. "We can try it!"

"*No.*" His rebuke was sharp. "We can't just…waltz in. We gather the others first. Our *uncle* may be waiting." He narrowed his eyes. "How exactly did you learn about this?"

"The wolves told me."

He blinked, then shared another look with Vivacia. But this time, it was a look of bewilderment.

Together, they asked:

"*What* wolves?"

Back in the barn, close to midnight, all gathered. And as fast as she had become the savior, bringing *literally key information to the table*, Molly was just as quickly cut back out. The group sat around the table, discussing how exactly they were going to tackle what Gabriel had named "the Uncle Gordo problem." Molly sat off to the side—forced to be a witness and not a participant.

Even though, hello, I'm the one who figured out how to get into the cemetery! she thought.

"Let's walk back. I'm still a *wee smidge* confused about these wolves," Ember said. "They aren't wolf-skins? Loops? Our cousins, the werewolves, is what I'm saying?"

"I've never seen them," Dustin said, looking a little lost. Sometimes he'd glance over at Molly, and they'd share a commiserating look—but then his face would sour and flash with a spike of anger. As if to say, *This is all your fault, Molly.*

He's never going to like me, she thought. *Not even if I save the day.*

Marsha leaned forward on her elbows, chin cupped in her hands, and said, "The Venerable Books show other instances of door-wolves: guardians of various gates. We've never seen them here, maybe because this cemetery wasn't in danger before? Question is, why didn't we know about the sibling thing? It's not in any of the histories. Is that true for just this cemetery or all of them? How the heck did we miss that?"

"Maybe we didn't," Dustin said. "Maybe Molly is wrong. It wouldn't be surprising."

"Thanks," Molly called from her corner, bitterly.

"I just mean, this isn't your world, so it's certainly convenient that you should meet magic wolves we've never seen and who possess secret information vital to our cause."

Molly's mouth dropped open. "I'm not making this

up!" she cried. "You're just jealous you didn't figure it out first."

Ember cackled. "I think she's got you there, Dusty."

"She doesn't *have* me there," Dustin stammered. "I— I know what I'm doing—and I'll remind you she caused this problem in the first place."

"It was *your* job to protect the key," Gabriel said nonchalantly as he leaned back in his chair. Behind his words was a smug *I told you so.*

"*Everybody*," Marsha said, clapping her hands as Molly had their first night in the barn. "Settle down, please? Maybe? Okay?"

"YES. EVERYONE SETTLE DOWN. FLORG IS BECOM-ING MOST AGITATED."

Dustin sat back grumpily. Viv placed a calming hand on his arm. Molly stared daggers at him.

"So *if* we can get in," Dustin said, "then we can handle my uncle."

"*Our* uncle," Molly chimed in.

"Aye, here's the plan: We go in," Ember offered, "we find mad Uncle Gordo Gorgoch Whatever Whoever, we kick him in the snack drawer, we come home. After we pay our respects," she added humbly.

"*No*," Gabriel said. The word was firm, like a fist. "We are each subject to the provisions of the Fivefold

Key—we can't just *wander* around the cemetery. First, the place is a maze. Second, there's a reason we're to be accompanied in the first place."

"You saying you don't trust us?" Ember asked.

"I'm saying I don't trust *you*."

"Well, maybe I don't trust *you*, Magic Man."

"Hey now. I'm just a simple chef. You're the fox-changer. A trickster at heart—all your *shenanigans* and *antics*."

"Oh no, not *shenanigans* and *antics*. Watch your mouth with such vulgarity—we've wee babes in the room." Ember looked around the room as if to garner visual support for her jab, but nobody seemed to care very much, so she waved it off. "It's funny, Gabe, you pretendin' you're some kind of slicker-than-goose-poop, new-wave, forget-the-old-ways maverick when really you're just a crusty old stick-in-the-mud."

"You don't know me."

"I know you fine. It's me you don't know. I'm trusty. Trustier than a good whack to the head," Ember said quite proudly.

"That doesn't inspire confidence. And the word is *trustworthy*, not *trusty*, Miss Felix."

"'Miss Felix.' Listen to you. As if we didn't *date* for three months back in oh-eight."

"Stop," Dustin said, raising his voice. Molly could

see that it took a bit out of him to be that assertive. He really *was* just finding his feet with all this, wasn't he? It almost made her feel for him. Almost. "It will be what it will be. All Five Watchers will go in together, and I'll come along, Viv, too—"

"And me," Molly said.

"Not this again," Dustin said.

"I'm going. Don't argue. I need this."

"You don't need to be a hero."

But I do.

"I messed up," she said. "I deserve a shot to fix it."

Eyes drifted from her, to him, and back again. He tried staring her down and she offered him a toothy smile. Her eyes did not smile with her mouth, though, and he could definitely feel that. Finally, he bent like one of Dave Peterson's straws and said, "Fine." Under his breath he added: "It's your funeral if anything goes wrong."

"Then good news—we'll be in the right place for that," Molly quipped.

A few beats of awkward silence stretched wide.

"**HA HA HA!**" Florg boomed. "**WE WILL BE IN THE RIGHT PLACE FOR HER *FUNERAL*!**" Florg paused for a few seconds. "**BECAUSE IT'S A CEMETERY.**"

"Very good, Florg," Marsha said. Not at all condescendingly, but rather like a proud big sister.

After that, everything snapped back into place,

and the conversation continued with Molly again at its edges (though Florg turned every once in a while to shimmer in her general direction).

Now the question was how exactly they would defeat Gorgoch—after all, a *kick to the snack drawer* would not suffice, it was pointed out. Marsha noted that if Gorgoch was truly in the cemetery for all the aggregate death energy, he would be *swollen* with the stuff at this point. "He'll be powerful," she said. "He might even be able to control the environment. There's simply no telling what he'll be able to do."

"We'll need something to slow him down. Weaken him," Gabriel said. "Something one and done. He might withstand a sustained effort."

"FLORG WILL WRESTLE HIM TO THE GROUND AND FORCE HIM TO RECKON WITH THE VOID."

"Florg," Marsha said. "I don't think it'll be that easy, sweetie."

"IT MIGHT BE THAT EASY. YOU DON'T KNOW."

Marsha patted the shimmering space with a gentle hand.

"We need more to go on here," Ember said angrily. "We don't have squat. If Gorgoch is gobblin' up all that death energy, he'll mulch us like autumn leaves."

"There's always the bee's oar," Dave Peterson said cheerily.

They all turned toward him. He noisily finished his blood smoothie with a gurgling slurp.

"What?" Gabriel asked.

"What what?" Dave asked.

"You said bee's oar?"

"Technically, she did," Dave said, pointing toward Molly. "She was trying to tell people about it yesterday but I don't think anyone was listening."

All eyes fell to her once more. She felt like a butterfly pinned to corkboard. "Gordo bought a bezoar. An elk bezoar. I found the receipt in his car. Here, take a look."

"A bezoar," Marsha said, her mouth forming an O as if she were silently whistling. "That's interesting."

"It sure is," Molly asserted, but then she didn't know what she was asserting and asked, "Wait, why is it interesting?"

"Well, that depends. Mostly, *mostly*, a bezoar is a...calcified hairball? A bolus of material inside the guttyworks of an animal—or person!—that forms over time. But there are other kinds, too. There are bezoars formed of cellulose or dairy products or, no joke, *unripe persimmons*. There's even a kind in the intestines that's called a *fecalith*—essentially a poo bezoar."

"**EW**," Florg said.

"It's nature," Marsha said, chastising them. "Everybody poops, Florg."

"FLORG DOES NOT POOP. FLORG'S EVER-SHIFTING FLESH IS AN ELEGANT MACHINE THAT UTILIZES EVERY OUNCE OF ALL THAT ENTERS IT. A TEMPLE WHERE EACH SACRIFICE IS SACRED AND—"

Vivacia interjected, ignoring Florg: "They're thought to have magical properties in some cases." She scowled. "*Usually* they're protective—amulets or rings meant to stop illness or poison. But to be honest with you, there's no evidence of their working like that. It's witless magic, just superstition."

"You'd think Gorgoch would know better," Ember said.

"Maybe that's it," Molly said. "Maybe it *is* superstition."

"Just superstition," Dustin echoed. "Hm. Afraid of being poisoned. Or just afraid of being sick. A hypochondriac."

"That's our way in," Gabriel said.

"I dunno," Molly said. "It feels a little shaky, doesn't it?"

Gabriel shrugged. "Big man in search of big power? Those are usually the people who are the most scared. It's what we have to go on. If we can unbalance him, make him act erratic, that makes him vulnerable."

"It also makes him unpredictable," Vivacia added.

"I mean, it *could* work," Marsha said, her eyes bright and excited—a little *too* excited, maybe—behind her big glasses. "A magical poison. To make him ill. To weaken him not just physically—but mentally. Emotionally! Gosh, even if it turns out he's not afraid to get sick— welp, a poison is still a poison. Especially if we use one that seizes on his magic. That interrupts his abilities— like disturbing an electrical circuit!"

Ember grumbled. "I'd still rather just kick him in the snack drawer."

"I'd have thought you would like the sneakier approach," Gabriel retorted. "We can do this—a poison that disrupts his magic. But it means we've got our work cut out for us."

"What kind of poison?" Dustin asked.

Marsha chimed in: "Mucus-thorn and mire-berry."

"Is that, like, some kind of alt-folk band?" Molly asked.

"Not as bad as that," Ember said, grinning like, well, a fox. "But as poisons go? Pretty flappin' bad."

28. and now: stress baking

"YOU HATE ME," MOLLY SAID.

Dustin was meticulously, gingerly folding dough onto itself. Grabbing an edge, tucking it into the middle. Every time he turned it into a doughy pillow, he then undid the doughy pillow by stretching it out once more.

It was night, and the others had left to find the necessary ingredients for the *pretty flappin' bad* poison. Dustin, Molly realized, had little to contribute to their efforts—or, worse, they didn't want him to.

"I don't hate you," he said in a way that suggested he pretty much totally did.

"We were, like, growing nicer to each other," she said, leaning against the fridge, gnawing on a carrot. That's how bad things had become: She was *eating* a *carrot*. "And then, all this."

"You mean, and *then* you stole a secret key using a ghost I'm not supposed to talk to and gave that key to our defalcator uncle and now he's loose in a magical cemetery."

"Maybe." She pouted. "Yeah."

He had no further comment and began slicking a steel bowl with a bit of olive oil, brushing it along the inside.

"Whatcha making?" she asked.

"Bread."

"Well, I mean, duh. What kinda bread?"

"A rustic sourdough boule. I have a starter I've been cultivating for two years."

"I don't know what most of those words mean."

"You can harvest wild yeast and keep it alive, then bake with it." Under his breath he muttered: "At least that's one thing I can control."

"Is that why you're salty? Because this is all out of your control?"

"No," he said sharply, but the way he clapped some flour onto his hands and roughly shoved the flour blob into the steel bowl spoke otherwise. "It's just—"

"Just what?"

He spun. "It's just, I was getting it together. I really was. I'm young and untested, and Viv has had to do a lot, but my mother—"

"Our mother."

"*My* mother left this place to me with the expectation that I could handle it. The burdens of the Solemnities Parlor and of the Mothstead Necropolis were on my shoulders and I was poised to carry that weight. I had accepted it. But then you show up. A fly in the proverbial ointment and now, *and now*, I look like a buffoon. Someone who can't handle anything. And you know what? They're right. Instead of proving I can control a difficult situation, I'm—" He angrily spun the steel bowl, and it whirled about like a top before almost falling off the counter—only Molly saw that a spectral hand darted out from the cabinet and buoyed it back to safety. *Lancaster*, she thought. "I'm baking bread," Dustin finished, looking curiously at the bowl, pondering how it didn't fall. "Because I have nothing more to contribute."

"Sorry," Molly said.

"Yes. Well. Aren't we all."

"Cooking is a cool skill, though. I bet you know how to make foods and other stuff that are part of laying monsters—er, you know what I mean—to rest."

Dustin didn't reply, just continued to stare at the bowl of dough.

Which made Molly nervous. Because a question had been nagging at her. No—nagging wasn't the word. It had been *haunting* her, like a poltergeist throwing itself around her insides. She wanted to ask, *Do you think, when all this is done, you'd have a place for me here? I could do costuming work because you said that was a part of bereavement and burial and I thought that was pretty cool, so, maybe I can stay?*

But instead, the question jammed up inside her throat. And a winnowed version—whittled down like a stick with a knife—came out. "What happens after? When all this is done? With you and me."

"Nothing," he said firmly and without hesitation. Answering both the spoken question and, she feared, the unspoken one, too. "When this is all done, you and I are done, and I shall be quite glad of it. As I'm sure you will be, too."

With that, he walked away with the bowl, and Molly skulked away.

Out in front of the barn sat a table of strange ingredients, each presented by those who had procured them.

The first was mucus-thorn: a fat, rubbery thorn the

color of smashed mulberries that did not look particularly sharp to Molly. Ember identified it with a game-show reveal when she said, "Taken from a bog in the Great Dismal Swamp. Plucked from a spot where neither moon nor sun ever shall shine. This one in particular grew under a haunted tree, a bald cypress that looked like a giant scarecrow, or so my mate says. Crowfolk live in that tree." Under her breath she added: "Long beaks. Love puzzles and dead things. Never make fun of one, or they go for your tongue."

Next up, an actual dead bird. Not a crow but a little songbird. Pale yellow. Eyes like puckered asterisks, beak the color of ash. Its little feet were curled up underneath it as if it were trying to hold on to a branch that wasn't there. Molly felt bad for it. Behind the bird, the air shimmered. Florg announced: **"BEHOLD THE DEAD BIRD."**

Marsha leaned in and explained to Molly, Dustin, and Viv: "It's a mire-bird. Technically, a prothonotary warbler who ate a poisonous mire-berry, then fell into some kind of bog, muck, or mire, and was thusly preserved. Like an old bog druid."

Florg bellowed: **"FLORG FOUND THE DEAD BIRD IN COAL SILT OUTSIDE THE RAMBLE ROCKS MINE. FLORG DID NOT EAT IT BUT WANTED TO. FLORG DESERVES A MIGHTY REWARD FOR SUCH RESTRAINT."**

Marsha flicked a Cheez-It into the air, and the mirrored air of Florg gleefully chomped it into oblivion.

Eyes turned to Dave Peterson, who seemed startled by the attention.

"Oh! Right." He cleared his throat and set down a small jam jar that contained...well, what looked like blood. "The sap from a bloodroot flower, mixed with the blood of the forager who plucked it." He grinned and said slyly: "I had a park ranger owe me a favor. Don't worry."

Now, it was Marsha's turn. On the table sat a little fabric pouch with a drawstring, which she delicately undid and overturned into her left hand. What looked like a red bean rolled out—a red bean with a big black spot on the one side. To Molly, it also looked like an eyeball. Marsha said: "*Abrus precatorius*, a.k.a. a rosary pea, a jequirity bean, or in the parlance of my people, an imp's eye. It is both poisonous and invasive, giving those who ingest it all manner of ill effects, including, but not limited to, heart palpitations, vomiting, diarrhea, lethargy, and hallucinations." She held it up gingerly, then slid it back into the pouch. "A real party, huh?"

Gabe stepped forward. "The knives are the last thing."

They looked to him.

"Well, I don't have them yet," he said, not in a way

that sounded apologetic, but in a way that possessed a kind of arrogant confidence—as if hidden behind his words was another word: *duh.*

"And why not, mate?" Ember asked, eyebrow arched.

"The Quack Mart doesn't open till weekends—Friday starting at five PM. And today is Friday, and it isn't yet five o'clock."

"The Quack Mart?" Molly asked.

Marsha offered a small smile. "It means he's going to go see One-Eared Earl."

Molly tilted her head: "That doesn't make it any clearer?"

Dustin said, with some tension in his voice: "One-Eared Earl is a collector of…hard-to-procure curios. Occult objects, reagents, and so forth, and he has a stall set up in a large so-called farmers market south of here by an hour or so, in Quaker Bridge." Stiffly, Dustin added: "We are not fans of his here in the supernatural solemnities business."

"I'm about to head over there," Gabriel said, "as I am of reasonable confidence that Earl has the type of blades we need."

"I'm going with you," Ember said.

"No, you are not."

"The hell I'm not. The hell I am! Who knows

what manner of *shady deal* or *tricky bargaining* you'll go through to get that blade. Probably sell one of our firstborn out from under us, you will."

"I'm not going to have you along for the ride, irritating me the whole way." Gabriel thrust a finger accusingly toward the fox-changer. "If anything, *you're* the trickster here. I am but a humble chef, and I've sought Earl's help in procuring certain ingredients time and again. We have a relationship."

"Oh, a relationship? We had one of those once, didn't we, sorcerer?"

"Ember, like I said—"

"I'll go," Marsha interrupted, like she was trying to be loud but failing. Then she said it again, more firmly: "I'll go. You all trust me?"

Nobody disagreed.

"Okay. Good. And Molly will come with me."

"Wuzzawha?" Molly said.

Dustin stepped forward, shaking his head. "No, I must protest—Molly isn't ready for this. She will remain here, out of the way."

"Maybe it'll be good for her," Viv interrupted, earning a glare from Dustin.

"Besides," Marsha added, "I think the kiddo wants to help. So she should." To Molly, Marsha said: "If you're cool with that?"

Wait, am I cool with that? Molly wondered. She wasn't exactly keen to hang out with Gabriel, though she did enjoy Marsha's company. More troubling was meeting anyone who went by the name One-Eared Earl.

But, she'd said she wanted to help.

So it was time to help.

"I'm in," she said. "I just need to change. I'll be back faster than you can say *elk bezoar*! I mean, like, not literally, though."

"You're not wearing that," Gabriel said when she came outside to meet him and Marsha on the front porch.

Molly looked down at the flowy gray-green cloak that touched the tops of her red-sneakered feet. Faux feathers made of felt lined the inside and outside.

"I clearly am wearing it," she said, declaratively.

"No, I mean"—he rolled his eyes—"go put on a different outfit, something *normal.* You look ridiculous."

"Says the *wizard*," she answered grumpily.

"Who are you supposed to be anyway?"

She flipped her hands forward so that the cards she had been concealing emerged, three in each hand, fanned out as if they were weapons.

"I'm *Cardiraptor,* the Bird Sorceress from the third

edition of the Card Captives game? Not the board game, and not the anime—though this outfit *pretty closely* matches the Sakura Journeys episodes, which in America is the third series, I think? Yeah. But I'm a purist; I really didn't like that, and mostly just played the card game—"

"I don't care," he said. "Go change."

"I think she's fine," Marsha said. "I, in fact, think you look *really cool,* Molly." The woman beamed. "Plus, no time. We gotta hit the road."

"Thanks, Marsha."

"It is *my pleasure."*

"Ugh," Gabriel said, then headed toward the driveway.

29. quack mart

THROUGH PINE TREES THEY DROVE. DOWN A LONG HIGHWAY, OVER HILLS that aspired to be mountains. Gabriel owned an SUV— an Audi e-tron, electric. "Good for the environment," he said.

Marsha added, chipperly, "That's why I ride a bicycle!"

Molly giggled from the back seat.

Gabriel ran a hand through wavy black hair. "All right. When we get there, Molly, you stay outside Earl's stall—just leave this to us."

"I think she should come in," Marsha said.

"Absolutely not. He doesn't like normies. And your outfit? No. We cannot risk ruining this at the last minute. These blades we seek? They're unique. Others can be forged but it would take too much time." He paused. "Stars only know how much damage your wannabe-Devourer uncle has done."

"Let her come in—she doesn't have to meet One-Eared Earl. She'll stay out of the way."

"Yeah, I don't actually *want* to meet One-Eared Earl," Molly said.

"Fine," Gabriel said, relenting.

"What are these *blades* anyway?" Molly asked.

Gabriel hesitated. Marsha sighed and said, "We can tell her. She knows everything else." And then Marsha leaned into the back seat and rolled her eyes. "Gabe here really likes to play everything close to the vest because he's a control freak."

"I am not a control freak!" he protested. "I just like things a certain way."

Marsha mouthed the words *control freak* and nodded.

Molly nodded back.

"I see what you're doing there," Gabriel said with some sourness.

"These knives," Marsha continued, "are daggers whose blades were forged from meteors. Meteoric metal is magical."

"Other metals resist magic," Gabriel explained.

"They repel it, expel it. But meteoric metal—ah-ha—soaks it up like a sponge. And thus can hold that magic, almost like a magnetic charge."

"Why five blades?" But before they could answer, Molly figured it out. "Right. One for each of you Watchers." She paused. "You don't trust each other."

"We trust each other fine," Marsha said.

"We don't trust each other, no," Gabriel said at the exact same time.

The two of them shared a look.

"We *trust* each other," Gabriel said, "except when we don't. A little lack of trust is good. It allows us to remain wary—so what is ours can stay ours."

Marsha made a scrunched-up face. "Gabriel really doesn't like anyone messing with his things."

"The *point* is," Gabriel continued, "we trust each other as far as we need to, and no further."

Marsha shrugged. "Well, I have plenty of trust for the both of us."

And again, she leaned back between the two seats to look at Molly.

"And I trust you, too, kiddo," she said with a wink.

Molly had seen a lot of movies and TV shows she wasn't really supposed to have seen at only thirteen years old.

Good or bad, that's just how it was—ol' Steve-a-roonie wasn't exactly monitoring her *media intake* (or her breakfast-cereal intake). And that meant she'd consumed more than an average diet of apocalyptic, end-of-the-world shows, and she was pretty sure all that had come to life in front of her.

The Quack Mart parking lot alone looked like the end-times.

Shattered asphalt, plants growing up through it; parked cars that were rusty and dirty. Then the market itself, which looked like a shopping mall that had died years ago but was still up and walking around—a zombie mall, its windows filthy and cracked, the sign out front hanging askew. It was also big. Bigger than she expected.

"You said this was a farmers market," she commented with some confusion.

"Eh," Gabriel answered. "That's what they call it."

"But, like, a farmers market has *kale* and *raw honey* and *weird apples*. This looks like a place you buy a muffler, a stick of dynamite, maybe a pair of camo pants, and a sick turtle."

Marsha shrugged. "Yeah, you can probably buy all that in here."

A rare laugh from Gabriel. "She's not wrong. I can even tell you what stall has the sick turtle."

"Why do they call it Quack Mart?" The sign did, in fact, have a weathered, rust-stained metal duck bolted to it—it hung loose and screeaaaked back and forth in the wind. *Screaaak, screaaaaaak.*

Marsha answered: "We're in the town of old Quaker Bridge, and somewhere along the way Quaker Mart became Quack Mart. Language is funny that way. Some locals just call it Q-Mart, or, 'The Q.'"

Impatience came off Gabriel in waves. "Can we go inside now, please?" he asked.

And with that, they went inside.

Expectations were everything, especially when they were roundly trounced. Molly had *expected* a farmers market and was shown a mall at the end of the universe. Upon going inside, Molly expected—well, she didn't *know* exactly what to expect, except that it was probably gonna be weird, and everything would smell bad, and she was gonna hate it.

She was wrong.

Quack Mart was a feast for the senses.

The air smelled like grilling meat, old books, and humid tropical plants.

Her ears heard a dull, murmuring roar punctuated by the sound of old cash registers (*cha-ching*), the clack of metal spatulas, aaaaand a squawking bird somewhere?

And the sights? *Oh the sights.* Stall after stall of junky wonderment and fantastical garbage. A creepy mannequin store! A used bookstore! A place that seemed to sell vacuums and vacuum parts from the last century! An Asian grocery that sold racks of never-before-seen Japanese snacks—these, Molly ran her fingers across, whispering promises of, *I'll be back for you, my sweets.* Then she saw a VCR store that, wait, whoa, *totally had* VHS tapes, too, and she spied not only fringe horror films from the 1980s (*Q the Winged Serpent, Tetsuo: The Iron Man, Pumpkinhead, The Bog Mummy, Underbite*) but also, *omg*, anime tapes like *Tenchi Muyo* and *Robot Pilot Gumball* and, ahhhh, was that a rare subtitled edition of the *Zero Flower* predecessor, *Honeysuckle Samurai*? Instantly, Molly darted inside, already conspiring to figure out what she could sell (shoes, cosplay, literal pints of her own blood) to buy that—

But then Marsha was next to her, hooking a bent arm around Molly's and gently easing her back out into the flow of market traffic. "Sorry, kiddo, kinda on a tight time limit," she said.

"But I waaaaanna go back in there, ahhhhhh."

"Maybe later, Molly. C'mon. One-Eared Earl awaits."

Fine.

And sure enough, ahead was a corner stall robed in curtains the color of mulberry—and hanging from them was a sign that read: EARL'S CURIOUS CURIOS. COMPELLING COLLECTIBLES! CLUSTERS OF (UN)COMMON CONTRIVANCES! COME IN, COME IN!

30. compelling collectibles

THE STALL ITSELF WAS BIGGER THAN THE OTHERS NEAR IT. A GOOD thirty-by-thirty feet, with long tables sitting in front of rickety, mismatched shelves. There existed no central theme to what was piled onto the tables and crammed into (and atop of) the shelves. Molly saw 1950s cookware, old blue bottles, political campaign buttons from people she'd never heard of, weird cameras, old Transformer toys, National Geographic magazines, a few janky Barbie dolls, a huge jar of golf balls. Nothing exciting, and nothing she would think of as being, like, *monsterish* or *occulty*. Just semicruddy antiques. Normal, human antiques.

This stall had no cash register, but rather, a sullen teen girl with a glittery nose ring standing by an iPad. Gabriel nodded to her. "Is he here?"

"Who's asking?" the girl said, her voice so nasal it was as if someone were pinching her nostrils shut when she spoke.

"Gabe. The chef. He knows me."

The girl did two slow blinks, then turned around and disappeared behind the dark scarlet curtain at the far end of the stall. Moments later, the curtain parted and she waved them in. "Okay. He'll see you."

And with that, they whisked behind the red curtain, leaving Molly alone with—well, all this junk.

"Welp," she said to no one.

What else was there to do? She started to poke around. Old Easy-Bake Oven. Box of vinyl records. A shelf of broken action figures. She picked up a Skeletor—one leg missing—and moved him through the air like he was walking. Er, hopping. "I'll get you for this, He-Man!" she said. When the sullen girl looked over at her, Molly laughed it off, hiding her embarrassment: "I dunno, is that what he says? I watched some old episodes on YouTube but, I mean, I'm not a fan. And jeez, he's pretty muscular for a skeleton man. I bet his muscles are just like balloons or something. Or grocery bags full of sausages."

The girl said nothing.

"Tough crowd," Molly muttered.

Her boot nudged something under the table, which made a familiar sound. A rattle-and-shuffle like—

Cards.

She knelt down, found a couple of old shoeboxes sectioned off with little dividers.

"Oh my god," she said.

The boxes were full of Card Captives collectible cards.

She began rattling off her finds as she flipped from one to the next. "Bishop Monkey. Squawkarr, the Cockatiel Corsair! *Commander Venomslice.*" She stood up suddenly and erupted with: "There are some *real* treasures in this box!"

Sullen Girl ignored her.

But then, she heard something. Something behind Sullen Girl. Something like—

Raised voices.

Behind the curtain came Gabriel's voice, then someone else's—gruffer, growlier. Then Gabriel's again. An argument was happening, and it was getting louder.

Molly took a step forward, and Sullen Girl snapped out of her dead-eyed stare and focused, like a laser turret, on her. Gingerly, Molly took yet another step, and this time, the other girl's eyes turned fire red, and she opened her mouth to show a pair of serpent fangs—a hiss slithering up out of her throat. Whoa! A clear warning. When Molly blinked again, the eyes had returned to normal and the fangs were gone.

"No," Sullen Girl said simply, as if she *hadn't* just turned into some kinda snake lady a second ago.

The voices grew louder. Protests by Gabriel from the sound of it.

"Hey, can I go back there?" Molly said in a sheepish voice.

"Yeah, still no," Sullen Girl said.

Now the voices turned into a physical clamor—a thump, followed by a loud growl. Then a muffled, gargled cry by Gabriel.

"It's just, I think my friends are in trouble."

"Yeah, no."

What do I do? She knew she was supposed to stay where she was. Gabriel was very clear about that. *But what if he's hurt?* Also, Sullen Girl had fangs? Didn't she? Was she just hallucinating that?

Now came a strangled cry from Marsha.

Oh god oh god oh god. Think of something, Molly. Think!

Nervously, she sauntered back toward the front of the stall, where again she found the huge jar full of golf balls.

It was heavy, or at least unwieldy—like, she had to circle her arms around it, that's how big the jar was. You could've stored three or four human babies in this thing. She struggled with it and said, "Hey, a little help over here? I want to buy this but it's heavy and"—the jar slid down a couple of inches through her grip—"it's slipping."

"Uggggh," Sullen Girl said, rolling her eyes. "Put that down." She hurried over, arms flat at her sides and head pointed forward (a little like a snake, Molly realized later), hissing even though she had not again changed her eyes or her teeth.

The mulberry curtains on the other side of the stall stirred like wind-swept waves, and Marsha's cries grew more urgent.

As Sullen Girl got closer, Molly said, "oopsie" and then—

Foisted the jar clumsily toward her.

Sullen Girl was not fast enough. The jar shattered. Glass went everywhere, and so did golf balls. Bouncing this way and that, *pock pock pock*. And rolling, too: a whole river of them, clattering in every direction.

That's when Molly made her move. She darted toward the curtain, and Sullen Girl charged after her— or tried to, but found herself surrounded by both glass and golf balls.

Ten steps and Molly was throwing back the curtain—

"Gabriel! Marsha!" she cried out, stepping into a cinder block–walled back room with cardboard boxes everywhere.

And that's when she saw the gray-skinned, long-nosed, tusk-mouthed thing that held both Gabriel and Marsha in huge, crushing, hairy-knuckled hands. The beast wore clothes: a raggedy yellow sleeveless shirt that said VIDELECTRIX on it, plus a pair of baggy brown cargo pants with stains upon them. The creature's face was elongated and strange, almost like a shaved goat? One of its ears was long and hairy, like a bat ear. But the other was gone, just a pucker of skin folded over into a puffy, inflamed cavern.

This is One-Eared Earl, she realized.

Gulp.

"Uhhh," she said, eyes darting between Marsha, who was swatting at the creature's arm, and Gabriel, who was digging into his pockets for something. His lips were turning dark. His eyes were bloodshot as he kicked uselessly at the air.

Behind Molly, the curtain rippled—she did not see this so much as feel the wind of it. And then in her ear came a serpent's hiss.

Sullen Girl.

Gulp, again.

She winced and did a pathetic imitation of the Cardiraptor battle stance, her hands trembling as they whipped out the Card Captives playing cards.

She felt Sullen Girl rise behind her—

And then the enormous gray monster gargled: "Stop."

Suddenly, Gabriel and Marsha were free, dropping down—Marsha landed on her feet, barely. Gabriel fell into a pile of cardboard boxes.

The creature Molly believed to be One-Eared Earl was suddenly not a creature at all. There came the sound of bones cracking, and a ripple sound like rubber sheets shook out on a windy day, and as quick as the snapping of fingers, there stood a paunch-bellied, pinch-eyed man with some chin whiskers and dark sideburns. Same yellow sleeveless VIDELECTRIX shirt, same cargo shorts. Same ear missing, except this time it was a human ear gone.

"Who's this?" Earl asked. Except more, *Whooz dis.*

Marsha, gasping for air, said, "Molly Grim."

"Grim. Grim, Grim, Grim." He snorted. "Stevie's kid?"

Gabriel finally managed to stand, albeit shakily. "That's right."

"You're dressed as Cardiraptor," he said. "Third Edition."

"Yyyyyes. Yes."

He nodded. "And whatcha got there?" Earl leaned in, unpinching one of his eyes to regard the cards in her right hand. "Middle card, there. That what I think it is?"

"It's a Gibbert."

"Gibbert, the Bone Bandit, from before he became—"

"The Skullihorde."

"The Skullihorde!" he said at the same time.

Gabriel blinked. "What is happening right now?"

"Gibbert," Molly explained nervously, "used to be a humble bandit working for whatever Dread Lord would hire him, but then one day he stole the Flesh Prism card and learned how to clone himself, and that's when he became the Skullihorde—like, basically a giant stampede of rolling skulls, and he took over the Wind-flip Provinces—"

"Enh, they don't care," Earl said. "*Gabriel* in particular is uninterested in what I have to say. Isn't that right, Mister Valverde?"

"Our disagreement—" Gabriel began.

"Our disagreement is actually a *debt.*" Now, Earl leaned toward Molly. "But maybe *you* can pay it." His eyes darted toward her hand. "I've been looking for a Gibbert card for a long time. Third edition—"

"Was the best edition," Molly completed.

Earl nodded eagerly. "So whaddya say?"

She did not want to part with her Gibbert. It was a foil card, shiny and iridescent. The art was the original by Galen Belledin. (Later editions changed it to computer-gen art done by the company.) She hadn't paid a lot for it—in fact, she'd gotten the card in a pack her father had bought at Javi's Pawn Shop, one of the few acts of kindness he'd performed for her. So this card was more to her than its value. It meant something.

But this situation meant something, too.

And she did not think fondly of her father, so to heck with it.

"It's yours," she said, and handed it over.

Earl gingerly took it from her. "Sssascha, if you please." Sullen Girl—Sssascha, apparently—appeared next to them and had a little card-protector slipcase already pinched open. He gently slid the card into its new home and she whisked it away. Earl put out his hand. "We have a deal."

Molly nodded and took it.

"Gabriel Valverde's debt is paid," Earl announced, as if to the whole market. "And as for the five meteoric blades, well—those I will *lend*, on condition that it is to serve our Celestial Protectorate from harm."

"Uh, it is. For sure," Molly said, nodding.

"Thank you, Molly Grim. And these two should thank you, as well."

Back in the parking lot, Marsha cleared her throat roughly and stopped.

Gabriel turned. "Yes?"

"Yes?" Marsha said, mocking him. "Gabe, don't you have something to say?"

Under his arm were the five meteoric daggers, the blades long and squiggly—wrapped in a swaddling of soft orange deer leather. "I…ugh…*fine*. Thank you, Molly. For saving us. Can we go now?" Without waiting for an answer, he headed toward the car.

"Uh," Molly said, "sure."

"You did good, kiddo," Marsha added.

"Thanks." Molly paused. "How did you know?"

"Hm?"

"You brought me on this trip. And before we even left, you told me to keep my costume on, which meant I had the card Earl wanted."

Marsha tapped the side of her nose. "I had a feeling."

"I thought Gabe was the one who knew everything."

"Gabe *thinks* he knows everything, which often

means he's not receptive to knowing new things. He'd let a lot more information in if he just opened the door."

"Thanks for believing in me."

"My pleasure. Now let's hit the bricks—then we can play with knives!"

31. suit up

ON THE NIGHT BEFORE THEY WENT TO THE CEMETERY AND TRIED TO OPEN the door, Molly assembled a new costume out of others: This one was Gunwitch Hera, a Freedom Inquisitor from the *Gunwitch* comic by Kirie Kate "K.K." Maggs. Long red coat, big chonky-heel boots, a Nerf gun painted to look like Gunwitch Hera's signature blaster, *Truth and Reconciliation*. (Or, roughly, anyway. She didn't have the right green, so she had to go with teal against the crimson, but honestly, she dug this more.)

It looked cool, at least in the mirror.

It helped her feel a teensy bit special and strong.

It also helped distract her from being scared witless. She didn't want to see Gordo again. She didn't want to go into Mothstead, the necropolis. Worst of all, she didn't want to disappoint anyone. Not Marsha. Not Vivacia. Certainly not Dustin. Nor the rest of the Watchers.

They had their blades now. They were all off getting rest or doing whatever it was they had to do. Dave Peterson was probably not sleeping, she guessed. Did vampires sleep? She'd seen him go out during the day under that black umbrella of his. Was that the equivalent of his staying up all night? A literal graveyard shift?

She sighed.

You'll be fine. Marsha believed in her and look what happened—she'd battled an ogre and won. That's what One-Eared Earl was, as it turned out: an ogre. Adjacent to the Goodly Neighbors, Marsha had explained during the car ride home as they'd chowed down on some Arby's. And okay, *no,* Molly did not truly battle him, not in combat and not even in a game of wits or anything, but she did talk him off the ledge of crushing Gabriel's and Marsha's heads like soft plums, so that was something, wasn't it?

You can do this.

"You're wearing that," came a voice from behind her. Dustin stood in the doorway. He seemed small, somehow—a sapling framed by a cathedral's arch, even though it was just the entrance to her borrowed bedroom.

"Yeah."

"What, ahh, what is it? Or who is it? Or what is it from? I'm sorry, I don't precisely know the right question."

"Gunwitch Hera. It's from a comic book and graphic novel. There was a video game, too, but it sucked pretty bad." She cleared her throat. "She's a witch but, like, with a gun that shoots these arrows of light, and when they strike people, they force them to tell the truth or give up secrets."

"Oh." He looked lost. "Good."

"Yup."

"Yes, indeed."

They stood there, awkwardly looking at each other.

"Thanks for helping secure the blades," he said, finally.

"Oh, sure. Yeah. Uhh. Thanks. I mean, you're welcome?" She laughed nervously.

"We'll open the gate tomorrow."

"Yeah."

"You shouldn't go in with us."

"What?"

"You should stay out here. You helped. You did your part. No need to do more."

"But there's a plan." Marsha had explained to her that Mothstead was simply too large for them all to stay together—the cemetery was called a necropolis for a reason. It was like a city of the dead. Each supernatural group had its own realm within the cemetery, because each had its own burial and grievance needs. (And, Gabriel pointed out, that way no group tried to grave-rob from another.) So the Watchers would go in one by one, each armed with one of the five poisoned blades. But, to appease the old traditions and treatises, some of the Watchers would have chaperones. Dustin, Molly, and Vivacia would go in with them.

Now Dustin was saying no to that?

"I'm going, Big Brother. Marsha is letting me go with her, so I'm doing it. You can't stop me."

With a stiff frown, he said, "So be it."

And then he turned tail and left the room.

She sat for a while in the quiet before another voice made itself known—whispering to her through a wall of tessellated quatrefoil:

"He's worried about you," Lancaster the Wallpaper Ghost said.

"If you say so," she answered with considerable grumpiness.

"I know him, and I know his voice, and I've heard that tone before."

"Oh? And what tone is that?"

"One that says he just wants you to be safe."

"Uhh, *doubt* that."

The ghost, now emerged halfway from the wall, gave a small, sorrowful shrug, and then again disappeared through the wallpaper and was silent once more.

They stood at the door to Mothstead: Dustin, Vivacia, Molly, and the Five Watchers, each with a sheathed poison knife around their waist. It was well past midnight, creeping now into the slow walk toward dawn, and Molly found herself looking around the forest, through and beyond the leafless trees. The door-wolves were not present. They did not come to send them off, or scare them away, or even watch from the shadows. She wasn't sure if that was comforting—

Or worrisome.

"So this is us," Dustin said crisply, looking to her. At first, she didn't understand but, duh, of course—the door. The handprints.

Fear was like a weight in her belly. So heavy it sank

all the way down past the core of her, into the ground. Now she thought, *Dustin was right. I'll open the door with him and then I'll run. I don't belong here. This was a mistake. I let Gordo in. I couldn't fight him then—how can I fight him now?* She wondered: What if she took off running? What if she bailed?

Besides, it wasn't like she was raised to be someone who stuck around. Steve sure didn't. And her mom didn't. And what did she even owe to Dustin? She'd done her part. Maybe it was time to get out of here. Let her brother handle it. This was his world, not hers.

But then she saw the look in Dustin's eyes. In Marsha's and Gabriel's and Dave's and even in Ember Felix's. They were all scared, too. (It was impossible to see Florg's eyes, but their form seemed to shimmer and shiver more than usual.) Even Vivacia didn't appear quite as confident and severe.

Then it struck her:

For once, she was a part of something. Okay, *sure*, it was something that came together because she'd royally borked it all up, but she belonged. They accepted her.

She hoped.

Molly gave Dustin a nod, and he gave her one, too.

Step by step, the two of them walked forward, in near-perfect tandem. (It was, Molly would admit later, the first time she really felt like his sister, like she had a brother.) Before putting their hands out, he gave his head a half turn and said, "I do like your outfit. I should've said so last night."

"Thanks," she said.

"Are you okay with all this?"

"I'm about as okay with all this as I am the existence of root canals, toe infections, and the color puce."

"Puce?"

"Puce. Like, yucky, pukey green."

"I think puce is a sort of…rust red."

"Really?"

"It has origins in the French word for *flea*—when you crush a flea, it leaves behind a little dark, mottled blot. A bloodstain."

"Puce. Flea's blood. That's fascinating. Thanks, dude."

"Of course." He smiled stiffly. "I've not been nice to you."

"No, you haven't. But I've made it easy to not be nice to me."

"We may die in there."

"Way to be a bummer about it." She gulped. "I kinda hope not, though. The dying part, I mean."

"Same here. That's why I didn't want you to go in. I…don't want you to die."

"I don't want you to die, either," she told him.

"Well, at least we have that in common," he said, a flicker of grim humor flashing in his eye.

From behind them, Ember barked: "Oi, we gonna do this, kiddies? The cemetery's not saving itself, is it?"

To which Marsha hissed in response: "They're having a *moment*, Ember. Jeez."

"**FLORG LOVES MOMENTS!**" florged Florg, nearby.

"Fine, fine," the fox-changer groused.

"Let's?" Dustin asked.

"Yeah. Let's."

Molly put out her right hand, and Dustin put out his left. Gently, they pressed their palms and fingers against the handprints on the wall and—

Nothing.

She winced and pressed a little harder.

Aaaand—

Nope.

"Um," she said.

"Well," Dustin said, and then pulled his hand away and pressed it again. "Hm."

And then Vivacia was behind them. Gently she reached out, and before grabbing Molly's wrist, asked: "May I?"

She shrugged. "Sure."

With that, Viv took her wrist and eased her right hand off the wall. Then she gently tapped the elbow of Molly's left arm.

Gabriel's smug, all-knowing voice called out: "In magic, sometimes it is the crossing of things that has the power. Lines joining. Like in the infinity symbol—the sideways eight they call the 'lemniscate.' It is the point where those lines cross that the power is strongest."

"What he said," Viv added.

"So just—" Molly started, confused.

Viv then urged Dustin to switch *his* hand, too. So now, Molly's left arm crossed under Dustin's right, their skin just touching as their hands pressed into the prints—

The locking mechanism made a deep, metal sound—

Ga-CHUNG.

With that, the door drifted open.

"We did it," Dustin said.

"We did it!" Molly yelled.

"Don't celebrate just yet," Ember said, sauntering past them with a walk that was somehow both jaunty and beleaguered. "You only opened the door. Now we gotta go in there and do the hard part, friendos. And Mothstead is a mighty big necropolis."

part three

MOLLY

THROUGH THE

MOTHSTEAD

GATE

32. a walking tour through the deadlands

THEY STEPPED INTO DARKNESS AS THICK AS PUDDING. IT WAS THE darkness of being trapped inside your own sweater, under a blanket, in a windowless room, on a moonless night. Molly felt the darkness steal her breath away and she thought, *Is this normal?* Not that anything was, but was this normal in the context of stepping into a supernatural cemetery?

That, she could not say.

Behind her, the door was still open—and the forest beyond it remained visible, somehow existing outside this primal, impenetrable black. Dustin moved to her side and said in a low voice: "This is normal. It'll brighten when the door closes."

She watched it do so. No one closed it. It simply eased shut on its own. And the lock mechanism reengaged with a whisper, not a clang.

Then the darkness brightened. Not all at once, as if flicking on a light switch, but rather, with the gentle growing glow of a sunrise. Though what settled in was not a sunrise, but a ruddy, gauzy half light of a world somehow between night and day.

As Molly's eyes adjusted to it, what she saw was…

Well, it was most certainly not a cemetery.

No headstones. No tombs. No flowers on mounded graves.

All she saw was a well-worn, mossy-stoned path, as uneven as a mouth full of uncorrected teeth. It cut its way through a purple grass meadow for about fifty feet, where it met and seemed to encircle a rather large, red-barked tree. Its branches hung in drooping twists, like ringlet hair, each marked with leaves the color of shined pewter patina. Beyond the tree, the path split into several routes, each winding and twisting into the far-off distance. And above all of it, little moths flitted about. White and yellow, brown and black. They seemed almost to glow.

Why moths? Molly wondered. There were moths

when Florg broke the table in the barn. Then there was the name of the cemetery—*Mothstead.* And now these.

It was like Marsha read her mind. "Moths are psychopomps," she said, as they watched the glowing whorl of moth-wing. "Shuttling the souls of once-living beings to the land beyond death."

"Oh," Molly said. *I wonder what kind of material would make great moth wings....* Then she blinked and gazed all around. "Um. I don't see our uncle anywhere."

"That's the problem; we don't know where he is," Dustin answered. "As noted, Mothstead is...not small."

Gabriel looked up, holding something in his hand. "Found the Fivefold Key. He must've ditched it the moment he stepped inside. Which would seem to indicate—"

"That he doesn't intend to leave," Marsha said, a chill in her voice.

Ember didn't hesitate. "Come on, come on, no rest for the wicked." She traipsed toward the tree and, as she got closer, lifted her nose to give an indelicate *sssniff* of the air, followed by more and more sniffs the closer she got.

Marsha hurried after the fox-changer with the eagerness and awkwardness of a hopping robin. She put both hands out and felt the bark.

"The Guidestone Tree," she said, but the way she said it was not wistful or happy in any way. Rather, Molly detected worry.

"What is it?" she asked.

"It's sick," Marsha said softly.

The woman's hand passed over a smooth opal—as big as a baby's fist—embedded in the bark, as if the tree had grown around it. A weak light danced inside the stone, like a firefly in a jar slowly dying. All around were carved sigils reminiscent of those on the locks: suns and moons and stars, in orbit around the opal.

"I still don't understand."

"This is an iron-red tree, y'see," Ember said. "From the Time Before. Infused with magic and souls. Contains a great deal of wisdom and all that, blah blah blah. It can help you find what you seek in a place like this, if you don't already know where—or what—that is. But the tree isn't doing so hot, is it?"

"It's not just the Guidestone," Gabriel said. He stood off to the side—in his fingers he held one of the seed-tops of the long purpley grass. With a pinch and a rub, he broke it apart. Gave the seeds inside a sniff. Then a taste. He spit out a few grassy bits and shook his head. "The magic that governs this place is fading fast. Gorgoch is draining it dry. He's become a Devourer, eating magic to fuel his own. Question is, why?"

"Question is," Ember said, "why does it matter? What he wants, who cares? We need to find him. Maybe the tree has enough juice to tell us."

"It does not," Marsha said with no small sorrow.

"FLORG WILL MAKE THE TREE TALK." The shimmering Florg stormed toward the tree, but of all people, it was Dave Peterson, the vampire, who stepped in front of them. **"TELL US THE TRUTH, TREE! FLORG DEMANDS!"**

"I don't think we can intimidate the tree into telling us what we want to know."

"FLORG CAN INTIMIDATE THE SKY INTO GIVING UP THE COLOR BLUE. FLORG CAN THREATEN THE OCEAN INTO GIVING UP ITS MOST SECRET SHARK. FLORG CAN DEMAND THAT ALL THE STARS IN THE SKY—"

"Florg, buddy," Ember said. "We like the tree. We don't hurt the tree."

"The tree's already hurting," Marsha added.

Florg sighed, their shimmering shoulders a-slump. **"FLORG WILL NOT HURT THE TREE. SORRY, TREE. FLORG IS JUST SO EAGER TO BE RID OF THE EVIL UNCLE WHO SULLIES OUR MOST SACRED RESTING PLACE."**

To Dustin and Vivacia, Molly whispered, "Are there other Florgs buried here?"

Dustin said solemnly, "There are no other Florgs."

"Florg stands alone," Vivacia said knowingly. "But they had friends. And those friends are all here."

Florg quietly wept, their shimmershape gently shuddering, the way one's shoulders might hitch when they cry.

Molly reached into the satchel she carried and pulled out a small baggie of Cheez-Its, which she handed to the shimmering hulk. For a moment, they went uneaten, but then they began to disappear into (presumably) Florg's invisible maw. *Cronch cronch.*

Marsha gave Molly a small, soft smile.

And then Molly heard a voice, also small, also soft—

But it didn't come from Marsha's mouth.

Molly…

A little sound, like wind chimes, came with the voice—and Molly was pretty sure it was only in her head, even as it echoed around her mind.

"Did you all hear that?" she asked.

"Florg's noisy chewin'?" Ember asked. "Aye, we all heard that."

"FLORG ENJOYS THE RESPITE OF SNACK FOODS."

Nobody else seemed to hear the voice, but Molly recognized it. It was the same one that had called to her from the lock when she was in the forest with the door-wolves. When she'd first found the gateway into Mothstead.

"Never mind," she said. "What do we do now?"

Gabriel pointed beyond the tree, to where the one path broke away into several. Molly could see them leading across lumpy hills, or through clusters of pine, or down around dark-water lakes. The last path led to what looked to be an ashen, blasted land. Gabriel said, "That way lies the many lands of Mothstead. Lands upon lands. Perhaps not all of them discovered."

"If the tree can't tell us where your bloody uncle is," Ember said, "then we're going to have to walk the paths. Which means the plan remains: We're going to have to split up."

"Right," Gabriel said. "We'll each go to our respective grounds." That left Molly wondering: If Florg stood alone and had no others like them, where would Florg be buried one day? Would Florg die? *Could* Florg die? She decided now was not the best time to ask. "Vivacia, you and Florg will come with me—someone has to keep an eye on them, and I don't want to do it." It struck Molly that he was the de facto leader of this group just by the act of choosing that role for himself.

"**HEY**," Florg protested, but that was the breadth and depth of their entire protest, as if even Florg realized the wisdom of needing a chaperone.

"Dustin," Gabriel continued, "you go with Miss Felix—"

"Oh, no, no, no," Ember said, waving her fingers about. "Not a chance, mate. I don't need a babysitter. Besides, I'm not just one set of eyes—I'm *five* sets of eyes."

Molly was about to ask what she meant—when suddenly, Ember's skin split open, not in a bloody gush, but more like it was just one of Molly's own costumes: It peeled apart, and stacked atop one another were a series of fuzzy, keen-eyed red foxes.

Five of them, as a matter of fact.

Five sets of eyes.

The flaps of human skin turned into glowing dust, then blew away.

Molly screamed.

"Bah, settle down," one of the Ember-foxes said in a growling version of her voice.

"It's just us!" a second Felix-fox barked, this one with a more boyish tone.

"You'll never catch us!" a third yipped, hopping off the top of the stack, which scattered them. All five foxes pounced around and upon one another, as if each were a vulpine trampoline. Marsha leaned over and said in a low voice: "Foxes. As the saying goes: Cat software loaded onto dog hardware."

Molly had to give it to her—that seemed exactly right.

With that, the five foxes bounded down the second

path, toward the pines. As they ran, they each seemed to steal moments from running to snap at one another's tails. Which made Molly wonder what it was like to be not just one creature, but several. Maybe she already knew, since she was trying to be Gunwitch Hera right now. Maybe that's just how people were, foxes or not.

Gabriel narrowed his eyes. "Well. Okay. Dustin, you go with Dave, as you two seem…compatible." To Molly's ears, that sounded like an insult. That was the thing with Gabriel, wasn't it? He had some ego on him, that guy. "Vivacia, as noted, you and Florg are with me. Finally, Marsha, you and Molly are together. Do we all agree?"

This last question seemed to pain him to say, as if Gabriel wasn't used to asking if people were okay with his suggestions—yet no one disagreed with his plan. It was all they had.

Marsha gave Molly a small smile. "You okay with this? Last chance to get off the ride."

"I'm okay," she lied.

"**LET US HUNT**," Florg said with a mad, gargling cackle.

33. marsha and molly

THE OTHERS DEPARTED INTO THE EERIE HALF DARK OF THE CEMETERY. Dustin paused for a moment and stood next to Molly.

"Are you going to be all right?" he asked her.

She looked him up and down. "You really *are* being nice to me. Why? What's up? First outside the gate, and now…here."

"This place is dangerous, Molly."

"So that's it. You don't think I can handle it."

He bristled. "No. What? Well. Maybe! I don't know what you can handle."

"And whose fault is that? You keep trying to shut me out of everything!"

He crossed his arms stiffly. "I—well—you—"

Gabriel appeared at Dustin's elbow. "Dustin, we should go."

"Yes. Of course." Her brother regarded her with a mix of frustration, fury, and worry. "You be safe is all I'm saying."

And then he hurried off.

"Yeah, well, you too!" she yelled after him, and though what she said was ostensibly nice, it didn't sound nice the way she yelled it. But, too late now, hm? "Jerk."

Marsha put a hand on her shoulder. "You okay?"

"Peachy. Dandy. Hecka awesome over here."

"Family can be tough," Marsha said.

"I'd take it one higher. Family *sucks*."

"Well." Marsha made an awkward face. "You know what? Let's walk and talk."

Molly nodded, and as they set foot on a path, it immediately felt like that moment of being on a roller coaster. Or in a sled at the top of a too-tall snowy hill. It was the feeling of gravity and danger, of a kind of deadly inevitability. Like once you started down, you wouldn't be able to stop. Marsha had said as much: *Last chance to get off the ride.*

The stones under their feet were cobbled and uneven and all different from one another: white flat ones, gray mounded ones, stones of smooth black, stones of fuzzy (and slippery) moss. The path cut through the tall grass, aiming them toward big, lumpy hills—hills banded by silver moonlight. The path did not go over the hills but between them, and they seemed to rise up on both sides like the shells of monstrous turtles.

"We're headed toward the burial mounds of my people," Marsha said. "They are, in a way, my family."

"You're all related?"

"Not exactly. Not like parents to children or…you know, a sister to a brother. But it turns out, we all share something. We share magic."

Ahead, the valley—and the path that threaded it— went up, up, up, and the hills got steeper and rollier. With them came trees, massive ones dotted here and there, trunks as thick as barrels, branches bent and twisty like the snakes of Medusa's hair. From where Molly walked, though, they were mostly silhouettes— black shapes against the twilight.

"So where does it come from, then? Your magic? Are you born with it?"

Idly, Marsha stopped walking. She said in a more distant voice now as she scanned the path, "No. It is often thought that we're born with magic, but that's not it at all. Birth matters very little among our kind.

It does somewhat with shape-changers, and certainly with your type: the Blooded. But the rest of us seek the magic, or the magic seeks us. We who join the Goodly Neighbors do so because we feel different, and so the universe calls upon us to…embrace our weirdness. We make our pacts and bargains with the Ones Behind the Thorns. And it changes us."

"So you all chose magic and that's how you found each other?"

"Like a family. We chose the magic and got to choose each other. Mostly."

Molly liked that a lot.

She was about to say as much, but she saw how Marsha continued to scan the hills and trees. "Hey, are you okay?"

"Something's wrong," Marsha said. "*Very* wrong." She hurried ahead, first in an awkward shuffle and then in a long, panicked, arm-swinging run. Molly trailed after, and as the path ascended and they ascended with it, she saw that along the sides were endless small mounds making the hills look extra lumpy. It took her a second to realize that these were where the—

gulp

—bodies were buried.

Each grave was covered with grass and a different assortment of plants and objects: big, red-capped mushrooms on one; a circle of brittle stick figurines on another; a spiral of white foxglove flowers; a pyramid of white stones marked with raven feathers; and on and on, each grave a unique space, far more unique than you'd find in, say, the average human cemetery. In the distance, too, Molly saw larger barrow mounds—some with doors cut into the rich, loamy earth, like ancient hobbit houses where (she assumed) only the dead lived. Out of these grew the massive trees they'd seen in the distance.

But she noticed soon that what was on the graves did not always look so healthy. Some of the mushrooms seemed black at the edges. Patches of grass had gone brown and dead. She saw veins of mold spreading across some. And those massive trees seemed to droop, lifeless and melty, as if their branches had softened in botanical sorrow.

"This isn't right, this isn't right," Marsha was saying as she hurried along. She'd stop for a second here and there, stooping to feel the grass, or touch a mushroom, or put her ear to the ground. "It's not supposed to be twilight. It's supposed to be dawn, everlasting dawn—"

"Marsha, what is it? Marsha! Wait up—"

Marsha spun around, heel-to-toe. Her face was frozen in shock. Her jaw worked as if she were a fish out of water. "I—I—I—I—"

"Marsha. It's okay. Breathe. Take a second."

A guttural, almost animal sound came up out of the woman. "He's…draining this place. Stealing its magic."

"That's what we thought, though, right?"

Marsha seethed, angrier than Molly had ever seen her. It took a second to realize where the anger was directed. "Yes, but to *see* it. To *feel* it. Everything is crying out in pain. This may be a place of death but it is a living place, too, living with the spirits of those who have been laid to rest. What your uncle is doing—what he's already *done*—is killing that." Her anger suddenly wilted, sure as the drooping trees seemed to be fast on the way to tears.

"We're here to stop him," Molly said. "Us and the others—maybe some of them have already found him."

Just then, they heard a crackling sound. The ground trembled just so, a light tremor that buzzed in Molly's feet, up through her teeth.

"Marsha," she said, suddenly worried.

"Oh," Marsha said, turning and looking back from whence they came. "Oh no. Run. *Run!*"

The woman grabbed Molly's hand and dragged her back in the direction they'd entered, the two of them bolting along the broken cobblestones, down, down, down toward the valley between the hills. Molly felt a strange lightness in her legs and a dizziness went through her. The earlier feeling of being on an amusement park ride was purely emotional, but this time it felt peculiarly real: Her stomach lurched as the ground seemed to move in front of her. The cobblestones began disappearing ahead of them, the path suddenly swallowed by a thick, hissing fog. It was no longer pointing them downward, either.

Marsha skidded to a halt. Molly kept trying to go, trying to run, toward the fog. But Marsha pulled her back.

"No" was all she said.

"But—you said to run—"

"The path is gone," Marsha said in quiet horror.

Molly looked down. Sure enough, the path had gone from beneath her feet. No more stones. No more walkway. It was just grass now: grown up and untrammeled. "I...I don't understand."

"He knows we're here. And he's trapped us, Molly."

34. lost in more ways
than one

IT WAS LIKE WATCHING A STUFFED ANIMAL GET ITS STUFFING RIPPED OUT.
Marsha plodded back to the burial mounds and sat
cross-legged between two of them. All parts of her
seemed to sink inward. She stared at her feet.

"Marsha," Molly said guardedly.

"Molly," Marsha responded, her voice distant.
"Hello."

"Hey. Hi. Yeah. So what's the plan?"

"I have no plan."

"What? We have to get out—we have to find Gorgoch. We have to *stop* him."

"He took away the path."

"So…we find another path. We pick a direction and we walk until we find something."

Marsha's eyes snapped to Molly. Not in an *omg, epiphany* way, but a *you naïve little child* way. "It doesn't work like that. This place, the cemetery, isn't like terrestrial space. The domains don't all click together like puzzle pieces. We call it *liminal* or *interstitial,* meaning: It's allllll in between. The paths are bridges between realms. Think of an island with one bridge going to the mainland. If that bridge is out"—with some horror she finished—"we're stuck."

Panic lanced through Molly. She hadn't thought of it that way. She'd just assumed this was like anywhere, like any map—but if it wasn't, then they really *were* stuck. And without food and water…

"You're scaring me," she said.

"You should be scared."

That sentence was not spoken by Marsha, but by a voice Molly knew all too well:

Gordo.

She wheeled around as Marsha backpedaled in a clumsy crabwalk. There, up from one of the burial mounds, rose a braid of twisting vines. At the top was a pulpy red flower, its petals like slices of fleshy fruit. In the center of the flower was Gordo's face. Or rather,

Gorgoch. For this was the monster's face: beet red, with shark teeth and vicious eyes. His mouth was twisted into a gleeful grin.

"Hello, *Molly*," her evil uncle growled.

But Molly's tongue was tied. Fear and anger warred inside her.

Marsha was hampered in no such way. She thrust her chin forward, defiant (though she had to pause to *also defiantly* push her big glasses up the bridge of her nose). "You are sullying this place, Devourer. We see you. We will find you. And we will kick you out."

Gorgoch chuckled. "Best of luck with that. Please, go ahead, scoot on out of here. Oh. Wait. You *can't*? The path has gone? Hm. Whatever will you do?"

Now Molly found her voice.

"Why are you doing this?"

The flower vine whipped toward her. Gorgoch's face suddenly became Gordo's again: round, human, both jowly and somehow cherubic. "You should understand, little girl, what it is to have something taken from you. Something that you should have shared in. Your father robbed me of that chance. He and your mother robbed you. Why, I just want what's mine. And if nobody's going to give me a slice"—he gargled a wet, yogurty laugh—"then I'll eat the whole delicious pie!"

Marsha grabbed hold of the vine and pointed her

finger into the flower's middle. "You may have side-lined us. But the others are coming for you, Devourer."

"The others?" Gordo asked, his face reverting to the monstrous, shark-mouthed demon. He laughed. "Oh, you poor, dumb fairy. You don't know. They're trapped, just as you are. Rats in jars. And I'm about to drown each one of them, followed by *you*."

Molly swallowed. If the others were really trapped, too…

It meant they'd already lost.

We should've never separated, she thought. *We should've stuck together.*

(*Like a family*, came a distant, uninvited thought.)

With that, the vine in Marsha's hand withered—going from green, to rust red, to brown, and finally to black. It turned to ash in her hand, and all that was left was Gorgoch's chuckle, a cruel echo that seemed to escape like a moth flitting up, up, and away.

"The others are in danger," Marsha said.

"I think we're in danger, too."

In the distance, a shrill scream cut the air.

Then another scream, somewhere north of them. (If *north* was even a direction here, Molly wondered.)

The two burial mounds near them began to quiver and quake. Each began swelling up, a berm of earth fit to burst. Roots crackled.

"What's happening?" Molly asked in a panicked voice.

But Marsha didn't need to answer. A hand thrust up out of a mound—a shadow-black forearm, like liquid darkness shot through with rotten veins of red blood. Another hand popped out and the thing began pulling itself from the dirt: It had a swirl of horns on each side of its head, like a ram. Its lower half was all goaty, too, with bent legs ending in pitch-black hooves.

The other mound erupted, too. From this one, a thing did not crawl, but rather, leaped out—it was a small being with a round moon face, little needle teeth, and big bulging eyes. Thin, shadowy arms flexed.

"Shades," Marsha said. "Shades of those buried here. No. *No.*" To the two shadows in front of her, Marsha pleaded: "Please. Don't do this. Go. Rest. Sleep!"

They hissed in response and leaped for her.

It was then that Marsha changed.

In the blink of an eye, she gained a full foot in height. Behind her big spectacles, her eyes formed shiny black almonds. Purple flowers bloomed from around her ears. Her fingers became long, like tree roots, and sharp at the end. With a whirl, she sliced one across the satyr shade's neck and thrust a finger from her other hand through the forehead of the gnomish shadow. When they were dispatched, the two shades wailed and melted back into the broken earth. Like oil pooling, the soil soaking them back up.

"Marsha, you look *awesome.*"

"Thanks, kiddo," came Marsha's reply—her voice now contained more than just a human sound—it contained cicada song, and rain showers, and wind through hollow reeds.

Behind them, more graves began buckling and bursting. The shades that crawled or jumped from their earthen barrows were creatures of—at least to Molly's eyes—impossible madness. Bulbous humanoids with many eyes; fish-faced, scale-bodied swamp monsters; lithe, beautiful, extraterrestrial beings; goat-men; winged sylph women; tangles of vines and roots forming human-shaped bodies.

"We need to go," Marsha said.

"But *where*?"

Molly's mind raced. Something had stuck with her about how Marsha described the bridge and the island. If a bridge was out, you'd be trapped on the island. But you wouldn't. Not really.

"You could take a boat. Or swim!" Molly said out loud.

"What?"

All around, the shades of the fallen Fair Folk searched until their gazes fell as one to Marsha and Molly. They began closing in.

A hundred feet.

Ninety.

"You said we're on an island and the bridge is out," Molly hastily explained. "But that wouldn't trap you on an island. You could steal a boat or swim across the water—there's gotta be a way."

Marsha flexed her too-long arms as the shades got closer.

Eighty feet. Seventy. Sixty. The shadows were running now. Galloping and gamboling.

"You might be right. It's the only chance."

Fifty. Forty. Hissing, snarling, cackling.

"Follow me," Marsha said, her sharp fingers dancing in the air. "Stick close. Let's see if we can find a way out of here."

Together, they ran.

Later, the escape would come back to Molly in flashes. Pulses of memory both waking and in dreams. She'd remember the pursuit of the shades, an unending pack of shadowy monsters rushing at them from all sides. She'd remember the graves and barrows, some erupting even as they passed, others swelling like earthen blisters ready to pop. The sounds, too, would come back to her: the straining of the ground, the hissing and shrieking of the shades, the way the rush and roar of them became a wave of noise that drowned out everything but her own panicked heartbeat.

She'd remember, too, coming up on what was clearly the border of this realm. Thorns and trees formed an impenetrable wall. Deep within, red flowers were already turning black. As if drained of life—exsanguinated.

Then she'd recall how Marsha stopped, reaching out with one of her root-fingered hands—those fingers splayed in a defiant gesture of power—and urged her will upon the wall. It crackled, the thicker and woodier vines of thorn breaking and stretching. A small path—a tunnel, really—opened. Almost too small for Molly. Almost.

She'd remember feeling the weight in her own hand of the meteoric knife, the blade they'd poisoned, pressed into her palm by Marsha. Her words to Molly:

Take this. You're going to need it to stop him.

Then:

Go!

The shades swarmed Marsha. She spun and thrashed. Molly remembered crying out, saying no, no she wouldn't go, but her feet carried her forward even as she denied it. Into the tunnel she went. She'd remember—and would carry the scars of—the thorns cutting through her clothes and into her skin. She'd remember Marsha's yells of defiance and triumph giving way to cries of pain and muffled yelps. She'd remember how the tunnel grew darker and darker and then turned downward into a slope and soon into a vertical fall, and then she was falling, falling, into open space, into nothingness, into a strange and starry void.

35. a whiff of amethyst in that strange and starry void

PURPLE.

That was what Molly noticed first. Arguably, she should've noticed a lot of other things before that: for instance, floating in what appeared to be outer space, yet being able to breathe. That was definitely something. Another something was the panoply of stars and *celestial* bodies found in every direction: pinpricks of light, gently turning orbs, comets with trails like fire and glitter, an oblong planetoid with strange rings around it.

But, no. The first thing Molly thought was:

Purple.

Because it was. The great void around her was not the deepest black or the darkest blue, but rather, a kind of cosmic, royal...

Well, *purple.*

The purple of kings. The purple of Prince. The purple of the Joker's jacket. Maybe a hair more pink to it than that—a whiff of *amethyst.*

Then, and only then, did all the other facts come rushing toward Molly like a horde of Black Friday shoppers. The floating, the breathing, the celestial bodies. Her mind flashed momentarily to all the glimpses of stars and planets she'd seen in the symbols on locks and upon one magic tree. And the cemetery was part of some Celestial Protectorate, according to One-Eared Earl, and Marsha had spoken of a common celestial ancestor, hadn't she?

Molly looked behind her, in the direction she'd just come from.

Out there was what looked almost like a planet— one she was drifting away from here in the weird void. That planet looked like a ball tangled in thorns: a landscape of carpeting, all-encompassing briar. It somehow felt both close and far away. Was that where she'd just come from? It was. It was the cemetery realm of the Goodly Neighbors.

Where Marsha still was, right now.

Molly reached out, tried to grab it—that was silly, though, because she was already far away from it, and it was shrinking away from her. Faster, now, than before. She kicked her legs, trying to swim back. But this wasn't water. It was *space*. Outer space? Inner space? She didn't know. Molly continued her drift in one direction and one direction only. She cried out. She wriggled like a worm. Even thrashing did little to alter her path into the void.

Panic ran through her like galloping horses.

Am I dead?

And if I'm not dead now, will I be soon?

After all, unless there was a burger joint out here, it wasn't exactly like she had food or water. It was the same problem as being trapped in the burial grounds of the Goodly Neighbors, but at least *there* they could've eaten weird mushrooms. Here, her only food was…what? Cosmic dust? Dehydrated emptiness? Voidburgers?

She looked at her arms, crisscrossed with fresh thorn scratches. Her Gunwitch Hera outfit was torn. Hopelessness seized her. She cried, no longer able to keep the tears back. She'd done so much wrong. *So* so wrong. If only she had just gone on her way after her father's death, if only she had just…let it all go. She squeezed her eyes shut so as not to stare through their teary veil at the purple void beyond—

Then something shifted.

She felt it.

Out there. In the great purple nowhere.

Eyes still closed, she sensed it but did not see it—it was movement, and presence, and *weight*. Something was here. Something *big*.

Reluctantly, Molly opened her eyes.

A face stared at her.

You do not belong here, a voice said.

The Big Purple Face did not say these words aloud so much as it said them in Molly's mind. She expected it to be like the voice that whispered to her through the lock that day—but it was not. This was different. Bigger, deeper. That voice was a fragile whisper.

"N…no," Molly said as she tried to reckon with and regard the thing she was seeing.

The face floating there was easily a hundred times the size of her own. Maybe a thousand. It was impossible to tell at that size, and it probably didn't even matter what the factor of multiplication was.

The face was made of light, but not so bright that it hurt her eyes. Its own eyes did not glow, but were like holes, literal ones—as if someone had taken a pair of giant scissors and *snip-snip-snipped* out two eyeholes in the fabric of light. And what lay beyond those black holes was not the purple void, but just an empty darkness. The mouth was not a mouth, really, but a circle with a hypnotizing spiral of light turning inside.

When the face spoke again, Molly saw that the spiral pulsed like lightning in dark clouds.

You have my blood.

"What?" Molly asked. Her eyes drifted away from the face but could find no body attached to it. Not that she could see much beyond it, anyway.

You are Blooded. Your human blood is mingled with starblood.

"I…only kinda know what that means."

The Face *hmm*ed inside her mind.

No, you truly don't. How curious.

A part of her was quite certain this thing—The Face—was going to eat her. Its hungry mouth would hoover her up, *shoomp*. And it would chew her into little oblivion bits.

She wiped some of her tears away. "Who are you?"

I am the First Ghost.

"You don't look like a ghost."

I look like the ghost of what I am. Which is not you.

"Fair point," she said, not really sure if it *was* a fair point or not. She just knew she really, reaaaaally didn't want to get eaten.

Then The Face lifted up as if taking a big sniff

of her—it was only now she realized the visage *had* a nose—a curved thing, sharp like a hook. Maybe like a beak.

You have work yet to do, don't you?

"I...do?"

There is a prophecy to fulfill. The Syzygy to complete.

"The sizza-what?"

You are Syzygy: One of Two. There is a reason you were kept apart. But now you are back together. And work must continue apace.

"What does my uncle have to do with all this?"

He was jealous. It poisoned him. He felt robbed of destiny, so he sought his own. He felt robbed of magic—

"So he sought his own."

Yes.

"I really don't understand all this."

You will.

"When?"

In time.

Something rose up beneath her. A great light in a bowl shape—no, not a bowl, but a cupped hand. With too many fingers that looked like insect legs or tentacles.

They closed around her.

Now you go back.

"Wait!" she cried from within the collapsing hand.

"I can't just go back! My uncle is there! I don't know how to stop him. Please help."

I didn't say I *had work to do. I said* you *had work to do.*

"Wait, no no no nonono—"

Goodbye.

And then The Giant Hand belonging to The Giant Face threw Molly through space, like a tumbling asteroid. *Whoosh.*

36. crash landing

MOLLY TUMBLED THROUGH SPACE, HER BODY TUCKING INTO A FETAL LUMP and cannonballing through a wall of brittle branches and dead leaves. They crackled and snapped as she fell. The purple glow of the spectral void gave way not to a soft twilight, but rather to a gray mist laid over blackest night. She hit the ground hard, the air horse-kicked from her lungs.

Gasping, she rolled onto her back. She stared at the skeletal network of dead branches above her, all twisting into one another. The mist that slithered around her was cold and damp—so much so it seemed swiftly to crawl under her skin like a worm, one that coiled around her bones.

Soon her breath returned. She blinked and sat up. Pain dug into her like a chisel into stone.

Her eyes adjusted, and though the mist made it difficult, she saw a gray stone path meandering through dark grass. And beyond the path, boxy buildings with the silhouettes of figures marking the tops.

Then she realized:

They're tombs.

Behind her, a distant hiss. And a scrape of something. Like the pad of a rough, bare foot on the stone walkway.

She spun and saw something fifty feet away: a lithe black shape. Like one of the shadows from the Goodly Neighbors' burial mounds. This one was tall, with a long neck and a head that craned round and round like an owl's. Spectral fingers tested the air, and she saw now that the eyes, *they glowed.* Bloodred, like brake lights on a foggy night.

Its gaze was roving, roving, looking for something.

Looking for me.

Another scuff.

Nearby, through the trees, came another tall shape. Same as the first. It hissed, and when it did, she saw something gleam in its mouth:

Wet fangs. Bone white and bright.

Teeth clacked together. A hungry sound. *Clack, clack, clack.*

More appeared all around her. Eyes searching the misty dark. Some seemed to be sniffing the air now, like animals.

Molly looked in the direction of the tombs. She saw nothing there—or, at least, none of the shadow monsters. She sucked in a breath, winced, and chased all the fears out of her head. *You just need to do this. Move your feet, Molly. Move. Your. Feet!*

And that's what she did. She broke into a hard run, feet whisking the grass and clopping hard on the walkway—

The shades spun toward her. Red eyes finding her. She *knew* because the shadows howled in unison: a harrowing, feral trill of rage and sorrow like a banshee that had just stubbed her toe on a river rock.

They came for her, *fast.* She glanced over her shoulder and saw their long black bone legs launching them into a terrifying sprint. Molly yelped and hurried into the tombs—past one, then another. Some sat alone, their doors barred with iron slats; others were lined with crawling gargoyles or perched skeleton sculptures. The shades funneled in behind her, forming a pack of wretched monsters, their arms reaching through the mist for her—

She ducked between two tombs, then another two—

And suddenly, she was off the path and off the grass.

She was in a maze. Or a mazelike series of tombs, the space between them forming a clumsy, claustrophobic labyrinth. Left, right, left she went. Then straight. Then again right. The wails of the coming shadows wound through the tight channels, making her ears ring and chill-bumps gather on her skin like an army of mourners.

And then—

She skidded to a halt.

It was a dead end. Two tombs met. She reached out and felt the seam where their walls were pressed together.

Behind her, the wails arose again. Closer now. And closing in.

No, no, no, no—

Something grabbed her from behind. Hands around her mouth. They pulled her backward even as she kicked and struggled. In her ear, something hiss-whispered: "*Shhhhh.*"

And then she was yanked backward—

Into one of the tombs.

Molly's eyes went wide with panic. She contemplated taking the heel of her cosplay boot and slamming it down on her attacker's foot. But before she could, again the voice hissed in her ear: "Shh! Follow me!" as its hand left her mouth and the owner shuffled past.

As he spoke more, saying, "I'm sorry about that. I didn't want to scare you or…grab you, but it seemed the only way," Molly realized she recognized the voice.

"Dustin?!" she said in a surprised whisper.

"C'mon," he said, ushering her deeper into the tomb, which she was sure wasn't much bigger than her bedroom in the last nasty condominium Steve had rented—but when Dustin said, "Careful here of the steps," she realized there was an opening. A large shape off to her right was suggestive of…well, the actual *tomb* part of the tomb. A massive stone coffin. What was the word? Dustin read her mind: "Also, mind the sarcophagus. Its edges are sharper than you think."

That was it. *Sarcophagus.*

And down they went, through a narrow channel in the stone. The steps underneath her feet felt dusty and home to bits of scree and other debris.

As they reached the bottom floor, Dustin moved past her and hurried back up the steps, saying, "Hold on a moment." Up at the top, he reached out and, grunting, drew the sarcophagus over the opening. This plunged them into a darkness deeper than Molly had imagined was possible, until—

Light bloomed ahead of her. A ghostly green-gold glow that she realized was bioluminescent, radiating from some kind of fungus. Not a mushroom, exactly, but a bundle of strange tendrils and tubules, each fringed at the top like a little squid. It had the shape of what a bouquet of flowers might look like on a whole other world.

Dustin's face was framed by the eerie illumination, which cast him in an even sicklier light than usual— deepening the lines and hollows of his face.

"Dustin, I—" she started.

He hugged her.

Tight.

Her first thought was: *What sorcery is this?*

Because he would have to be mind-controlled to exhibit *this* magnitude of kindness in her general direction. Sure, he seemed to have warmed up to her a little before, but this, *this* was different. This was…a brother's hug.

And she didn't know what to do with it.

So she did what felt best: She hugged him back.

"I'm so glad you're all right," he said. "I thought—I thought I dragged you into this. And then, it was so much worse than we knew."

"I know." After a nice while, they broke the hug. "I was worried about you, too. I think…Marsha…"

Dustin's brow darkened in the fungal glow. "Oh no."

"I left her." Molly's eyes welled up. "These shades came and—"

"Yes. They're the specters of the dead interred here. Seems our demonic *uncle* has found a way to force them out of their graves to serve him as shades of what they once were. He controls this whole cemetery." With anger and sadness so palpable you could chew on them, he added: "Every realm of it."

"That's what he told us."

Dustin harrumphed. "He spoke to you, too, hm?"

She nodded. "He appeared to Marsha and me. And…" She cried out, hands balling into fists. "It's my fault if she's hurt. I shouldn't have left her." It occurred to her: Marsha meant a lot to her. She was like a big sister.

Or a mother.

She was really racking up family members all of a sudden.

Dustin sighed. "If it's any help, Marsha can take care of herself."

"I saw. She…changed." *Maybe she'll be okay.*

Only now did she take a look around. They appeared to be in another maze: this one subterranean. Gray walls lined with capillaries of moss surrounded them on all sides, carrying off in two directions—though she could see various other corners and bolt-holes in the glow of the fungus.

"You came with Dave. Is this the—"

"The Tombs of Undeath. Where the Children of the Night—the vampires—are buried, yes."

"Is Dave okay?"

He sighed. "I don't know. We got separated. Woefully, I've not seen him."

"I hope he's all right." She blinked. "Also, is *now* a bad time to ask why vampires need cemeteries? It seems like they'd need the *opposite* of cemeteries."

He chuckled darkly. "Yes. Well. They do sometimes die. As in, *die* die. The True End, they call it. Many things can kill them: the sun, a stake to the heart, fire. It's why I'm holding a glowing wad of fungal pods and not a torch. If they are turned to ash, their ashes can be interred here. But others become lost to their vampiric natures—and as their last wish of sanity, they can ask to be buried here instead. Entombed."

"The shades. They're the ghosts of the dead-dead ones? The ashes?"

"That is correct."

"What about the Entombed? The ones going insane but... still alive. Er, undead? Unalive?"

He paused. "I don't know. They don't seem to be free. Not yet, at least. And thank all the gods for that."

Hm, she thought.

Hm, hm, hmm.

"What do we do now? We have a plan, right?"

But the lost look on his face gave her the bad news. He forced a smile. "Come on. I have a place down here. A little food. Some water—not easy to come by in the land of the truly dead."

"You have a place?" she asked, following along. "Dude, how long have you been here?"

He paused to think about it.

"A couple of weeks, I'd say."

"Wait. A couple of *weeks*?"

37. a plate of bugs and feelings

TURNED OUT, YEP, HE'D BEEN HERE A COUPLE OF WEEKS.

They wound their way through some tunnels, around a few bends and corners, and down another set of steps, until they ended up in a small antechamber—this one home to twisted tree roots pushing through the stone walls. Here, Dustin had marked the days on the wall—not that the sun ever came up, but the moon rose and fell, and that, he felt, marked a day. She noticed, too, in his gathered bundle of glowshrooms, that his jawline was speckled with soft stubble. Time had passed for him in ways it had not for her.

"I don't understand it," she said. "I feel like I haven't even been here for a whole day. How have *you* been here for two weeks?"

He *hmm*ed at her as he pulled out a copper plate gone aquamarine with patina. "I don't know, I just have been. How did you get here?"

"I crawled through the thorns at the edge of the cemetery. And then I ended up in, like, I dunno. Outer space. And I met a—"

A ghost.

A face.

A faceghost.

A ghostface.

But she couldn't quite bring herself to explain. She wanted to say, *it told me I had work to do,* but that sounded cuckoo bananapants. She bit her tongue and said: "I don't know. Next thing I remember, I was crashing back down through trees, not thorns. And I was here."

"You went outside the cemetery," he said in a hushed whisper.

"I. Uh. Yeah? I guess I did."

"What was out there?"

A big face, and a lot of purple.

"Not much," she said stiffly. "A void. Stars." *A big hand that threw me back here.* Why was she reluctant to tell Dustin about this? Because it was just too much in a time that was already spectacularly extra? Because The Face told her things about him, too, that she and Dustin were some kind of cosmic pairing? She didn't know. All she knew was—now was not the time to get into it. "That's it."

"Do you know the word sidereal?"

That word, he pronounced it *sy-dee-re-ull*.

"No, but it's cool-sounding. Should I?"

"It means something that comes from the stars. The supernatural inhabitants of our world believe their magic comes from the cosmos, far beyond the solar system or galaxy we know."

"So their magic doesn't come from *our* stars. But rather—"

"Those stars," he said. "The ones in that void."

For reasons Molly couldn't pin down, a shudder galloped through her. Dustin broke the silence by holding the plate toward her. "It's an old offering plate. The vampires put them outside the tombs and altars of their friends and loved ones—even their enemies, as they tend to consider even their greatest foes sacred—and others are encouraged to leave tribute. Coins and jewels and blood—or blood amber. It's a bit of a heresy to take one and use it like this, I'm afraid, but it's not like I brought a tote bag."

Molly wasn't quite sure what he was using it *for*, until she looked a little harder.

The plate seemed to be moving.

Squirming, more like.

She heard the gentle *tick-a-tack* rasp of legs upon legs upon shells upon mandibles, and she saw that what was collected before her was a whole plate full of *beetles.*

Red-black beetles. Each with a crown of little spikes above prodigious eyes. She blanched.

"You have to twist the heads off first," he said. "Then you pop them into your mouth. They're crunchy mostly, except for, ahhh, the goo."

"The goo."

"Yes. The goo. Less like pudding, more like toothpaste."

With a gentle push, she eased the plate back toward him. "I think I'm good."

"I promise they taste better than my sales pitch. Nutty, almost."

"Bad news, brother. I don't think they're vegetarian."

He winced. "I tried eating the glowy fungus. It, um, didn't go well. Sure you don't want some?"

"Maybe when I get hungry." She sighed. "Please tell me you have a plan? You're smart. You're thoughtful. Please."

Dustin sat back on a fallen stone pillar. His chin sank to his chest and he set the beetle plate next to him. (The beetles began escaping.) And then it was like a storm rushing upon the land with little warning—his head tilted back, and he let slip a dread wail and began openly sobbing.

Molly stared.

"Oh. I. Oh."

Suddenly, she snapped to it and hurried to sit next to him on the bench formed from the collapsed pillar. Molly put her arm around him and rested her head on his shoulder.

"It'll be okay," she said, not sure if she was doing this right.

"Will it?" he moaned. "I'm supposed to know what I'm doing, Molly. I am the caretaker of this cemetery! But nothing I know has prepared me for a situation like this! And I know *a lot*. You cannot have *one whit* of iron buried on or near a Goodly Neighbor! Under the right, or wrong, circumstances, a vampire can reconstitute itself from its own ashes! Werewolf bodies must be shellacked in a slathering of special hallucinogenic honey! Why? I don't know! They don't know! They just do! Do you know how *hard* it is to procure said hallucinogenic honey? *Very incredibly horribly hard.*"

He buried his face in the bowl of his hands. His shoulders shook as he wept. "I just wish Mom hadn't died. I wish she hadn't left this all on me. I wasn't even sure I *wanted* to do it once I was old enough! And now…I've got you. A little sister. What kind of a big brother am I?" He yanked his head out of his hands, his eyes puffy and red—and he pointed those puffy peepers right at her. "A terrible one, that's what. I've lied to you. Led you astray. Here I was acting all high and mighty but I'm so lost. I've just been sitting here, eating…bugs."

His mouth trembled. He blinked back the tears.

"I'm lost, too," Molly said plainly.

His mouth formed a bewildered squiggle. "What?"

"I'm just as lost as you are. And jealous, really. You had a mom who loved you and believed in you. And despite being a little, uh, high-strung, you seem like someone who has it together. You dress well and you know who you are, and I don't think I know who I am. I dress up in all these costumes because it's easier than being me, I think. Whoever 'me' is." She sighed and looked down at her outfit, which had been torn asunder by her transit through the thorns. "I'm not Gunwitch Hera. I'm just me. Bleh."

"I *wish* I could be someone else. I envy you, Molly."

"It kinda makes me feel good to know that."

He laughed a little and sniffled. "Two peas in a pod, we are."

The Syzygy, she suddenly remembered. Was that about them?

She stood up and mussed Dustin's hair. "Big brother, it's okay you don't have a plan. There's no good way to have a plan for all…this. I let our nasty uncle into this place and now he's let all the monsters out, and…"

"Not all the monsters."

The way he said it sounded like he had an idea.

She arched an eyebrow.

"The Entombed," he said, leaping to his feet, finger thrust in the air.

"The feral vampires?"

"Yes."

"What about them?"

He hesitated. "I think I want to let them out."

"What? *Why?*"

"Because, besides us, they're the one thing our uncle does not control. We let them out, he'll have to come deal with them. And then…we strike."

"What are the chances he actually shows up?"

Dustin offered a small shrug. "I can't say. But it's a better chance than we had before."

"Only if the ancient feral vampires don't eat us first. And Dave, wherever he is."

He offered a small, tight smile. "Well, yes, there's that." But then his smile broadened, and in the deep of his eye was a flicker of anarchy—one that, Molly had to admit, she saw in her own eye now and again. "Shall we go cause some chaos?"

"Oh, we *gotta*."

38. one more lock to open

OF COURSE, THE ONE PIECE MOLLY DIDN'T UNDERSTAND—HOW EXACTLY they were gonna *free* a series of Entombed vampires— was no mystery to Dustin. He told her to follow him, and off they went, deeper into the catacombs. Around bends and corners, down one set of steps, then another, then another, until the last set was a dusty spiral stair- case cut into the stone—so tight that it made Molly's breath catch in a fit of claustrophobia.

"It's here," Dustin said, holding the glowing fungal bouquet ahead of them like a torch.

They stepped into an octagonal antechamber. Down from the ceiling stretched old, dead roots—red as rust and blood, and thrust through with dark veins. Dustin said they were the roots of the trees she fell through to get here. "They're like that iron-red tree at the start of all this," she said. "The Guidestone."

"That's exactly right, they are. But different, too. *These* iron-reds are dead—well, undead, I suppose."

"So they're…vampire trees?"

"Of a sort. They feed on blood—that's, in part, what the beetles are for. It forms a kind of *ecosystem*, I guess you'd call it. Sometimes they feed from the interred or the Entombed, too. The iron-reds are the first wizard trees. Supposedly created from a graft of an ancient magical tree known as the Charitable Thorn. Which, in turn, is where you get that other famous tree, the Glastonbury Thorn—the one reportedly grown by Joseph of Arimathea, who planted his staff in the ground."

"I don't know, like, any of what you're talking about, but it sounds real smart." She patted him on the shoulder. "See? You got this."

He sighed. "I don't know a lot of actually important things, though. I've absorbed so much of this *strangeness* that I scarcely have room to learn about math or science or any of that." He lowered his voice to a whisper, as if to confess a sin: "I don't know how to do taxes!"

She shrugged. "I don't think anyone knows how to do their taxes. They sure don't teach it in school."

"I guess that's good. For me, not the country." He stepped forward. "That is a concern for another time. As for now—" He swiped his foot left and right, clearing off some of the dust on the ground. There he exposed what looked to be a sandstone brick, separate from the rest of the smooth, seamless floor.

No, not a brick, she realized.

A button.

Dustin toed the stone button, and the brick sank a few inches, grinding as it did. It settled into place with a *ka-click.*

With that, the room lit up in an eerie golden glow. Threads of fungus along the wall began to pulse with light. Then, in the center of the room, a pedestal corkscrewed up from the floor—a square of brick topping it like a hat—and stopped at a height of six feet, no longer a pedestal but a pillar.

Said pillar was peppered with carvings of the moon in all its phases. No stars, no suns, no planets. Just moons.

She noted as much to Dustin.

"Yes," he said. "The governing celestial body of the vampires. The moon, symbol of night. Symbol of the vampires."

"I would've thought that was the fox-changer

symbol." She explained: "Because the moon changes faces so often?"

"But the moon is always the moon. It doesn't actually change, but what we see does. The fox-changers on the other hand—and the werewolves, and the Crowfolk, and the Hivetenders, and so on and so forth—all literally change their bodies. Their symbol is that of Mercury, the quicksilver planet. Ever-shifting." He went on: "Magicians and sorcerers count their symbol as the sun-in-splendor, and the Goodly Neighbors are represented by a globe with meridian and equator—some believe it's the Earth, or an Earthlike world whence their magic came."

"What about Florg?"

Dustin shrugged. "Florg is Florg. An anomaly, like so many. Represented only by the star shape, for so many of the celestial denizens cannot chart their magic from any origin point, and instead it's just…from out there. Somewhere."

Poor Florg, Molly thought. But maybe that made them special, too.

"What about the comet?" she asked.

"What?"

"The comet. On the padlock to your libroratory. I saw those other symbols, I think, but then there was also a comet."

"I honestly can't say. I assume it's someone's symbol, lost to time, lost to the books. I've never found much about it."

"Oh."

Then, in the center of the moon symbols, she saw another familiar sight:

Five keyholes.

"For the Fivefold Key," Dustin said. "Which we don't have."

"But we do have these," she said, holding up her hands, fingers tickling the air. "Think they'll work again?" She led him around the pillar, finding a handprint on two opposite sides. Red, like on the gate to enter the cemetery.

"Once again," Dustin said, "it seems that together we are more powerful than alone. I wish I'd known that a few days ago. Even years ago."

"I wish I'd known all this. Or none of it."

"Same."

She held up her hand. "Shall we?"

He exhaled deeply and said, "We shall."

They pressed their hands against the prints, and a faint tremor buzzed through the stone. A few threads of dust fell from the ceiling above their heads, whispering as they hit the floor.

Then it was done.

"Did we—?" she started.

"—do it?" Dustin finished.

"I heard a sound. Or maybe I *felt* the sound?"

"Yes." He nodded, uncertain at first but then faster and surer. "I suspect that was the sound of sarcophagi opening. And the tombs within. They're all connected here by the stone from which this realm is carved."

"How long will it take for them to—"

An inhuman wail cut the air, somewhere up above them. They heard it winding its way through the tunnels like a serpent made of terrible, terrible sound. A mix of rage and hunger.

"Uhhh, Dustin. That sounds like it's down here."

"As I just noted," he said a little testily, "the tombs all connect here."

"But won't they come for us? Here? I mean—" She gestured at herself as if she were a lobster in a lobster tank begging to be picked. "We are full of blood. And I expect their vampire tum-tums are heckin' empty."

"Oh. Yes. Right. We're safe down here—or, we will be."

He hurried back to the door whence they came, running his hand alongside the frame, again wiping away dust. Once more, a button was revealed, inset against the otherwise unbroken stone. He pushed on it, and it didn't budge. "Um."

"Dustin."

A scream rose louder.

Not just louder. *Closer.*

"Dustin."

He pushed the heel of his hand against it. "Oh no. Oh no no no."

A new noise now to accompany the next scream: a scrambling sound, running from one length of the ceiling to the next. Like hearing a rat in the wall, except this sounded like a *very* big rat, indeed. A second scream rose to join the first. Then a third.

Molly bolted across the room. Halfway there, she began hopping clumsily as she struggled to unzip a long boot—one with a big, chunky heel. She nearly fell, toppling past Dustin and thankful for the wall that stopped her.

"They're coming," he grunted, trying again to push the button.

"Move!" she yelped, popping the boot off her foot and calf. She spun it around, grabbing it like a weapon—

Just as something began scrambling down the steps toward them.

She heard claws on stone.

And hissing.

Molly took the heel of the boot and—

Wham. Used it like a hammer against the button.

The button *moved.* The sound again came like stone grinding against stone, and as the button sank into the wall, pale white bricks began falling out of the left and right sides of the doorframe. They did so in a way that at first she was sure meant it was broken—

But she saw how neatly they landed upon one another, stacking with a loud crunchy clap. *Clonk, clonk, clonk,* they went, one after the next, swiftly forming a bricked-up wall.

Molly staggered back—

And as the portal closed, sealing them in, she saw the face of the first Entombed to reach them. A pale, brutal face—its skin like a moth-eaten bedsheet drawn across a hard-angled skull. Its fangs were as long as her index fingers.

It screeched, and long, hooked fingernails scraped at the top of the doorframe. A brick fell upon them— snapping them off. The nails clattered against the floor as the wall finally closed.

She stood, panting.

Dustin made no sound at all. His hands were clasped in front of him. His lips were pursed, his eyes as wide and wet as ponds.

"Thank you," he said in a small voice.

"Thank my boot."

"Thank you, Molly's boot."

On the other side of the brick wall they heard screeching and scraping. A fierce madness lurked just outside. The stone only somewhat muffled the roars of rage.

"They can't get in here, right?"

"I don't believe so. This entire place is made of the same material that built their sarcophagi. It is a blessed, sacred stone called Purestone. Mined from the ossified remains of a fallen god. Or angel, or star-titan, depending on whom you ask."

"That's weird."

"Welcome to the supernatural solemnities industry."

"Are we okay here, then?"

He swallowed. "Yes."

"Can we get back out?"

On that, he did not answer.

"Okaayyyyy," she said. "Let me ask a different question: Why does a place like this even exist? Why is there a switch to open the graves? And, like, a safe room to protect yourself?"

"I asked Mom that when she took me around. Her answer was vague. Frustratingly so. It has to do with the end of the world."

"The what now?"

"You know. Apocalypse, Armageddon, Ragnarok, the end-times."

"We didn't just start the end-times, right?"

He blinked and chuckled. "What? Oh no. Of course not." But his face showed a sudden and distinct lack of certainty. "I mean, I *hope* not."

She shuddered, remembering that the Void Face seemed very interested in Dustin and her being together. *Work to do.* Best to think about it later.

"What exactly is the outcome of this plan?" she asked. "I mean, the monsters are free and now we're trapped in what may end up being our own tomb. I'm starting to think this wasn't a plan as much as a, I dunno, *random flailing* in a dangerous direction."

"The plan, or its consequence, is that the Entombed lose our scent and begin going after the food they know: the iron-red trees, which are full of blood. But we have evidence that Gordo is also feeding on them to claim the magic for himself. And if *the vampires* begin pilfering his magical food source…"

"He'll go after them."

"Yes. And though Gordo may be strong, I do not know that he's strong enough to take on a hundred elder vampires. Each starving and mad."

Suddenly, all the fungus in the room pulsed so brightly it made Molly wince. Dustin, too, shielded his eyes. When the light dulled anew, they saw tendrils peeling away from the walls, as if animated. Threads of fungus met other threads, and they braided together, forming—

A face.

Not *that* face. Not *The* Face.

This was the face of their wretched uncle.

Gordo the man. Gorgoch the Devourer.

He sneered. "You two."

"Uncle," Dustin said, swallowing hard. He tried to step back but Molly caught him. *We're not shying away from Gordo. Not now.* Dustin seemed to take some power from that, and he lifted his chin (however trembling) and thrust out his chest (however swiftly it rose and fell like the panicked heartbeat of an espresso-addled hummingbird).

"Hey, *turdbutt*," Molly said.

His fungal nostrils flared. "What did you do? You let them out, didn't you? All those musty, old vampires."

Dustin summoned some bravado. "You'll find that you're confusing *old* with *elderly*. They're quite spry. And quite hungry."

"Neither of you deserve the fruits of this place. Neither of you even *see* the power it generates. Your rat-faced mother, your shiftless, thieving *father*—they wouldn't give me even a *whiff* of what they had, but now—"

Suddenly he winced, as if in pain. Some of the fungal threads that made up his face went suddenly black.

As if dead. He snarled and formed a fungal hand, which he clutched just below his neck. The darkness in his face shrank—

But some of it remained. Some parts of him never lit up again.

And that's when Molly understood.

She understood it all.

What this was.

What had happened.

And how to defeat him.

She let him go on about how he would deal with the crusty, old vampires, become even more powerful, and then make her and Dustin wish they'd never been born. Typical big bad villain stuff. But it was the last thing he said to Molly that really sealed the deal:

"*You*, of all people, should understand."

The threads of fungus broke apart, brittle, and crumbled to the floor. They no longer glowed—though the rest of the room again grew illuminated.

"We're in trouble," Dustin said.

"No," Molly said, turning toward him, a big smile on her face. "For once it's not us who's in danger. It's him. It's Gordo."

"I don't follow you, little sister."

"I know how we beat him, big brother. I know *everything*."

39. bee's oar

"IT'S THE BEZOAR," SHE SAID.

"Yes, we know. The bezoar is a symbol of his fear, and it showed us his weakness. But it doesn't really *do* anything, Molly."

"I disagree."

He narrowed his gaze. "Oh?"

"We don't have to poison him. He's already been poisoned. These?" She held up the meteoric blade. "Useless."

"I still don't follow."

The Giant Face said it, she thought to herself. And here, she reiterated those words: "His jealousy poisoned him. That's not, like, a metaphor. It's *literally* poisoning him. Did you see what happened when he talked about Mom and Dad not giving him a piece of the pie? He seemed suddenly in pain, and he grabbed at his neck. The bezoar must be the only thing stopping the poison from killing him."

Dustin's eyes narrowed as he remembered. "When the fungus blackened."

"He's sick with a disease of his own making, Dustin."

"Jealousy," they said in tandem.

She continued, almost theatrically, like a detective revealing the solution to a dread murder: "He's so jealous of our parents—his own brother—that it's killing him. The bezoar is somehow stopping the sickness, I bet. Or slowing it. I remember—when he was using me to open the door to the cemetery—I saw a necklace. I thought what was hanging from it was some kind of rock or stone, but I think it was this."

"So if we steal the bezoar—"

"I think the jealousy overtakes him."

"We've no way to know if that's true."

She shrugged. "We just gotta trust our guts."

Dustin nodded. "And each other." He lowered his head. "A lesson we could both have learned earlier, I guess."

She slugged him in the shoulder. "Now is not the part of the story where the music swells and we Hallmark movie our way to a big, weepy hug."

"So what part of the story *is* it, then?"

"The part where we go out there, kick his butt, save the other Watchers *and* all the cemetery realms."

"That's a little vague. And we're probably going to die. But okay. I'm in."

"I'm sorry I got you into this, dude."

He smiled softly, not stiffly. "I think this is as much my fault as it is yours. Let's just call it a wash. *Dude.*"

"Oh. Oh no." Her mouth pursed, her nose rankled as if she'd just sniffed a bucket of rancid cabbage. "Don't say *dude*. It's just not good in your mouth. It's not right."

"But they say it in Hawaii. Dude. *Brah.*"

Molly faux-gagged. "Please. You're hurting me. It's like orange juice and toothpaste, man. Can we just get to work?"

"Of course we can," he said.

"Thank you."

"Dude."

"No."

"Brah."

"Dustin, why are you like this?"

"I learned it by watching you."

Dustin pressed his ear against the pale bricks that walled them in.

"I don't hear anything anymore," he said.

"You sure they're not just waiting out there for us?"

"In my experience, starving vampires are neither patient nor quiet. They are messy hunters, single-minded and noisy in their pursuit."

"You gonna hit the button?"

"I am going to hit the button."

"It's gonna open the door?"

"I believe it will open the door."

Dustin pushed the button.

Molly flinched.

Nothing happened.

Seconds passed. He hit the button again. Still nothing.

Molly shoved past him and whacked it with the boot again. With that, the button made a grinding sound before clicking, and one by one, the bricks retreated, as if tugged by invisible hands, back into the wall whence they came. "Boot magic," she said, to explain.

"I guess there is a world of small magic I haven't considered."

And with that, the portal was open. The way was

clear. Dustin thrust the bouquet of glowing fungus pods ahead of him, and they saw claw marks etched into the stone stairs and walls that had not been there before. Molly shuddered, thinking of the force and fury required to carve stone. Not to mention a whole lot of *sharpness.*

They could hear the vampires' howls and wails more clearly now. But they were far off—somewhere above, in the cemetery. Not down here, which was good, Molly thought, until she reminded herself that they had to leave *here* and go *there.*

"Ready?" Dustin asked.

"No."

"Me neither."

And yet they went.

They moved through the tight, twisting passages and tunnels of the subterranean labyrinth. This time they passed funerary masks set in the walls, each showing a different vampire's face: a lady vampire with one eye and a mouth full of shark-teeth fangs; a gent with long hair and a twisted grin, his tongue poking out almost playfully over thin lips; a third with skeletal cheeks and deep-set eyes and a ridge of bony spikes riding its too-wide, too-tall forehead.

As they went, there came a sudden tectonic shift: a

grumbly rumble in the walls, floor, and ceiling. More streamers of dust hissed to the ground.

"The vampires?" she asked in a loud whisper.

"No. I think it's *him.*"

Gordo. Gorgoch. Uncle Turdbutt.

The Devourer.

Ahead, a shaft of moonlight shone down from above. The way out, Molly realized. And then, from up there, a sudden howl arose. Similar to before, when the vampires were swarming toward them—but now louder, more malignant, with a far greater *mad hunger* factor. It reminded her of the worst storms: like the few times she'd experienced a tornado warning and the sky went black and the rain went horizontal and hail broke branches off trees.

"I don't want to go out there," she said, having to raise her voice over the din.

Dustin nodded. "You stay here. I'll do it."

"Dustin, no."

He met her gaze. "You're my little sister. This isn't your responsibility. And—it's my job. Literally!" He held both of her hands as the screaming in the world above grew louder and louder. "I've got this. I'll come get you when it's done, Molly."

Then he turned and went toward the staircase.

She stood still, her feet rooted to the ground like a tree.

Her brain told her: *Stay here, he's right, this is his job, you're too young, too foolish, just a stupid little girl playing dress-up.*

But her heart said differently: *He needs you, you figured out how to beat Gordo, you're a team, and by the way you're dressed as Gunwitch Hera and do you remember in Issue 14 how she went up against her own boss, Governix Kell Cargoom, and he gained power from the Books of Illumination and became this big, horrible monster and she got her butt kicked but still beat him in the end, yeah, duh, you're dressed as Gunwitch Hera for a reason, so quit listening to your brain and trust what's in your dang heart.*

She took a deep breath, gritted her teeth—

And ran to Dustin, catching his elbow. She yelled at him over the storm of screams. "Hey! I'm in! You don't do this without me!"

He nodded.

Together, they returned to the night, entering the storm of screams.

40. the monster mash

MOLLY AND DUSTIN EMERGED INTO A GROVE OF LEAFLESS IRON-RED TREES.

Reluctantly, they turned toward the origin point of all the vampiric shrieking.

And that's when they saw a lone figure. Familiar in his suit, now ragged and torn. *Gordo.* Looking more like a man than the red-faced, many-eyed demon he had become (or, Molly feared, truly was). He emerged from a wall of tombs, hands hanging by his sides as if in wait. And ahead of him, galloping less like humans and more like rabid beasts, were the vampires. A hundred of them at least, their long, many-jointed limbs carrying them toward their prey with alarming speed.

From here, they were little more than pale, rampaging juggernauts. Few wore clothes—what material was left had gone rotten, worm-eaten, threadbare.

Dustin said, "My gods."

"It's like watching a tsunami."

"A tsunami about to hit one man."

And that's exactly what happened.

The beasts, in waves of their own, pounced—mouths open. Jaws distended. Claws out. Screaming, hissing, wailing. The first wave slammed down upon Gordo like a fist made of monsters, and they swarmed him just as the second wave crashed down, and the third, and the fourth, until Gordo disappeared beneath a hill of starving vampires.

Well, that ended quickly, Molly thought. Because surely there was no way that Gordo had survived—

That's when the *pile of vampires* erupted. No longer a hill. Now a volcano.

Monsters flew through the air—their broken bodies pinwheeling in the darkness. What emerged from their center was an arm—impossibly long and segmented, like a centipede. It lashed about, plucking elder vampires off the pile before flinging their thrashing forms into the night. A second arm joined the first and aided in the eruptive extraction.

Then the trees around Dustin and Molly crackled.

"What the—" he said.

One by one, the trees bent over, pushing their branch tops into the dusty, ashen earth. Then they *pulled* at the ground, hauling their roots out of the brittle clay. And one by one the iron-red trees began *handspringing* toward the fracas. Molly and Dustin had to duck and scurry away from one that landed right where they'd been standing.

"Whose trees are these?" Molly asked.

Dustin didn't need to answer. Because the trees—clumsily vaulting themselves forth with great haste, bough over roots, then roots over boughs—began pinning whole *clumps* of writhing vampires to the ground in claws of brutal branches.

"The trees are Gordo's," Dustin answered.

In the distance, their uncle's body emerged—his torso still roughly human-shaped and human-sized, but his legs as long as the tallest ladder; his arms, too. His face shone blister-red in the moonlight, and his mouth opened big, bigger, biggest—Pac-Man mouth with a wet lashing tongue that squirmed and gleamed. He spun about like a tornado as he slashed at his attackers, cutting some clean in half, flinging others into tombs, smashing more into their cohorts. Cackling loud enough that he could be heard over their bloodthirsty shrieks.

And then something changed. When enough of the

vampires had been felled, he began picking up their broken bodies, one by one...and cracking them in half like sticks. From them emerged a red, glowing mist, which Gordo seemed to inhale through the flappy slits that served as his nose-holes. After each inhalation, he shuddered, and a little pulse of thunder kicked off him with an air-shaking boom.

Dustin blanched. "He's eating their spirits. He is truly a Devourer."

"We can't get close to that," Molly said. "It's just... chaos."

Dustin gripped his chin with thumb and crooked forefinger—a gesture so stereotypical of a man in thought Molly didn't think anyone actually *did it*; she just assumed it was something movies made actors do.

"He's by the tombs. We need to get behind him," Dustin said. And with that, he pulled her back down into the tunnels. She was thankful Dustin seemed (mostly) to know where to go. He hurried to one passage, then took a left, and another left, then a right, and on like that, moving from hall to hall. And as they moved, the sound of mayhem above grew louder and louder, until suddenly—

It stopped.

Dustin skidded to a halt. He held up his hand. "Wait."

"What is it?"

"The sound."

"I know, it's quiet." Molly felt her hands shaking. "Is that good?"

"I don't know." He paused, panic flashing in his glow-lit eyes. "Let's continue. I think there's an exit—"

There came a great crashing sound, and Molly found herself on her butt, her vision swimming, her ears ringing. Above her head, the world had opened up—the moonlit sky glowed silver, fringing the edges of the hole that had been ripped in the tombs in a soft luminescence.

Near her, she heard a sound—a squeaky utterance of her name:

"Molly."

Her body ached too much to sit up properly, so she tucked her chin to her chest and tried to follow the voice—

Dustin stood enveloped in tomb dust. Through the haze, she saw a hand was around his throat—or, rather, around the back of his neck, the fingers pushing in on his trachea. Those fingers were long and raw-red, attached to a chitinous hand that was itself attached to a crab-like arm that disappeared up through the hole.

"Dustin," she said.

Above, Gordo's head—

(No, *Gorgoch*'s head.)

—appeared at the opening, hovering on a massive neck that looked like a monstrous anaconda the color of a boiled hot dog.

He laughed.

And then he hoisted Dustin out of the hole with terrifying swiftness. *Whoosh*, and her brother was gone. Taken up into the night.

"No!" she cried, and scrambled to stand. It was hard getting her feet under her, but Dustin was in danger, and so she pushed past the pain that throttled up her tailbone and urged herself onto the pile of rubble and earth that had mounded underneath the hole. From there she leaped up and caught the edge of the fissure.

And then she just sort of…hung there.

She'd never done a pull-up before.

She'd *tried*, of course. In gym class they always made you try. Jump up, grab the bar, try to pull yourself up. But she had the upper-body strength of a plate of fettucine. So mostly in gym class her legs would kick fruitlessly at the air as if she were trying to karate her way up. It never worked.

And it wasn't working now. Her legs kicked. Her shoulders and arms burned like match-tips. Dizziness rushed over her in a wave—

Above, she heard Dustin screaming in pain.

He's hurting my brother.

Now, Molly had heard tales of moms who had found their children trapped under, like, a cement truck, and had somehow manifested Mom Strength and gone *hnn-nnrrrggh* and lifted that cement truck off the child in a feat of impossible parental might.

Molly had always thought that was pure nonsense.

But now she wasn't so sure. Because Molly, with a feeling in her arms like lightning (so sharp and so sparking it felt like her arms were about to tear out of their sockets), hauled herself up—

Hnnnnnrrrgh!

—out of the hole.

Mom Strength? Nope.

Sister Power? *Heck yeah.*

Up on the ground, Gorgoch's monstrous, spiderlike legs hoisted his round torso in the air, his gut swaying left and right. It was comically bloated, pregnant with what Molly had to guess were the souls of the blood-thirsty damned. His swollen, strained belly had pushed apart his jacket and had popped the buttons on his shirt, exposing that rash-red chest of his.

And there, she saw it hanging from his neck. Gleaming in the moonlight. *The bezoar.*

Dustin dangled thirty feet up in the air, held by the

scruff of his neck as if he were an errant kitten. He cried out, and Gorgoch shook him hard.

"Quiet, *boy*," he roared. "Your plaintive cries are so pathetic they actually hurt *me* more than they hurt *you*." But then Gorgoch burst out laughing, his massive mouth opening wide as the guffaws jiggled his moist mouth fringe. A forked tongue slid along rows and rows of razor teeth. "Oh, I kid. Nothing hurts me, you sad, little *ferret*."

Then Gorgoch wheeled his head on his stalklike neck to face Molly. "And *you*, little Molly. Such a disappointment. Here I have your brother in my grip. And you've come to...what? Save him?"

The bezoar gleamed.

I need him closer.

"Nah, kill him," she said, broadcasting it loudly.

Dustin's eyes went wide.

"What?" Gorgoch asked.

"Can I tell you a secret?" she said, this time lowering her voice just so. Just enough that his body shifted and he moved his head closer.

"What are you playing at?" Gorgoch asked her.

"I get it. I know why you're doing all this."

Again, she pitched her voice just a bit lower. Grimacing viciously, Gorgoch swept in closer still. *Just a little more.*

She continued:

"Something was taken from you. Your brother got all the chances. But Steve was a worthless, shiftless jerk. A basic slacker with no prospects in life, and then? He's the one who marries up. Gets a piece of all this. And does what with it? He *flames* out. All the while you, the smart one, were kept from...the uh...gates of heaven. So to speak."

"Yes. *Yes.* Who went to law school? Me. While *Steve* went to parties! But who won the heart of the pretty lady? Who ended up with a stake in a business that could've afforded him ultimate power? Who had it all? *Him.*"

"And I feel the same way about my brother."

Dustin cried out: "Molly—no! It's not like that! It's not—*grrk!*" The words died in his mouth as Gorgoch thrust him downward suddenly, pressing his face into the dead gray earth.

"Shhh," he said. "The adults are talking."

Molly forced a smile. As if to act like, *Aww, that's sweet of you, Uncle Gordo.* She kept on: "Dustin was given everything. And he doesn't even know what he's doing. He doesn't *deserve* this. But I do. You do." She turned away now and muffled her voice just enough: "We both deserve what was given to others."

She *felt* him come closer, heard the wet, slithering

crickle-crack of his neck bones as his head eased near. Near enough? She didn't know. But it would have to do.

"Yes, Molly. Let's kill your brother. *Together.*"

"Molly?" she asked, tilting her head as if she didn't understand. "I don't know who that is."

"What?" Gorgoch asked, puzzled.

"My name is—"

She whirled around, the Nerf pistol out of its holster.

"*—Gunwitch Hera.*"

Then she pulled the trigger and the dart flew true. Toward Gorgoch. Toward the bezoar. It hit the stone around his neck and—

41. flight of the gunwitch

THE DART BOUNCED OFF THE BEZOAR AND FELL LIKE A STUNNED bumblebee to the ground below.

Molly gritted her teeth and pulled the trigger five more times, emptying the dart clip. Each one hit the bezoar around his neck (she'd practiced target shooting with these darts countless times in her many bedrooms), and every time, the dart bounced off like she'd been shooting ping-pong balls at the Batmobile.

She blinked.

Gorgoch blinked back.

"That was supposed to be cooler," she said, shrugging.

"You little scab," her uncle hissed.

Then he backhanded her with his free hand. It hit her with the force of a speeding minivan. The world whirled around her, end over end, until she hit the ground, the air clapped from her lungs. And all went dark.

Reality roared back in fits and starts. Her eyes opened, and she saw them: shades. Creeping closer. Claws out, eyes red. She tried to move, but—

Darkness claimed her once more.

Then a gasp and a shudder and her eyes popped open again. Consciousness visited her like a sunbeam in a rainstorm. But what the light showed her was not welcome, for the shades were upon her now, their crimson ember eyes glowing, their talons reaching. And then, *no no no, stay awake, get up, get up*—

She was swept away on another current of unconsciousness.

But though she could not see, she could still *hear*. The sound of something vicious entered her ears. A snarling. A *chewing*. A rending, as if someone were ripping a flimsy bedsheet in twain. *It's me*, she knew. She was being rent apart.

And then, like a fist to the gut, she awakened again.

She blinked. And in between blinks, she saw something whipping about, rushing through the shades, slicing them to wisps of darkness that turned to ash on the wind.

The *something* doing all that rending looked very familiar.

It was a monster, to be sure. Yellow lupine eyes. Jaw distended like a snake's—and with a pair of vicious curved fangs on the top and bottom. A vampire. But the outfit of a humble office worker? The mop of mostly combed (though now slightly messy) chestnut hair?

This monster was Dave Peterson.

Dave Peterson, the vampire, the monster, the beast. Whirling about like a carousel straight out of hell. And then she blinked again and it was done.

Dave Peterson stood before her, his body racked with shudders of what she feared might be pleasure. Then he turned toward her, smiling a fang-riddled smile, and his yellow eyes narrowed with what she surmised was a lust for her blood.

"Hey, Molly!" he said, rather unexpectedly. It was said in the same sort of chirpy, mildly pleasant voice he usually exhibited, except this time with a faint *growl* underneath it.

"Hi, Dave Peterson," she said, her voice small and hoarse.

"Here, let me help you up."

He offered her a hand, and she took it.

She staggered, wobbly on her feet, but the chonky heels of those Gunwitch boots kept her firmly on the ground.

"There's a problem," Dave said, in what Molly felt was the understatement of her lifetime, if not all time. Because there, in the distance, she saw Gorgoch with both hands on Dustin. Twisting him like a washrag. Which, given that he was *not* a washrag, would not end well for her newfound brother. It would tear him in half like a stale baguette.

"I need to get the bezoar," she said.

Dave frowned curiously, which was somehow extra upsetting given his currently monstrous visage. "I still don't know what that is?"

"The necklace! I need Gorgoch's necklace." Her brother screamed in agony and she winced. "Can you throw me?"

"Throw you?"

"Are you strong enough to throw me? At him."

"At him?"

"At him."

Dave shrugged. "Golly, probably! I'm always game to try something new, it's my motto that—"

"Now!" she screamed.

The vampire shrugged, grabbed her under the arm-pits, and then swung her around and around before finally—

Letting go.

I'm flying.

An absurd thought, yet true just the same. Because she was flying. Less like a bird, more like one of the Nerf darts.

Ahead, Gorgoch rose before her like an apocalyptic pillar, a demonic cyclone the color of beet juice and popped zits. He saw her coming, his long neck and wretched face spinning toward her.

She began to lose altitude in her arc of flight—

Which put her right on target.

Dustin cried out for her—

Gorgoch let go of her brother and he fell down, down, down—

Dustin hit the ground with a *crunch* and a *snap*—

Her uncle grabbed ahold of her, stopping her flight—

No, no, no! I'm so close!

She yanked forward, caught as he grabbed her. No—he grabbed her *coat*. Quickly she bent her arms back and freed them from the sleeves. And as she did so, she planted her boots firmly on the long, flat underside of his forearm and *kicked off* as if she were an Olympic swimmer. Her hands reached out. The bezoar was there, right in front of her.

Her hand closed around it as she fell.

Gorgoch's hands grabbed her, tried to pull her away. Molly would not relinquish her grip.

"Let *go*," he seethed.

"No!" she cried. "Not a chance."

One of his hands wrapped around her face, the claws digging in behind her ears. She felt something wet slide down her neck. Blood?

As her demon uncle pulled on her, *she* pulled on the bezoar—but the cord was too taut, too strong, and it would not break.

Then she remembered what Marsha had said:

Take this. You're going to need it to stop him.

The knife. With its magic poison she did not need. But the blade? The blade she could use. Her one free hand flew to her side, unsnapped the sheath with a thumb, pulled out the blade, and slashed at the hand around her neck. It opened like a blooming flower and recoiled—and when it did, she could see her target.

She hooked the blade under the leather cord that held the bezoar around Gorgoch's neck. Then, with a fast tug upward—

The cord sliced in two.

The necklace was free.

"Choke on your jealousy" was what she *would have* said, if she'd had half a chance. Instead, Gorgoch writhed, letting go of her entirely. She tumbled downward, hitting his bony knee and rolling off it, landing hard against her brother. The blade dropped, too, sticking into the ashen earth only inches from her head: *kchuff.*

Gorgoch towered over the siblings, his face swelling and distending, livid with pure rage.

"YOU FOOLISH GIRL. YOU GIVE THAT B—"

But that word seemed to lodge in his throat, because the rest of it came out a strangled gurgle. His forked tongue lashed at the air like a whip. A blackness like bubbling burns spread across his chest, down his legs, across his limbs, and up his neck. It sizzled and crackled as bits of his skin swelled like a tortilla left too long on the skillet—flexible at first, then turning hard and charred before flaking away.

The burns crept over his face then, but Gordo's gaze found Molly, and in that look was something both contemptuous and pitiable. And in a voice that was small, that had returned to sounding like her uncle's *human* voice, he said, "I thought you were on my side. I thought you'd understand."

She had no answer for him that would satisfy either the man or the monster.

The burning darkness, which she knew to be jealousy, formed vicious fingers that closed around his face, and it was like watching a pumpkin rot on fast-forward. His head collapsed in on itself. There was no blood, no brains—only a gassy gush of green steam. Then the rest of Gordo fell to the ground like a house of cards—a *fdddt* of papery pieces that quickly all blew away.

"Dustin, please be okay," Molly said, hugging her brother.

"Nnnngggmmh," he said, facedown in the dirt.

"Oh gods, you're alive."

"I think my—" He rolled over and then cried out through gritted teeth. With one arm he pulled the other, limp, toward his chest and held it there. "Indeed, my arm is broken."

"Are you okay otherwise?" she asked.

"No. But yes? But no."

She laughed a little. "Same here."

"You did it."

"*We* did it."

A shadow fell over them. She flinched, fearing her uncle had returned in some way—

But it was just Dave Peterson. Still looking monstrous.

"Hey, you two," he said, rather chummily. "We should probably go? All the vampires you woke up? Well, Gorgoch put them back to sleep…but I don't think it's gonna last."

Dustin gulped. "Yes. Go. A good idea. But the path—"

Molly stood with Dave's help, and then she helped her brother up, being careful of his arm.

"The path is back," Dave said, his voice suddenly dark and crisp, with what might've been a vague British accent? "I can feel it in my blood. It sings for exeunt! Through the deathlands we again carve our ineluctable *path*."

They stared at him, puzzled.

He shrugged and grinned. His voice was back to normal when he said: "Sorry, us vampire types tend to get a little purple in the prose sometimes. I think it's a supernatural power. Or maybe a curse. Anyway, looks like with Gordo gone, we're free to go!"

"Then," Dustin said, "let's get the *heck* out of here."

42. singing for exeunt, as dave said

THEY WALKED THROUGH A GROVE OF UNDEAD IRON-RED TREES THAT twitched and crackled as the group moved past. No shades pursued them. Far behind, the ground remained littered with the bodies of the Entombed— some of whom had been broken in half, their souls eaten by Gorgoch the Devourer. Many remained, however, moaning and hissing.

As yet, the Entombed had not yet again caught their scent. And they quickly spied the way out—an uneven path of rough-hewn stone that seemed to head off into shadow.

"The Entombed," Molly said. "How do they…get put back in?"

Dave Peterson, who now had returned to his goofy Dave Peterson face, said: "I'll meet with the Blood Vicar and they'll convene the Ministry of Night who will invoke the Crimson Precepts to deal with them."

"Those are a lot of gothy words. Can't the elder vamps just…follow us? Leave the same way we are?"

Dustin answered that one: "No. The pathway is carved from Purestone. They cannot abide it."

"Oh. Good. Because I sorta was afraid we let out something…well…if not as bad as Uncle Gordo, at least still really, really bad."

"No, they are trapped in this realm," Dustin said. And he said it with confidence.

Dave Peterson smiled.

They hurried past tombs and sarcophagi and urns, many busted open and broken. And as they reached the edge of the vampire realm, darkness swallowed them.

The journey through the deep dark was not an immediate one—it was a strange, unsettling walk where they could see the Purestone path ahead but nothing beyond it. It was as if they were walking on a plank extended over oblivion, and it made Molly feel a sudden fear of heights—even though, when she tapped a foot off the path, she found ground there. Soft, spongy ground. Just black as the blackest ink, is all.

Onward they went. The journey took them maybe five minutes—not a long time, but long enough to make it feel completely off-kilter when they finally emerged into the half-glow twilight of the cemetery's beginning. In the distance they saw the same iron-red tree that they'd found at the start of this journey. The Guidestone Tree.

And even from here, Molly could see others standing beneath it.

She broke into a run, legs pistoning hard. The path underneath her was bumpy and she nearly tripped a few times (her Gunwitch Hera boots were not made for sprinting), but she couldn't stop now!

As she got closer, she recognized those who had gathered—

Gabriel Valverde, his dark chef's attire torn nearly to shreds—

A faint glimmer-shimmer of what must surely be Florg—

A mussed and exhausted Viv, who sat by the base of the Guidestone Tree—

And there, *there*—

Molly slammed hard (too hard, for which she apologized later) into Marsha Skullcap, who had clearly survived her encounter with the shades back in the burial mounds of her people. Marsha looked as bad as the others: bruised, thorn-scratched, clumps of dirt and root-tangles in her wild hair. But she was alive. And she hugged Molly back.

"You made it!" Marsha squawked.

"*You* made it! I thought you were dead."

"Guess no one's worrying about me," came a voice that was both foreign and familiar to Molly. She spun and found a redheaded individual sauntering up with an easy swagger. A man. Shock of red hair. Long ragamuffin's coat.

"Em...ber," she said, confused. "I thought you were a woman."

"I am what I am when I am" was all Ember said. And it was then that Molly remembered what Viv had said: *Ember Felix, or sometimes Felix Ember.*

Both a she and a he, it seemed. Depending on the day.

"Yeah, nice to see you, too," Ember—or was it Felix?—grumbled.

Molly turned to the others and offered a surrendering hand. "I'm sorry—no, I mean, yeah, I'm glad you're all okay, I just, with Marsha—"

She hugged the Goodly Neighbor again.

"I made it, kiddo. No worries. Those shades, they

buried me in one of the mounds!" She shrugged. "I don't know how long I was down there, but then...then it was over. They were gone. The way was clear once more." She stared at Molly with a know-it-all look. Pushing her glasses up the bridge of her nose (they were even more wonky and crooked now), Marsha said: "Did you do that?"

"Because none of us did," Gabriel said, almost disappointed.

"**FLORG MAY HAVE**," said the shimmery space. "**YOU DON'T KNOW. MAYBE FLORG FIXED EVERYTHING. IT IS POSSIBLE.**"

"It was us," Molly said, gesturing toward Dustin and Dave Peterson as they approached. "We stopped Gorgoch." She sensed disappointment in the shimmering shape. "But Florg probably helped."

"**SEE.**"

They all took a moment to revel in that. To look upon one another's bedraggled faces and realize they'd survived, and they'd won. Vivacia stood before Dustin and Molly and said, "A change has come over you two. I can see it."

"I decided Dustin's not so bad," Molly said.

"And I decided to embrace the chaos of a little sister."

Sister, Molly thought. It felt good to hear him say it. It was a nice moment.

And then Felix ruined it.

"Well, good job, team. Now let's faff off. I'm starving, I'm tired, and I want to watch Netflix until my god-blamed face falls off."

As they left Mothstead, the great door groaning open to a forest whose trees were budding anew, Molly did not see the door-wolves waiting for her. But as the others kept on going, she hung back for a moment. Something compelled her to—she simply felt like she *should,* and so she *did.*

It was then that the wind, gentle as brushing fingers, swept up around her and only her, stirring leaves, stirring her hair. The others did not seem to see it.

And with it came a voice. A familiar one. *Thank you, Molly.*

It was the same voice that had called to her the day she found the door, and when she first came upon the Guidestone Tree. It was stronger now, less a whisper and more bold and deep, almost matronly. In it was a rustle of leaves and a gentle hum.

Molly knew then it was the voice of the Guidestone Tree itself.

She didn't know how she knew this. Or why no one else heard it.

"You're welcome?" she said.

We'll talk again, the voice of the tree said to her.

"Did you say something?" Vivacia asked. The others were continuing on, but Viv was walking toward Molly, concern on her face.

"What? No. I was just—" *Talking to a tree, I think.* "Saying goodbye. To all those still in the cemetery."

"Paying your respects," Viv said. "That's good." She paused, regarding Molly with a careful eye. "I see her now in you."

"Huh?"

"Your mother. For a long time I saw only your father and that was my fault. I didn't much care for him. He liked your mother. Loved her, even…but I was close to Polly. I was her best friend, her confidante, and I suspect I couldn't ever believe anyone would be worthy of her *or* her work here. She had a kindness, a deep well of empathy. You have it, too. I see that now."

Molly forced a smile and chewed on the inside of her cheek.

"What is it?" Viv asked.

"Why did she get rid of me?"

"She didn't."

"What?"

"I did."

Molly's guts clenched up. She felt weird. She felt…

angry? Sad? Confused? This wasn't what Link had told her. Not exactly.

"But she was my mother. She had to make the final decision, right?"

"She did, but only after I pushed and pushed." A sad smile crossed Vivacia's face, like a lonely boat drifting upon a glass-water lake. "I knew what we were doing here was important, Molly. Of utmost importance, in fact—life and death, and in fact, beyond both life and death, as you've now seen. Polly's was a sacred responsibility, and two children...it was too much. Especially since, really, she had *three* children—" At that, Molly's jaw dropped, but Viv clarified: "Your father. He was basically a third child. Needed a lot of attention. It distracted her. She lost focus. So I felt it best that she leave your father, and he take you with him."

"I think I'm mad at you," Molly said, but in a way that was very un-mad. Because she didn't *feel* mad. Just sad and resentful and more than a little lost.

"That's okay. You should be. I'm sorry."

"It's okay."

It wasn't okay. But maybe it would be one day.

"Shall we catch up to the others before they come back for us? And I'd...I'd be happy to tell you more about your mother, if you'd like. Whenever you want."

"Yeah. Okay."

Molly thought for a moment to mention that the tree had spoken to her. But she held her tongue. She didn't know why she kept it secret. Maybe because it felt so special to have the tree talking to her and only her. Maybe because she was tired of mysteries and didn't want to provoke another one. Maybe she was just *tired* all around and wasn't sure that she trusted Vivacia. Not all the way. Not yet.

With that, they left Mothstead, left the forest, and headed back home.

43. summer's end

SUMMER KEPT ON KEEPING ON, UNTIL IT WAS NEARLY OVER.

One morning late in August, Molly came downstairs, her hair a-tangle, sleep boogers still crusting the inside of her eyes, and she saw through the front window a shadow standing on the porch.

She knew who it was, and what he was doing.

So that's where she went.

"Hey," she said, the word trapped in the middle of a yawn.

Dustin did not look at her as she stepped out the door, but rather, continued staring past the driveway, toward the road.

"Good morning," he said, his voice as far away as his stare.

An enormous suitcase sat next to him.

"You ready for the big trip?"

He exhaled. "I don't know. I really don't." *Now* he looked at her, and she saw the lightning flash of panic in his eyes. "I've never been on a plane before. Did you know that?" He moaned. "I should've really taken a small flight first. Something to wet my beak, so to speak. Not this...behemoth."

"Dude. It's, like, ten hours. Less than a day." She grinned sloppily, like her mouth was still half asleep. "Besides, at the end of it: tropical bliss."

"Hawaii is for work, not for pleasure."

"Yeah, yeah, I know." He was going to procure iron-red acorns for replanting purposes—Gordo had, after all, hurt their supply of magical trees considerably. And as Molly had researched, she'd found there were certainly much closer occult botanists who could provide acorns or saplings. But when she found someone on the Big Island of Hawaii, well...why tell Dustin about the others? "Be sure to have some fun, though. Look at some turtles. Toes in the sand. Some fancy juice in a tiki mug."

"The Hawaiian culture is far more robust than that, I'll have you know. The ancient *heiau* temples are fascinating, and they have a complex system of magic and belief that I look forward to investigating." He cleared his throat. "Again, for work. Not for pleasure."

"Of course. Pleasure is the devil's playground."

"There is no devil. Just many devils."

"Even now, you can't stop lecturing me. I mean, *teaching me.*"

His face went pale—er, paler than usual. "Oh gods. You're not going to be okay, are you? This place takes a lot to run, and the supernatural community's faith has been shaken in us, and now *I'm* leaving and putting all the pressure on your shoulders—a burden! You're not ready for this. That's it. I'm not going. I'm canceling my flight—"

He started to drag the suitcase toward the door.

Molly stepped in front of him.

"Ah-ah-ah. No. You stop right there, scaredy-boy. I got this. Or, at least, *Viv* has this." Molly had been studying ever since they left the cemetery. How to run a funeral home and maintain a cemetery for monsters. (*Not monsters,* she chided herself. *The denizens of the supernatural world. Supernatural citizens.*) She imagined it was hard enough running a funeral home for humans. But there were so many rites and rituals, so many bereavement methods and grieving signals. Then there were ceremonial dances and music and on and on. She wasn't expected to know it all, but Vivacia would be here for her, as she had been for Dustin.

He sighed—a bit contentedly, but also with hesitation. As his shoulders slumped, he said, "Are you sure? Molly, you had plans. Plans to go away to school. And I know we…messed up a lot of that."

"It's cool, bro. Good news is, the denizens of the dark? They all have very particular costuming needs. I mean, blah blah blah, *ritual raiment.* Like, the vampires alone, *whew.* Already the Blood Vicar has said he needs new Taurobolium Robes to honor the Great Crimson Mother, whatever those are, so I think I'm on deck to help out. And the Knockers need new helmets. Something called an Uriska apparently needs a new cloak, but also they make cloaks out of peat-mulch? Which I don't think I can do. But I can learn! I can definitely learn. See? Lots of opportunity."

She smiled. "And, you know, maybe instead of dressing up as other characters in other stories, I'll get to have my own story now. Er, not that I'll stop all the cosplay. And you're back in time for Liberty Bell-Con, because I have a Baroness from G.I. Joe costume that I'm noodling on and I swear if you make me miss it—"

"I'll be back in time." He smiled. "Thank you. For everything."

"Go. Do all your *very serious work* in the horrible hellscape of miserable *Hawaii.*"

A small smirk played at the edges of his lips. "It will

be nice, won't it? Hawaii. I really get to see it. Here I thought I'd have to stay here forever and I'd never have help."

"And here I thought I'd get to go to costuming school and not have to babysit a funeral home for monsters."

He arched an eyebrow. "Oh, pish. Viv will do the heavy lifting." He smirked and jabbed her in the rib with an elbow. "Besides. It's not so bad, is it?"

It's not, she thought. But she sure wasn't going to let him know that. She thought to tell him that it was good he was running away for a little while, and it was good for her to *stop* running away for a little while, but instead she turned her eyes to the horizon as a black SUV turned off the road and onto the driveway.

"Here's my ride," he said.

"Have a safe trip, bro."

They hugged.

He took his suitcase and headed to the car. The driver, a thick-necked man in a black suit, took the bag for Dustin and opened the back door. But as the man hauled the suitcase into the back—

Molly saw a head poke out.

Not a solid head, but rather, translucent—invisible at certain angles.

It was a familiar face. Bone white and sallow. But

not sad-looking. A cheeky, mischievous smile was there. Lancaster Bauman Jr., the boy in the wallpaper, saw her looking, and he winked at her and held his finger to his lips. *Shhhh*. She rolled her eyes.

But she let it go.

Dustin's vacation was going to be quite interesting. And those two weeks would be interesting for her, too.

She turned back to the house.

To the funeral home.

And my home, too, now, I guess.

She waved one more time to Dustin as the car pulled away. He looked happy. Which made her happy, too.

Molly then looked at the meadows, the road, the forest in the distance, and, though it was concealed from view, the cemetery beyond. She'd found her place. There was work to be done. And for the first time, she felt like she was the right one to do it.

acknowledgments

As writers, we are who we read. And so I must acknowledge first the writers who made me who I am very early on, writers and cartoonists like Lloyd Alexander, Judy Blume, Beverly Cleary, Douglas Adams, Jane Yolen, Roald Dahl, Christopher Moore, Bill Watterson, Gary Larson, Jim David, Berkeley Breathed, Stephen King, James and Deborah Howe. But then I must also acknowledge those who guided me to those books, via bookstores and libraries, which means talking about my mother and my sister, both of whom encouraged my reading (and inevitably, my writing) at a very early age. Thanks too to my agent, Stacia Decker, and editor, Deirdre Jones, for allowing me to take you all on a guided tour of Mothstead, and helping make that tour as awesome for you as it was for me. And finally, thanks to Jensine Eckwall, who brought these pages to life in a way I could not have imagined, with her wonderful, inimitable artwork. I am a lucky writer. I hope you are lucky, too, dear reader.